SUMMER OF THE BIG BACHI

"Hirahara has a keen eye for the telling detail and an assured sense of character uncommon for a first-time novelist. . . . [Her] compassion for her characters and evident love of the region where they live and work keeps the heart of *Summer of the Big Bachi* whirling and purring as strongly as the engine of Mas's cherished Ford. Both mystery fans and readers of L.A. fiction will eagerly await her characters' further adventures."—*Los Angeles Times*

"Packs a considerable wallop."—*San Francisco Chronicle*

"An original and exciting mystery."—*Chicago Tribune*

"A unique voice in a genre cluttered with copycats."
—*Rocky Mountain News*

"Hirahara has crafted an intriguing mystery, full of earthy, subcultural richness. . . . An impressive first novel."
—*Old Book Barn Gazette*

"Debut novelist Hirahara's prismatic writing nails a Japanese American subculture and a troubled past few of her readers have ever confronted directly."—*Kirkus Reviews*

"[A] poetic, affective and artful debut novel."
—*Orange County Metro Magazine*

"Naomi Hirahara's story of forgotten men who share an unforgettable past sweeps the reader into a world most of us know little about. . . . A complete original."
—S. J. Rozan, Edgar Award–winning author of *Winter and Night*

"Naomi Hirahara is a bright new voice on the mystery scene. *Summer of the Big Bachi* presents an intriguing puzzle written with a true insider's eye for Japanese American life."
—Dale Furutani, Anthony Award–winning author of *Death in Little Tokyo*

"A novel about social change wrapped inside a mystery . . . Reveals the hopes and compromises that lurk on the fringes of the American Dream."
—Denise Hamilton, author of *Last Lullaby*

Naomi Hirahara

Gasa-Gasa Girl

Delta Trade Paperbacks

GASA-GASA GIRL
A Delta Trade Paperback / April 2005

Published by
Bantam Dell
A Division of Random House, Inc.
New York, New York

Cover design by Royce M. Becker

Book design by Lynn Newmark

Library of Congress Cataloging-in-Publication Data

Hirahara, Naomi.
Gasa-gasa girl / Naomi Hirahara.
p. cm.
ISBN 0-385-33760-4
1. Japanese Americans—Fiction. 2. Millionaires—Crimes against—
Fiction. 3. Parent and adult child—Fiction. 4. Fathers and
daughters—Fiction. 5. Gardeners—Fiction. 6. Gardens—Fiction.
7. New York (N.Y.) I. Title.
PS3608.I76 G37 2005
8134'.6 22 2004056923

Printed in the United States of America
Published simultaneously in Canada

www.bantamdell.com

BVG 10 9 8 7 6 5 4 3 2 1

To Jimmy,
the real artist in the family

ACKNOWLEDGMENTS

Thanks to Professor Kendall Brown and Yukiko Yanagida McCarty, for sharing information about Takeo Shiota. Quotes from Takeo Shiota were taken from his essay "The Miniature Japanese Landscape," written for the Newark Museum Association and available at The New York Public Library. For more information on Japanese Americans in New York, I can recommend two nonfiction works, Mitziko Sawada's book, *Tokyo Life, New York Dreams: Urban Japanese Visions of America, 1890–1924*, and Scott T. Miyakawa's article "Early New York Issei: Founders of Japanese American Trade." To learn more about the history of Seabrook, see Charles H. Harrison's *Growing a Global Village: Making History at Seabrook Farms.*

Regarding the writing of *Gasa-Gasa Girl*, I am indebted to both my editor, Shannon Jamieson, and my agent, Sonia Pabley, for their perceptive advice in making the story as sharp as possible.

I also acknowledge the help of Anne Winthrop Esposito, Patrick Huguenin, and the agency of Rosenstone/Wender.

For other tangible help, whether it be providing a bed for a weary traveling writer or making refreshments for book parties, I thank my parents, Mayumi and Isamu Hirahara, and their friends; my brother, Jimmy Hirahara, and his friends; my homegirls (you know who you are); Lewis Kawahara and Akiko Takeshita; Paul Kroner and Sharon Ozzolek; and New Life Christian Church. Attorney Mike Yamamoto fielded questions about criminal law. I also give thanks to the Japanese American community in both New York City and New Jersey, whose members were so welcoming during past research trips for other writing projects.

Last of all, but most important, appreciation and love go out to my husband, Wes, who has provided a nurturing environment for me to write in.

A real person, Takeo Shiota, and real places are mentioned in this novel, but the story of *Gasa-Gasa Girl* is completely fictional.

Gasa-Gasa Girl

BEFORE

Gasa-gasa. That's what Chizuko called her. Their *gasa-gasa* baby, constantly restless, constantly moving. Once, when Mas Arai returned from his gardening route to their home in Altadena, California, he found her in the living room chewing on the leather case for his favorite pair of pruning shears. Five minutes later she had gotten into his bowls of Japanese *go* playing pieces, a spray of black and white stones all over their linoleum kitchen floor. And five minutes after that, she had moved into the hall closet and pulled down all of Mas's long-sleeved khaki work shirts.

"She movin' all the time," said Chizuko. "Can't watch her every minute; I have enough to do around the house."

Mas didn't dare criticize Chizuko's mothering skills, because what could she say about him as a father? It was one thing when they were at home, when the walls of their McNally Street house could contain her. But out in the larger world, Mas and Chizuko had to keep their eye on their daughter at all times. If they didn't, Mari would have for sure stumbled into a dry ravine in Elysian Park during a gardeners' association picnic, or run away with a band of ravenous deer at the old Japanese Deer Park, in Orange County. Mari always seemed to be on the move, yet she still somehow escaped falling off the edge. Where, Mas often wondered, would the *gasa-gasa* girl end up next?

chapter one

To go far from the noise of civilization, to live the simple country life and breathe deeply of pure air—that is the cleanser of life.

—Takeo Shiota
New York City, August 1, 1915

March 2000

Mas knew that New York City wasn't for him as soon as he saw that its gardens were under lock and key. Even in the best neighborhoods in Beverly Hills or San Marino back in Southern California, lawns lay open like luxurious carpets to the edges of sidewalks, beckoning guests and the glances of envious passersby. Of course, back home there were also visual threats and warnings—the blue and yellow Armed Response signs on metal stakes. But it was one thing to pierce grass with a sign, and quite another to put a garden behind bars.

"It's called a community garden," Tug Yamada

explained. "Everyone pitches in to make it green." They were stuck in traffic on Flatbush Avenue. Tug had picked Mas up in a white Mercury rental car, a pearl amid the black Town Cars that had circled JFK Airport. Mas could always count on Tug to help him in a pinch. But then again, Mas guessed that Tug was behind this recent turn of events. It would take an outside force—specifically a six-foot Nisei, a second-generation Japanese American—to push Mas's daughter, Mari, to place a call from Brooklyn to his home in Altadena.

"Community? Like Japanese ones back in Los Angeles?"

"No Japanese gardeners over here, Mas. At least no more than you can count on one hand." Tug stretched out his palm, magnifying the missing half of his forefinger, a remnant of his war injury in Europe.

This was no place for Japanese gardeners and no place for a Kibei like Mas, who was born in the U.S. but raised in Japan. *Kibei*—"ki" meaning "return," "bei" referring to America—was a word made up by Japanese Americans to explain their limbo. So while America was actually home for the Kibei, many of them weren't quite comfortable with English; on the other hand, they weren't that comfortable speaking Japanese, either.

Mas was used to not belonging, but he felt an especially strong sense of displacement the minute he'd gotten on the plane. A bunch of *hakujin* and blacks, and a few young Chinese. There were a couple of Japanese, but they were business types who wore blue and black suits with ties and hard shoes even on the airplane. They sat in the front, behind a curtain that separated the first class from the rest of the plane, called economy but really meaning *bimbo*, for the passengers with no money, like Mas. Even when Mas returned to America from Hiroshima in 1947, he bought the third-class boat tickets, which turned out to be a large open room full of other teenage dreamers lying on *goza*, straw mats, on the bottom of the ship.

In the streets of New York, there were black and brown teenagers with the same look in their eyes. Wrapped in puffy jackets and their heads topped with knit caps, they seemed to hold their dreams casually, maybe recklessly, as if those dreams could never dry up.

"Everyone *gasa-gasa* ova here, huh?"

"Yeah, everyone moves around in New York, Mas. You should see where Joy lives in Manhattan. It's like rivers of people walking at night."

Tug had been in New York for a couple of weeks now before the opening of his daughter Joy's art exhibit. In Mas's eyes, Tug was the closest thing to an expert on Manhattan. "Joy live close to ova here?"

"You have to go over the Brooklyn Bridge, but it's just a short subway ride away."

"Fancy place, dis Manhattan?"

"Well, Joy lives in a postage stamp of an apartment. The water comes out all brown." Tug stroked his white beard. "And you know how I love baths, Mas."

Tug, in fact, had installed a Jacuzzi tub, his and his wife Lil's only extravagance, in their modest home just two miles east of Mas's. There was no doubt that this love for baths started when Tug was a child simmering nightly in the family *furo*, the huge Japanese wooden tub, on their red chili pepper farm.

Mas asked a few more perfunctory questions about Joy, then cut to the chase. "So you knowsu whatsu goin' on with Mari?"

"I'd better let her and Lloyd explain."

Lloyd? Mas had barely thought of his new son-in-law. "Not the baby—?" Mas couldn't even say the name: Takeo Frederick Jensen. It was too long; and why had they named the child Takeo, anyhow?

Mari had sent a photo back in December of a little red monkey-faced infant with fists curled up like cooked shrimp. You couldn't tell if the baby looked more Japanese or *hakujin* or something in between. Mas remembered when Mari had been that small. He was almost afraid to touch her, and even Chizuko told him to keep his distance. But, in time, he got the hang of it—support the neck, watch the soft spot on top of the head. The first and only time he gave Mari a bath, he noticed a dark-blue mark above her buttocks and thought he had done something wrong. "Masao-*san*, most Japanese babies have that," Chizuko said, laughing. Later Tug's wife, Lil, explained that doctors called it a Mongolian spot, which seemed like a fancy term for a temporary birthmark on a baby's behind.

Tug stopped the car at another light, and Mas noticed another one of the community gardens. This one was a triangle of green trapped next to a fancy white store that looked like it sold overpriced basketball shoes and jerseys. Mas could make out a Japanese cedar, and even some kind of makeshift pond. It was still cold in New York, a good thirty degrees lower than L.A. Were the people of New York City so hungry for trees and flowers that they had to create this spring oasis in the middle of melting snow?

Tug seemed to read Mas's mind. "Lloyd was telling me about that place. Even has a name, Teddy Bear Garden, or something like that."

Teddy bear? Kids' stuff, thought Mas.

"A developer was going to get rid of the garden, so the whole community, even Lloyd and Mari, protested. Early on, somebody had thrown a teddy bear into the area, so I guess the name stuck. You know about these community gardens, Mas. There's one across the freeway from Dodger Stadium, I think."

Tug was a die-hard Dodger fan, so it was no wonder that anything remotely involving his baseball team would stick in his mind. Mas himself recollected seeing the small clumps of flowers and vegetables against a hill right above one of the tunnels of the Pasadena Freeway. And there was another garden in Alhambra, a few towns south of Altadena, where Chinese immigrants dressed in cotton pants and sometimes straw hats tended stalks of corn and vines of cherry tomatoes. But those gardens were primarily vegetables, while these ones on Flatbush Avenue were filled with trees and flowers struggling to bloom. In L.A., everybody had pride of ownership in their personal flower gardens—a concept that had led Mas and several thousands of other Japanese Americans to get jobs as gardeners, whether they could actually grow anything or not. Everyone assumed that Japanese had green thumbs. If only they knew the truth: that most of them starting out could hardly tell the difference between a weed and an impatiens plant. But they had caught on fast enough, making money to feed their families and send their kids to fancy schools as far away as New York.

"How long youzu gonna stay?" Mas asked.

"Well, Joy's exhibition opens in a couple of weeks. You, Mari, and Lloyd are all invited, you know. I don't know about the baby, though. I don't know what people do at art gallery openings."

Tug's daughter, Joy, had recently traded in her white coat and stethoscope for poverty and paintbrushes. It had been a bad blow, but in typical Yamada fashion, Tug had bounced back, in full support of his daughter's new career. Mas had never been much into support; at least that's what both Chizuko and Mari told him time and time again. That's why he had been surprised to hear Mari's quavering voice on the other end of the line from Brooklyn: "We're in a bit of trouble, Dad. We might need your help." Help? When had Mari ever asked for help? Mari didn't want to get into the details but told him that she and her new husband, Lloyd, were going to buy him an airplane ticket. "You'll need a driver's license to board. And don't forget a credit card, just in case," she said.

But there was one problem: Mas didn't have a credit card. He'd had one briefly, when his wife, Chizuko, was alive, but that had been about fifteen years ago. So he went to the bank, and within a week, he had his own shiny piece of plastic bearing on it his full name, MASAO ARAI.

Now, with his driver's license and new credit card in his worn leather wallet, he had both an identity and money. He wasn't sure whether they were enough to help Mari, but he knew if he didn't come through this time, he probably would never get the chance again.

They passed a few more corner pizza shops, a line of leafless trees in a brown park, and some small grocery stores that looked like the old produce stands in Little Tokyo. Tug finally turned right onto a smaller avenue called Carlton. On both sides of the street were three-story brick buildings—brownstones, Tug had called them. They all had heavy metal gates on the doors, but no Armed Response signs. These Brooklyn people chose to fight their crime the old-fashioned way, thought Mas.

Cars were parked bumper to bumper along the curb, so Tug double-parked in front of one of the brownstones, pressing down a button to open the trunk. "I'm sorry I can't wait with you," Tug said. He left the car running while he got out and lifted Mas's hard plastic yellow Samsonite suitcase from the trunk. Mas clenched his arthritic hands as he waited out on the curb in the cold.

Tug handed Mas the suitcase and a set of keys. "Lloyd asked me to give these to you. One's for the gate and the other's for the door. He'll come home right after work."

And Mari, what about her? Before Mas could get any more information, Tug was back at the driver's-side door. "See you, old man. I'll call you tomorrow."

Mas hesitated for a moment in front of the brownstone. Clutching his suitcase and keys, he started up the concrete steps, only to have Tug honk his car horn. Shaking his head of white hair back and forth, Tug lowered the passenger's-side window. "No, Mas," he said, "not up there. Down."

Mas pointed to a gate on the right that seemed to submerge below street level, and Tug nodded in response. With that, the white rental disappeared down Carlton Avenue, leaving only a brief trail of steam and exhaust.

This was worse than Mas had imagined. He knew making ends meet for a freelance filmmaker and—could he even say it—modern-day gardener in New York must be tough, but was it tough enough that they had to live underground? Even the small window, no higher than Mas's knees from the street, was heavily barred. You couldn't tell if it was meant to keep people out or keep people in.

Trying the keys a couple of times, Mas was finally able to open the gate. Beyond the gate was a dark and damp entryway leading to a large door. Mas's eyes had trouble adjusting to the dim light, so he pulled out his new Rite Aid reading glasses from his shirt pocket to pick out the key for the door.

The apartment was cool and musty, much like his garage

after a winter rain. There were layers of smells: the familiar staleness of old newspapers and books, a lingering memory of meals made by Mari and Lloyd, and maybe decades of households before them, and a faint sweetness of talcum powder. Mas felt the side of the wall by the door—wood paneling, but no light switch. He could make out the outline of a lamp shade, found the knob, and turned it two times.

The front room was small, about fifteen feet by fifteen feet. There was a long couch along the wall on the left side, but what caught Mas's eye first was a set of wooden stairs that led not to a door or room but to another wall. Stairs that went nowhere, an underground apartment—what *was* this house? Tug had explained that the neighborhood was called Park Slope, but Mas hadn't seen any sign of anything green other than the Teddy Bear Garden. He noticed that unlike in typical Japanese American households, no shoes were left anywhere near the doorway, so he went ahead and stepped onto the hardwood floors, leaving his suitcase on the threadbare brown rug.

There was a mini kitchen in the corner, a wire dish rack holding a couple of coffee cups, a plate, and a few upside-down baby bottles. A desk by the hollow fireplace was overburdened by papers and books—it seemed almost as if it were spitting out and rejecting the weight of the information it carried. Mas turned on another lamp by the desk and peered at the books. Most were in English, but a couple were in Japanese. A Japanese-English dictionary, the fat kind that Chizuko had used when she was writing official letters, sat on a shelf. Even though Mas and Chizuko had sent their daughter to Japanese school every Saturday, Mari wouldn't have anything to do with the language and had forgotten the little that she had learned. Chizuko was offended and sometimes hurt when the teenage Mari had hissed at her in public places: "Speak English, Mom, speak English."

These couldn't be Mari's books: but then again, who else's would they be? The son-in-law's?

On the shelf next to the dictionary were a couple of photographs: the same one of the baby Takeo that Mari had sent to Mas, and a large one of Mari with her pale and scraggly husband, Lloyd, standing on some cement stairs leading to an official government building. Mas had not seen Lloyd for years, and that absence hadn't done Lloyd any good. Instead of looking more refined and clean-cut, his hair was down to his shoulders and barely combed. He wore wire-rimmed glasses and a tan suit, but he wasn't fooling anyone. He was a no-good gardener, just like Mas. But while Mas was a Kibei, Lloyd was a *hakujin* man, over six feet tall. He had absolutely no excuse for falling into the same line of work as desperate men.

Taped to the wall over the desk was a grainy photocopy of a man's image. Mas adjusted his Rite Aid glasses. A Japanese man wearing a straw hat and suit. A shadow fell on half the man's face, but he looked important. *Erai:* a big-boss type. The image was black-and-white and had obviously been taken more than half a century ago, maybe in the 1920s or 1930s, about the time Mas was born.

The disorganized books and papers on the desk didn't make much sense: Mari had always been like Chizuko, who'd kept their home in Altadena spotless. Every kitchen knife was sharpened (that part done by Mas after much nagging from Chizuko) and arranged by size in one of the kitchen drawers. The bills were paid immediately and filed away. When she was a child, Mari herself had lined up her pencil erasers by size at the top of the pink desk Mas had built for her. A few of them were those strange white Japanese ones wrapped in colorful cardboard sleeves. At one time they smelled like sugary flowers, but now, still left on the pink desk in Mas's silent house, they were virtually odorless.

Something else was wrong with the Park Slope apartment. Mas had taken on a new customer a few months ago, a young couple with a baby, in Pasadena. Their wood-framed house had a sloping front yard—something Mas would have never taken on in his heyday. But now competition was worse than ever and he couldn't afford to be choosy. Every time he waited at the door to talk to the missus, he noticed the trail of blocks, overturned plastic toys, and abandoned blankets. A disaster that only a baby could create. This front room had little sign of that.

Mas went into the back room, the bedroom. Again he turned on a light, the lamp beside the bed. Sure enough, a small crib stood in the corner. A few stuffed animals and packages of disposable diapers. By the crib was a large fluorescent lamp, almost like the ones Mas had seen in orchid greenhouses. What kind of strange life was Mari leading with this giant *hakujin* gardener?

A door in the bedroom led to a small backyard outside. Through the bedroom window, Mas could see that it had started to rain. He turned the double lock and opened the door. Finally, a faint patch of green, mixed in with dirt and gray.

Mas let the drizzle wet his hair, which had been combed back with Three Flowers oil, like always. He drew up the collar of his jacket and went up the steps to the miserable garden. Its condition didn't surprise Mas. Most gardeners were too busy with other people's gardens to put much energy into their own. Mas's front yard had its share of dandelions, and the backyard would have been completely grim if it had not been for Chizuko's leftover buckets of cymbidium. As he stumbled over some icy gravel, he thought he heard the ringing of a telephone in the distance. Not my phone, he thought, going over to examine a fancy iron bench and some metal rabbits and ducks. The square of green looked like last season's Bermuda grass.

Someone had attempted to plant a few daffodils, and they were bravely breaking through the chocolate brown soil. The plum blossoms on the garden's sole tree were still tightly closed, awaiting the warmth of the spring sun.

Before Mas could take further inventory of the hibernating plants, he noticed a figure at the open door. The son-in-law, a skeleton of a man, his dirty blond hair hanging down his head like seaweed. His face was ashen gray. Mas shoved his hands in his coat pockets and walked back to the apartment, preparing himself for the fake niceties that relatives who were virtual strangers said to one another at holidays and funerals.

But the son-in-law didn't even bother to smile. "Mari and Takeo aren't here," Lloyd said. "And I'm not sure exactly where they are."

chapter two

The son-in-law was on the phone, sitting on the stairs that led to a wall. Mas remained seated in a beat-up easy chair in the bedroom and recalled the telephone message that Lloyd had just replayed for him in the kitchen. It was an old answering machine, the kind with a large dial for *play* and *rewind*.

"I'm not sure how I ended up here." Mari's voice, which had once been as solid and defined as polished stones, now sounded limp and flimsy. *"I was taking Takeo for a walk, and before I knew it, we were*

on the subway, and now we're in Manhattan. I think we'll just stay the night over here. I'll call you back later."

In the other room, Lloyd had apparently gotten up from the nowhere stairs and was pacing on the hardwood floors in his work boots. He was still on the phone, perhaps with one of their friends. "She turned off her cell phone," Lloyd was saying, "or else forgot to charge it again. I don't know what's going on with her." And then in a hushed tone that Mas could still hear: "Her dad is here for the first time, for God's sake. Why would she just take off like that?"

Mas pressed the palms of his hands against the arms of the chair. He ached for a cigarette, but hadn't had time to stop by a grocery store.

Lloyd ended the phone call soon afterward and then stepped into the doorway of the bedroom. "Our friends in the Village are going to call as soon as they see or hear from Mari. I'm sure they'll turn up somewhere." Lloyd's words were spaced out far apart from each other, as if he didn't quite believe them.

Lloyd ran his hand through his hair, and Mas noticed that instead of a gold or silver wedding ring, he had a black and blue tattoo around his ring finger like a modern-day *yakuza*. Mas shuddered to think that Mari might have branded herself as well. "The thing I don't get is," Lloyd continued, "why would she pull this on the day you're supposed to arrive?"

Mas traced the back of his dentures with his tongue. This Lloyd Jensen was an amateur. For the length of his body, it seemed that his brain should be much bigger. Obviously, Mari wanted to make sure that her father got a big dose of *bachi*, retribution, for all those times he had left the house with no word.

"Sure she come back," Mas said.

Lloyd didn't seem comforted by Mas's words. "Takeo needs his light treatments. What the hell is she thinking?"

Mas stayed silent.

"You don't know what's been going on, do you? Not any of it."

Mas shook his head, not knowing if he wanted to.

They went into the tiny kitchen, where Lloyd boiled water for tea and Mas sat at a small wooden table. Lloyd removed a flowered canister from the refrigerator—a cylindrical tin that reminded Mas of one that Chizuko once had. He poured loose green tea, which looked like dried grass cuttings, into a small teapot. Mas was surprised. He thought for sure the son-in-law would have thrown a couple of tea bags in boiling water.

"Jaundice," Lloyd finally said. He put two large ceramic cups, the kind that sushi bars use, steaming with hot tea on the table.

"Huh?"

"Takeo was born jaundiced." Lloyd sat back on a wooden chair that creaked from his weight. "His liver was unable to break down his bilirubin, so we've had to use an ultraviolet lamp."

Mas couldn't figure out what his son-in-law was telling him.

Lloyd tried again. "It's a disorder where the skin, eye whites, are all yellow."

Mas nodded. "Sure, Mari had that."

"But this was a serious case. He may even need a blood transfusion."

Blood transfusion? A little baby? Mas took a sip of the green tea. The heat burned his tongue, and he was happy for it. Mas couldn't help but wonder if his being a *hibakusha*, an atomic bomb survivor, had anything to do with his grandson's health problems. Two generations removed from the Bomb—could there still be a connection? Impossible, thought Mas.

"So dat why Mari call me in the first place?"

"No, it was the garden. It's all about the garden."

Lloyd went to the overloaded desk, shuffled some papers, and finally drew out a skinny book and a stack of photographs looped together by a rubber band. He leafed through the book and held two pages open toward Mas, who pulled down his glasses from the top of his head. It was a drawing of a curved light-blue pond surrounded by green and pink trees, most likely cherry blossoms.

In the center of the pond was an orange *torii*, a giant gate that reminded Mas of the one at Miyajima, an island not far from his family's house in Hiroshima.

"Brooklyn Botanic Garden," Lloyd said.

"Your garden?"

Lloyd laughed. "No, I wish. It was built a long time ago. One of the first Japanese gardens in the U.S., around 1915. It's only about five blocks from here."

Mas traced the outline of the pond with his left index finger, a week's worth of dirt still left underneath his fingernail. "*Kokoro,*" he said without thinking.

"Yes, yes." Lloyd almost dropped his tea mug. "The shape of the pond."

"Dis *kokoro* shape famous." At least that's what Mas learned from a few classes attended at the gardeners' federation in L.A.

"*Kokoro,* the Chinese character for heart, right?"

Heart? Mas didn't put *kokoro* in the same category as heart. *Kokoro* didn't live in the chest, but in the gut, and from there, it burned throughout one's body. "You knowsu Japanese?"

"Never really studied in school, but I'm going to have to take at least two years' worth for my doctorate—that is, when I can go back to school again. I'm planning to do my dissertation on Takeo Shiota, this garden's designer. That's his photo up there." Lloyd pointed to the image of the Japanese man in the straw hat.

Mas couldn't follow all of Lloyd's words, but recognized the name. "Takeo?"

Lloyd smiled. "Yes," he said, "like our Takeo." He then paused and narrowed his eyes. "Damn, it's one thing for her to have a meltdown, but why take Takeo with her?"

Mas didn't know whether to defend Mari or add his two cents about his daughter's mood swings. He chose instead to play it safe and keep his mouth shut.

"She doesn't sleep well, you know," the son-in-law continued. "Has nightmares but can't remember any of them. She says it runs in the family."

That it did, with both Mas and Chizuko. Chizuko would periodically wail and cry in her sleep, but wouldn't recall anything the next morning. It was as if she exorcised all her demons from her life in Japan in the other world behind closed eyes. Lately Mas was remembering more and more of his own nightmares, which he considered more of a curse than any kind of illumination.

"Garden, youzu talk about garden." Mas attempted to change the subject.

"Oh, the garden." Lloyd removed the rubber band from the stack of photographs. "This is my garden."

The first shots were of a dirt hole, a residential excavation next to an odd mansion with a pagoda-style roof above a frame like the Craftsman houses in Pasadena. In later photographs, the cement bottom of a koi pond had surfaced, and cherry blossom trees, their roots bundled in burlap, had been brought in. A pile of rocks was stacked in a corner. Where had they gotten their rocks? wondered Mas. These days even rocks were worth a premium.

"This Japanese garden had been covered over during World War Two," Lloyd said. "It's part of an estate that was once owned by a shipping magnate, Henry Waxley."

Apparently Henry Waxley was one of those men who owned companies that owned more companies. Lloyd even had a book about Waxley's life. It didn't matter that Mas had never heard of him. Men that powerful chose to rule in the shadows—that way they could move around and make their deals without much public fanfare. By the time regular people figured out what had happened, it was too late.

To be closer to his business empire, Waxley, his wife, and their newborn daughter had left the estate to move to Manhattan in the thirties, Lloyd explained. Distant relatives moved in and bought the house, but lost the property after a particularly nasty divorce.

Happened all the time, thought Mas. He had heard about farmers losing their acreage after these family breakups.

"So new owners took over in the forties." Lloyd took another sip of his tea. "After one of their cherry blossom trees was cut down in the middle of the night, they decided that it might be better to get rid of the entire garden, during the war at least. Too many people against anything Japanese."

The next photo showed a tall, Asian-looking elderly man in a tasteful gray suit, the brim of a felt hat darkening the left side of his face. "This is the man who took over the house last year. My boss, Kazzy."

"Kazzy?" That was a nickname only an American-born Nisei would own.

"Short for Kazuhiko. Kazuhiko Ouchi. They also call him K-*san*. The Waxley estate is where his parents had worked. His mother was a maid; his father, the gardener."

Mas looked closely at the man's face. "Don't look Japanese."

"He's *hapa*."

"*Hapa*," Mas repeated. He was surprised that Lloyd

knew the term, which meant half Japanese, half something else. There were tons of *hapa* today (Takeo, for example), but from Mas's generation? He didn't know of any in L.A., but then hadn't there been laws in California against Japanese marrying *hakujin* before World War II?

"Even has blue eyes," added Lloyd.

A blue-eyed Japanese? Mas took a second look at the man's face. Sure enough, the right eye seemed to have a glint of silver metal in it.

"His mother was Irish. His father was from Nagano Prefecture, Japanese Alps. Kazzy was born in the Waxley House. His mother died when he was young, and then his father shortly thereafter. He was on his own at age twelve. Became a multimillionaire in textiles, mostly silk. All after the war."

An orphan and a self-made millionaire. This type of man is different from the rest of us, Mas said to himself.

"But he's a hard man to deal with."

"Naturally," said Mas. "You make it big, have to be hard." Especially being Nisei in the 1950s, he thought, but he knew that this giant gardener probably wouldn't understand.

"He has his own private group, the Ouchi Foundation, to fund the restoration of the garden and make the house into a museum."

"Museum?"

"It's going to tell about the Japanese in New York. The garden will come first, and then the museum. Kazzy handpicked me to be the director of landscaping."

Mas almost started to laugh. Fancy title for a low-down gardener.

Lloyd must have noticed Mas's grin on his face. "No, really. You can even ask Mari. I was working on a special project for the city in Central Park. Mari was there, bringing me lunch. And then this *hapa* man in his felt hat comes over and tells me that he'll match my salary and more, with full medical benefits, to be his landscaping director. I checked him out, of course. His company, Ouchi Silk, is still in business, but not as big as it used to be.

"He took me out to dinner and told me about his grand plan: to document the history of Japanese Americans on the East Coast. He said that I was part of the Japanese American community, too, because I was married to Mari."

Mas scoffed inside. Why would a *hakujin* person want to be anything other than *hakujin*?

"Mari even turned down a documentary project to help out on the fund-raising video. Waxley Enterprises and Miss Waxley, Henry's daughter, have given a substantial amount of money, but we are filing for nonprofit status soon. Mari and I feel really strongly about this project. We've even pledged some money ourselves."

So they had everything riding on this Japanese garden. Mas was a savvy enough bettor that he would have told Mari never to put your money on such a dark horse. But then he hadn't been around to tell her and she wasn't in a place to listen.

"I look at it as something I'm building for the future. Our future. And Takeo's."

Lloyd was a dreamer, his head not on practical matters.

Mas pushed his top dentures hard against his gums. This was not a good sign. With the addition of Mari, there were two dreamers leading the family.

"We're supposed to open in a couple of months, but recently there's been vandalism." Lloyd went through more photographs, which revealed the half-planted garden full of garbage and splattered in white paint.

"Teenagers?" Even at Evergreen Cemetery in East Los Angeles, where Chizuko was buried, somebody had knocked down some of the older tombstones, apparently a youngster's prank.

"Probably. But the police can't figure it out. And Kazzy hasn't been of much help. He's accused the whole staff; well, he's fired three of us so far. There's only the administrative assistant—his daughter, Becca—and myself left. Kazzy said that between the two of us we should be able to take care of the garden, which is crazy. If I could get out now, I would. But with Takeo being sick and all, we need the insurance. Times are tough; it's not like these jobs are easy to come by.

"That's why Mari called—to ask your help. Kazzy doesn't want to pay for extra workers; somehow we've already gone over budget by thousands of dollars. I have friends who might have come out, but we figured that they would get tired of it. We were talking to Mr. Yamada about our problems, and then he mentioned you. Said that he thought you'd be open to helping out."

Mas bit down on his dentures. So that explained it. Mari

had cried out to him—not to be a father or even a grandfather, but to serve as a common laborer. Only worse, because they wanted him to work for free. And to top it off further, it had all come from Tug—just like he had thought.

"*So—ka,*" Mas finally said.

"It's not that we wouldn't pay you eventually," Lloyd added. "I know that you're neglecting your own customers to come here."

Mas grunted. He had asked his best friend, Haruo Mukai, to look after his nine customers back in L.A. But since Haruo had gotten a part-time job selling chrysanthemums at the Southern California Flower Market, Mas had to also depend on a no-good gardener, Stinky Yoshimoto, who cut down bushes and trees so severely that their forms looked like the bodies of amputees.

"We'd just pay you later, when Kazzy sees that all is going well. And quite frankly, the fact that you're Japanese may calm his nerves."

"Nerves?" This Kazzy-*san* was sounding more and more like a man gone *kuru-kuru-pa*.

"He's just a little on edge. The opening is supposed to be in May, but the vandalism really set us back. Now Mari wants us to walk away from the project."

Not a bad idea, thought Mas.

"But she seems to forget that my work at the garden paid for her insurance when she was pregnant, the rent, and other bills. We've used up our savings. She thinks that we can live on nothing, on air. Maybe we once could, but not now, with Takeo."

Mas hadn't known Mari was hanging by a financial thread, in spite of the fact that she had some kind of fancy degree from Columbia University. To live from paycheck to paycheck—like father, like daughter.

Lloyd pulled back his hair behind his ears and cradled his head, as if he had been physically battered. He finally looked up, and Mas noticed that his son-in-law had black flecks, like splintered glass, in his muddy-colored eyes. "Here you are, on your first night in New York, and I should be taking you out to dinner. But I have to go look for Mari and Takeo."

Mas wanted to join Lloyd in his search, but he knew that he would only slow down his long-legged son-in-law. And besides, Mari had probably disappeared because of him. Mas figured he would be the last person she would want to see.

"There's salami in the fridge and a baguette by the toaster oven. And there's plenty of restaurants in the neighborhood within walking distance."

"No worry about me," said Mas. "Youzu just find wife and kid."

❖ ❖ ❖

After the son-in-law left, Mas opened the refrigerator for the salami, but opted for a six-pack of strange beer instead. Made somewhere in Europe, the beer was as thick as syrup and dark as Coca-Cola, but it still did what it was supposed to do: help ease Mas's troubles. Lloyd had placed a couple of blankets and a futon covering on the couch, as well as two limp pillows. Mas turned on their rickety television and watched the news. The anchors and reporters looked more subdued than the ones in Los Angeles. They didn't seem to force fake smiles and banter, and instead of bright-blue skies and palm tree backgrounds, the sets were simple, painted in basic blue, red, and black. The stories, however, told of the same kinds of shootings and gang violence, only in neighborhoods he had never heard of. Mas switched from one channel to the next. Unlike L.A., there were no Japanese American reporters, reminding Mas that he was in territory where he didn't belong. He drank another beer and then a third, feeling the alcohol loosen the tightness in his neck and shoulders. Soon the couch in the Park Slope apartment became his friend, cradling him to sleep amid the muffled noise from outside, where his daughter, grandchild, and son-in-law were wandering somewhere, loose and separate.

A crab was pinching Mas's big toe. It appeared out of nowhere, and then dozens of minicrabs descended on Mas's body from cracks in the floor, the walls, the ceilings. As they traveled, their spindly legs made clicking sounds. Soon the sounds became louder and louder, merging together into a shrill pitch.

Mas woke up and shook his head to clear his mind from the dream of crabs. He paused a moment to get his bearings. The phone by the nowhere stairs was ringing. Mas didn't know whether to answer or not, but it could be important. News about Mari.

"Hallo."

"Mas—?"

"Hallo," Mas repeated. The voice on the other line sounded familiar.

"Itsu Haruo."

Haruo. Mas's skinny friend with the fake eye. At first Mas was going to ask how he got Mari's number, but then remembered that he had given Haruo the number in case of emergencies. "Whatsu the time?"

"Youzu just get up? Itsu four o'clock ova here. Izu at the Flower Market. Itsu a slow day today—just wanna make sure you got to New York *orai*."

"Izu here," Mas said. But nothing was all right. "Mari's missin'. Son-in-law gone to find her."

There was a pause on the other end. Haruo finally murmured, "Missin'. That makes no sense. You say sumptin' to her, *deshō*?"

Mas didn't like what Haruo was trying to say. "Haven't even seen her. Or the grandson." Mas didn't want to get into Takeo's health problems right now.

"You call the police?"

Mas couldn't imagine getting them involved. "She left a message, Haruo. No funny business, Izu sure. Just a lot of stress right now, money and work."

"I see," said Haruo. Mas could imagine Haruo nodding his head, his shock of black and white overgrown hair barely covering the keloid scar on his face. Since going to a counselor in Little Tokyo for his gambling addiction, Haruo considered himself an expert on anything troubling somebody's mind.

"I gotta go, Haruo."

"You callsu me when they find her. You promise, Mas? You gotsu both my numbas, here at the Market and home."

"Yah, yah. Got work to do, Haruo."

Before Haruo could ask what kind of work, Mas hung up the phone. There was no sign that the son-in-law had returned to the underground apartment during the night. The heater had been left on, so the front room was now uncomfortably warm. The futon and the two blankets, apparently kicked off by Mas during the middle of the night, were crumpled on the brown rug beside the scratchy wool sweater he had been wearing—a hand-me-down from a customer's teenage son.

Mas tore pieces of the French bread and balled up the soft insides for his breakfast meal. He noticed an old jar of Nescafé and warmed water in the teakettle over the stove. After sipping a strong cup of coffee (two heaping teaspoons of Nescafé) sweetened with another two teaspoons of sugar, Mas made a decision. He couldn't just sit there and do nothing. Pulling on the wool sweater, he stumbled to the desk and waded through the papers. Beside the stack of photographs were some brochures of the Waxley Garden sponsored by the Ouchi Foundation. Taking a brochure and a map of Brooklyn, Mas headed out from the underground apartment in search of Lloyd's garden.

✣ ✣ ✣

Tug had told him that most New Yorkers survived without cars, and Mas believed him. It was barely eight o'clock and the sidewalks were filled with well-wrapped men and women holding briefcases, duffel bags, tabloid newspapers, and disposable cups of steaming coffee. Mas stopped by a sycamore tree growing in a dirt square and studied the map. There was a diamond of green labeled Prospect Park, where Takeo Shiota's Japanese garden lived. A few blocks north was the Waxley House.

Before Mas could tackle any real work, he needed reinforcements. He walked across Flatbush Avenue toward a grocery store, its facade covered in thick plastic strips like those of a car wash. Bright orange and red gerber daisies were bunched up, their stems soaking in water next to a large open refrigerator holding plastic containers of cut-up cantaloupe and honeydew melon. Inside, the small market reminded him of his neighborhood liquor store back in Altadena. Boxes of cereal and cans of soup were stacked high up to the ceiling—no space was wasted. Behind the front counter were a young Asian girl and a man about Mas's age, perhaps her grandfather. The man studied Mas for a moment, and Mas stared back. The man wore a light-blue button-down shirt and a puffy vest. His graying hair was parted to the side. He looked respectable. Mas figured that he was meant for better work than he was doing. "Marlboro," Mas said to the man.

"Marlboro?" the man repeated as if he didn't quite understand.

Mas nodded, and the man drew out a pack from a line of cigarette cartons organized against the wall.

"You Japanese?" the man finally asked, after Mas pushed a ten-dollar bill across the counter.

Mas didn't know if it was a trick question. He knew that the Japanese weren't much loved among other Asians, especially those straight from the Pacific. "Yah, but Izu born here." Mas waited for his change. "California."

"Oh, California." The man slid the change from the curved slots of the cash register. "My sister in California. Los Angeles."

Mas nodded. "Me, too."

"Los Angeles a very good place."

Mas agreed. It didn't matter that L.A. had been hit by its share of riots, earthquakes, fires, and even tornadoes. Most city folks knew little of the tornadoes, but Mas knew enough nurserymen to have heard about the plastic roofs of their greenhouses flying off in the wind, leaving behind only a twisted metal frame. L.A. was for the toughest of the tough, and apparently this store owner's sister qualified.

Mas shook the package of cigarettes over his head in appreciation and made his way through the plastic strips to the sidewalk. With a fresh cigarette finally in his fingers, Mas couldn't help feeling a little optimistic. Mari, the baby, and the son-in-law had to be together by now.

The Waxley House was a strange blend of styles, looking a lot like a child who didn't know how to dress. On the bottom, the house was all dark wood, simple and clean lines. But on the top, it was brightly painted with swirls of red, green, and yellow, reminding Mas of those Chinese-influenced temples in Japan. He thought he even spotted a wooden dragon where the peaks of the roof met.

The grass in front was freshly seeded, and the familiar smell of steer manure burned Mas's nostrils. He was surprised that Lloyd didn't use chemical fertilizer pellets—odorless and definitely high-technology. Mas didn't want to admit it, but he was impressed that Lloyd had opted for the old way instead of the new. Stuck in the steer manure was a rectangular sign:

> Waxley House and Garden
> est. 1919
> Operated by the Ouchi Foundation

The door to the front seemed to be ajar, but Mas felt funny about going through the house. Seeing a gate to the side, he chose instead to enter the garden through the back way, his favorite approach to a strange place.

A large, leafless oak stood on one side of the property, making it look nothing like a Japanese garden. A couple of dozen cherry blossom trees had been introduced to the property, but their branches drooped as if they were in mourning. Mas went forward for a closer look. What the hell? The trees had been massacred—the branches pulled down and broken.

Mas also noticed the outline of the koi pond for the first

time. Undoubtedly because of the weather, the pond was dry, with no signs of either fish or water. It was, however, filled with debris and trash; the vandals had indeed hit again.

"The police were already here; you just missed them."

Mas turned to face a woman who was the size of two Maris—at least widthwise. She had a round face and short reddish brown hair that was chopped at an angle. She must have been around forty but had at least three sets of earrings dangling from one earlobe. Something about her eyes seemed Japanese.

"You must be Mari's father, right? Lloyd mentioned that you'd be coming—you look just like Mari. I'm Becca Ouchi. I work with Lloyd." She reached out her hand, a heavy silver ring around her thumb. Mas tentatively squeezed the woman's hand. It was soft yet firm, like a slightly overstuffed pillow.

"Lloyd and Mari have been so great. My father's not the easiest person to work for, but they've really been so devoted. And we're all wild about Takeo. He's like a member of our family. My brother, Phillip, says sometimes it seems like K-*san* and I favor Takeo over his children." Becca laughed and then glanced at her watch, which was shaped like a sundial. "K-*san* should be here soon—I'm sure he'd love to meet you. He must be running a little late. And Lloyd, too. Is he on his way?"

Mas grunted. He didn't know how to answer the woman's question. He took stock of the damage again. "Terrible," he muttered. The woman, on the other hand, didn't seem that rattled at first glance.

"I'm used to it now. It's quite an adventure: what havoc will I discover at the garden today?" She was trying to make a joke, but Mas noticed that her eyes were filled with tears. "K-*san* is going to be so pissed. This is the last straw; he's going to close it down for sure now. Phillip will be happy to hear that."

Becca went on. "He doesn't understand how important this place is, to both K-*san* and me."

K-*san* was this Kazzy Ouchi, so this was the daughter? Why was she calling him by his nickname? Must be a strange New York practice.

Becca must have picked up on Mas's reaction. "I didn't grow up with my father, so I never really called him 'Dad' or 'Daddy.' K-*san* just worked out better."

Mas didn't know why women—at least those not related to him—always wanted to tell him their troubles. He was usually minding his own business, raking leaves by a customer's back door or buying cigarettes and beer at the local liquor store, when some lady would appear right next to him, ready to spill her guts. Was it because they knew that he would keep his mouth shut or that he had no one, at least no one who mattered, to reveal their secrets to?

Mas looked over the garden once again. It wasn't large, maybe fifteen hundred square feet, but Lloyd seemed to have put up a valiant effort. Azalea bushes and sculpted pine trees had all been arranged artfully around the dry koi pond. A thatch of bamboo was planted in the left-hand corner—Lloyd should be careful that the bamboo didn't crowd out the rest of the plants, Mas thought. Bamboo, which could spread as fast as wildfire, was hell to deal with. A *toro*, a cement Japanese lantern, had been placed on the north side of the path next to three good-sized rocks. By a wooden shed in the other corner was a pile of smaller rocks, most likely to be eventually used to outline the edge of the pond. The pond itself was shaped like a *hyotan*, or gourd—not the classic *kokoro* shape, but a popular choice nonetheless. It was simple and uncomplicated, almost like an hourglass figure of a shapely woman. A bridge, trimmed with cut bamboo poles, stretched over the pond.

"You should have seen it—all covered over," said Becca, obviously noticing Mas's study of the pond. "It had been used as a badminton court. When the Waxley House recently came back on the market, K-*san* bought it and unearthed the pond. He's restoring it the way his father would have wanted it to be."

Mas nodded.

"My grandfather was Mr. Waxley's gardener. He built this garden in K-*san*'s honor. Look, there's even a dedication to him carved into the base of the pond."

Becca began to push through the debris with her bare hands, but Mas waved her off. No matter how much he didn't want to get involved in this mess, it wasn't right for a lady—even one with three holes in her ears—to go through trash. He removed a pair of work gloves that he had stashed in his inside pocket. He'd figured that New York would be cold, and he'd had no time to buy proper gloves. He told Becca to bring over a shovel and some gauze or tape from a first aid kit. Becca seemed confused by the second request, but went dutifully anyway toward the toolshed in the corner.

Meanwhile, Mas wheeled a couple of plastic trash cans from the gate to the pond. When Becca returned, Mas brought her to the trees and showed her how to tape the cut branches together again—a grafting technique that he was very familiar with from years of work for Mrs. Witt, a former customer who had a passion for hybridizing different types of persimmons. Mrs. Witt had moved and the grafted trees had been pulled out months ago, but Mas had taken a few seeds from a persimmon mix and planted them in his backyard. You'd never know what Mother Nature would bless and what she would curse.

As Becca attended to the trees, Mas shoveled out the trash from the pond. Plastic tofu containers, empty cartons of soy milk, orange peels, coffee grounds, balled-up Kleenex, Pepto-Bismol bottles—a strange mix of the health conscious with the sick. With each shovelful of trash, Mas could better appreciate the pool maker's handiwork. The pool was shallow on the outside edges and progressively deeper toward the middle. Since koi, which sometimes grow heavier than cats, need a lot of water to swim around in, the pond was at least four feet high at its deepest point. Kazzy Ouchi's father had obviously known what he was doing.

With one trash can overflowing, Mas squatted on the

bridge and dug toward the middle of the pool. The tip of the shovel hit something more solid, but it wasn't the concrete bottom. Mas kept poking, but he couldn't come up with anything besides coffee grounds. He finally jumped down and reached into the debris with one gloved hand. Funny. A black shoe. But not the kind of shoe that you'd normally find thrown away. It was fancy leather and, aside from the coffee grounds, not at all damaged. Mas pulled at the shoe and then immediately dropped it. Heavy, as if weighted down—no, it couldn't be.

Mas waded through the trash, suddenly spurred on.

"Mr. Arai, what are you doing?" Becca turned away from one of the cherry branches, the medical tape still in her hands.

As Mas pushed away some dead leaves and more coffee grounds, he could now see a man's face. Mas had seen his share of dead people years ago in Hiroshima during the aftermath of the Bomb, but they had been scorched, not frozen like this in the cold. The man's skin looked like old chicken skin, and his eyes were still open, a funny gray color, like steel wool smeared with cleanser. Mas knew who it was even before Becca came over and gasped, "K-*san*."

chapter three

The police came within fifteen minutes—stocky men stuffed in blue uniforms and windbreakers. They spent most of their time speaking to Becca, whose nose and eyes had become red and swollen from her crying. They barely acknowledged Mas, who was used to and even happy being overlooked.

The policemen took Becca into the house. Mas stayed outside in a corner of the garden and watched as more men and women, their hands gloved and mouths covered with cloth masks, came in to retrieve the body. They walked into the concrete pool, and as they lifted Kazzy's shoulders, Mas noticed that a piece of the back of his head was missing. A woman wearing rubber boots waded into the trash, picked up something the size of a smashed peach and stained with the color of chocolate syrup—no doubt blood—and placed it into a plastic bag.

Mas felt woozy, his mouth raw as if his teeth had been extracted again with a double dose of novocaine. He welcomed the numbness, postponing the time when memories of dead bodies, both past and present, would haunt his mind.

Kazzy was wearing a fancy gray suit, and even with bits of trash stuck to it, Mas could tell the suit was at least five cuts above the black polyester funeral version hanging in the back of his closet in Altadena. As the body lay on the gurney, Mas noticed that Kazzy had been tall for a Nisei, probably around five feet eight or so. Workers wearing jackets that said CORONER on the back covered the body in cloth and then lifted the gurney, causing something white, as large as Mas's fist, to flutter down to the ground. Mas was ready to say something, but then thought better of it. It was probably nothing, another balled-up Kleenex. No sense in calling attention to himself now.

After the people from the coroner's office left the garden, Mas knelt down to get a better look at the white object. Wasn't discarded tissue paper but a flower. A huge gardenia, whose edges were still white. Mas took out an old pen from his jeans pocket and poked the back of the pen gently into the center of the flower. The petals were stiff, not from the cold but from wax coating. There was a dark hair in the middle, much longer than an eyelash, but shorter than a regular strand of hair. "*Okashii*," Mas muttered to himself. Strange.

"Hey, you, get the hell away from there!" It was a tall man with a heavy moustache and full head of hair. Some kind of shiny badge dangled from his black jacket.

Mas backed away from the gardenia. He looked both ways for a place to escape back into anonymity, but it was too late. This man wasn't going to forget about him. A couple of the uniformed officers were stretching yellow tape across the now empty pond. Even the trash had been bagged and taken away.

"Come over here, sir. We need to have a conversation," the man said.

Mas felt his hands grow sweaty. I didn't do nothing, he told himself.

"I'm Detective Ghigo." Strange name, thought Mas, accepting the detective's business card. The card said Ghigo worked for the Seventy-seventh Precinct—wherever that was. "I understand you were the one to discover the body."

Mas nodded.

"You can speak English, right, sir?"

Mas cursed in two languages in his mind. He wanted to sneer, but instead bit down on his dentures. He nodded his head again.

"What's your name?"

"Mas."

"Mas? M-A-S? That's Spanish, right?"

"Japanese," Mas spouted out. "Izu Japanese."

"Your full name?"

"Masao Arai."

"Arai? So how do you spell that?"

"A-R-A-I."

"Okay, so what do you have to do with this garden? Is this your place of work?"

Mas paused. Was it or was it not? "First day."

"Well, what a way to start your first day of work, huh? Address?"

"Izu live in California."

"California—that's a long commute, Mr. Arai."

Mas shook his head and took out his wallet. "Izu livin' here now." He took out a scrap of paper with Lloyd and Mari's name, address, and phone number.

"Lloyd and Mari Jensen; I'm looking for them. What is your connection to them, Mr. Arai?"

"Daughter and son-in-law."

"Well, where might they be? They were expected here this morning. In fact, about an hour ago."

Mas hesitated. He knew by the tone of the detective's voice that both Lloyd and Mari were under suspicion.

"They comin', they comin'. Problems with their kid. Their son, Takeo."

"Well, I called their house, and no answer. Cell phone, same thing."

Mas licked his lips. It was so damn cold in this Brooklyn place.

"I don't want you going anywhere, Mr. Arai. You just stay put here for a while."

Mas had to warm up his joints, so he went into the house through the back door. There was a small room with a photocopy machine and shelves holding office supplies, most likely once a bedroom for the servants. Then a large tiled kitchen and, beyond that, an open living room with bright-colored paintings on the wall. At a long table sat Becca, who had been crying so hard that half circles of black makeup shadowed her eyes. A man in his mid-thirties was pacing the hardwood floors. "I told him that this project would only mean trouble. I told him, I told him. Now he's fallen off the bridge and killed himself."

"We don't know that, Phillip. He was covered in trash. Somebody buried him. Probably the same people who were vandalizing the garden."

Phillip's face turned a chalky white. He suddenly noticed that Mas was in the room. "Who's this guy?"

"Phillip, this is Mr. Arai, Mari's father. Mr. Arai, this is my brother, Phillip."

"What's he doing here?"

"He's come to help on the garden. To make sure that it's ready by May."

"Well, there won't be any opening." Phillip finally looked

straight at Mas, who made note of the familiar steel gray eyes. "So we won't be needing your services, Mr. Arai, or Lloyd's."

"You don't know that, Phillip. The garden is part of the foundation, and it's the foundation's decision to make."

"Well, we're two of the five board members, not to mention Dad, and he's not around to say one way or the other."

"And I'm not for canceling anything. This was K-*san*'s dream. And I'm not going to let him down, especially now." Becca began to cry again, and Mas was amazed that more tears could come out of her swollen eyes.

Phillip gripped Becca's shoulder and glared at Mas. "Can you please give us some privacy?"

Before Mas could explain that he had been ordered by Detective Ghigo to stay put, Phillip practically pushed him out of the living room and then the kitchen and laundry room. Before Mas knew it, he was outside behind the closed back door.

Mas sat on the cement steps and sucked on another cigarette. The coldness from the stairs soaked through his jeans into his *oshiri*, but he didn't care. He blew out smoke and was grateful for the quiet, aside from the steady hum of cars on the street. Detective Ghigo was back inside the house, questioning Kazzy's two children. Where the hell were Mari and Lloyd? This didn't look good, them disappearing and a dead man in Lloyd's place of work. Mas didn't know what kind of relationship Kazzy had with Lloyd and Mari, but knowing how his daughter felt about authority figures, it couldn't have been too good. And where was the wife? Becca and Phillip acted like a pair of siblings who seemed unanchored to each other. Mas had a hunch that their mother was already dead—without the mother, the family was never the same.

Before Mas could start on his third cigarette, a young *hakujin* man came through the back gate. He was dressed in a black suit and black tie, but he was no businessman. First of all, he wore tennis shoes—the modern kind, with bright-red wafflelike soles and silly white swoops sewn into the leather. To top it off, his hair was whipped into tiny cones that dangled like baby sea eels stuck in a piece of coral.

"Hey," the man said to him.

Mas just grunted back. He wasn't going to waste any extra energy to say "hallo" to someone who was going to "hey" him.

"Got an extra smoke?"

Mas studied the man. He wasn't homeless; some kind of working stiff. Mas held out his Marlboro package.

"Thanks." The man slipped a cigarette into his mouth and returned the package to Mas. He flipped open a shiny metal lighter and leaned the cigarette into the flame. After a few puffs, the man attempted to make some conversation. "I've never seen you before."

Well, never seen you before either, Mas thought. He had little patience for small talk, but here he had little choice. "Help wiz garden."

"Oh, yeah? Were you here when they found—"

Mas nodded his head.

"No kiddin'. Right over there?" The man pointed his cigarette to the empty pond, the yellow police ribbon stretched across from the bamboo to a broken-down cherry blossom tree.

Mas nodded.

"Shit, gives me the creeps. I guess the police want you to hang around."

Mas exhaled smoke from his nostrils. "You knowsu him— Kazzy?"

"Yeah, real nice guy. He lives in Manhattan on the Upper West Side, but he seemed to hang out here the most. Anytime I gave him a ride, he always gave me a good tip. Twenty dollars, even, for taking him a couple of blocks." The man extended his hand. He wore ragged knit gloves with the tips of the fingers cut off. "I'm J-E. Miss Waxley's driver."

"Jay," Mas repeated, not bothering to shake the man's gloved hand or introduce himself.

"No, no. Jay-Ee. The letter J, hyphen, then E. J-E."

Mas paid little attention to the driver's detailed instructions on how to spell his name. What did he care? "Your boss live ova here?" Mas gestured toward the Waxley House.

J-E shook his head, causing his twisted tufts of hair to tremble. "Nobody lives there now. Just offices. Used to be Miss Waxley's father's place way back when, though. Miss Waxley's here because she's a member of the foundation board. By the way, how's Becca taking it?"

Mas shrugged his shoulders. He didn't know the daughter that well, but from the looks of it, her response was not good.

"I call her 'sweet,' her brother 'sour.' Have you met the brother?"

Mas nodded.

"He thinks that he's all that, you know. Conceited bastard. He thinks that he's the only one who knows what's going on. Becca and the rest of us are fools, he thinks."

Mas didn't care to listen to family gossip. He brought the conversation back to the garden. "Somebody must be out to get dis Kazzy. Or at least his garden."

"Well, he's a rich guy. Must have had his share of enemies. But the garden, what would anyone have against that? Doesn't hurt anyone, you know?"

The back gate to the garden swung open and slammed shut. A bald *hakujin* man in an oversized sweater walked over to the stairs, his legs spread wide and his elbows out, as if he were challenging them to a gunfight at high noon. "Is that your damn Cadillac parked outside my house again?"

"Hey, it's a free country. The street is public property," said J-E.

"I'm expecting a special delivery today. I need the street clear today for my delivery guys."

"Well, that's not my problem. You don't own the street."

The bald man's face flushed red, his head now a distressed lightbulb. "You move your damn car, or else I'll be telling Miss Waxley to do it."

J-E rose, dropped his still-smoking cigarette on a step, and swore under his breath. "Asshole. Makin' trouble all the time. Wouldn't surprise me if he offed Kazzy himself."

Crushing the cigarette with his waffle sole, he looked apologetically at Mas. "I'll catch you later, man."

Mas nodded back. He knew the sting of *urusai* neighbors complaining about the volume of a gas blower or lawn mower. The thing was, they had a job to do, and nothing was going to happen in America without some kind of inconvenience to somebody.

The driver never returned, but two other people came through the back gate a few minutes later. *Hakujin* men, again in fancy suits. One was short, almost Mas's height, in a brown suit and an orange tie the color of a sea urchin's guts. Even the front of the man's reddish brown hair was splayed out like the spikes of a sea urchin. The other man was taller, with a solid body like a mini sumo wrestler's. His gray pin-striped suit seemed a little tight on him, as if he had recently gained weight or muscle.

"Oh my God, look at that." The sea urchin pointed to the yellow police tape fluttering in the breeze across the pond.

"The last resting place of Kazzy Ouchi." The sumo wrestler spit on the concrete. It was so cold out that Mas noticed the man's spit came out slow and even seemed to harden right there on the cement walkway. "Good riddance."

"This isn't going to mean the end of the garden, right?" The sea urchin's voice went up an octave higher.

"No. Don't worry about it, Penn."

The men noticed Mas for the first time. Examining Mas's brown, leathery face and worn jeans, they must have figured that he was no threat to them. "Are Becca and Phillip inside?"

Mas nodded. "Wiz police."

The men exchanged glances. They didn't seem too eager to enter, but with Mas sitting out on the stairs as a witness, they didn't have much choice.

Finally, after about forty-five minutes, the back door opened again. It was Detective Ghigo, his tie loosened and eyes bloodshot. "Okay, Mr. Arai, we're ready for you."

Mas followed Ghigo through the dining room into the living room. A gloomy gray light from the large picture window in the front cast a pall over the surroundings. On the large couch sat the son-in-law, wearing the same work clothes as yesterday, and Mari, carrying the baby. They must have come through the front door, thought Mas, grateful that everyone was back together, safe and sound. Another older woman, a *hakujin* with silver hair piled on top of her head, sat in a high-backed armchair. Miss Waxley, the driver's boss, Mas figured. Both the sea urchin and sumo wrestler were standing awkwardly next to the picture window.

"This is your father, is that correct?" Ghigo asked, pulling at Mas's coat as if he were a piece of old furniture found in the trash.

Mari glanced down at the Oriental rug in the middle of the room and then lifted her head toward Mas. She had gotten much thinner; her face was now angular, much like during her teenage years. But she had also aged—her eyes had lost all their sharpness, and her skin was as sallow as raw fish that had been left out too long. Her hair had been clipped short like a boy's, and poking out from the top of her head were quite a number of gray strands.

Mari licked her lips. "Yes, he's my father," she said.

"Well, your father verified your story. That you were at home taking care of the baby this morning."

Takeo was sleeping in Mari's arms. His face was no longer so red as in his earlier photograph, and even with his eyes closed, he somehow looked more Asian.

"So we can go?" asked Lloyd.

"Yes." Detective Ghigo nodded. "You all can go. But don't be planning any trips to California."

As Lloyd went to retrieve a baby stroller left in the hallway, Mas patted down his coat pockets. Empty. "Gloves, forgot my gloves," he told the son-in-law. Mas went through the back door, and sure enough, he found the gloves on the stairs. What a sonafugun mess, thought Mas, taking one last survey of the garden. He expected to see the pure whiteness of the gardenia left in the middle of the dirt path. But the path was completely empty, as if it had been swept clean.

❖ ❖ ❖

"I think they are going to close down the whole project, the garden and the museum," Lloyd said. Mari pushed the stroller, one of these elaborate kinds with patterned cushions and even a holder for drinks.

"What do you expect? Kazzy's dead." Mari bent down to adjust the blanket over Takeo. He was starting to fuss, making hiccupping noises. Mari then noticed Mas at her side. "It's a real screwed-up situation," she said to no one in particular, followed by a couple of double-dose bad words.

Mas hated to hear his daughter curse, much less in front of the baby (who knew what he could absorb?), but it wasn't anything new to him. Ever since she had moved to New York for school, it seemed that the East Coast had coarsened her, stripped her of any good manners learned from their detached single house in Altadena.

A large truck was parked outside the neighbor's home, a two-story white building with columns. The back of the truck was open, revealing some fancy wooden furniture. The man with the lightbulb-shaped head was now shouting instructions to some deliverymen who were raising a load ramp from the back of the truck.

When the neighbor spied Lloyd and Mari, he switched his focus to them. "I can't have all these cars here," he told them. "Miss Waxley's Cadillac was parked outside my place again."

"Dammit, Howard," Lloyd said. "Kazzy's dead."

The neighbor didn't register any emotion. "I know, I know. I've already spoken to the police. I'm the one who called them when I heard a gun go off at nine last night. They couldn't find a thing wrong; they didn't take my call seriously, I guess. But all this ruckus proves what I've been saying: that garden and museum thing has no place in this neighborhood. Take it over to downtown Brooklyn, or Manhattan. But not here."

Mari looked like she was going to verbally slash the neighbor, but Lloyd pushed her forward. "C'mon, Mari. We've had enough excitement over the past twenty-four hours. Just let it go."

They made it a few doors down until Mari apparently couldn't hold it in any longer. "He's a damn racist," she muttered, tightening her grip around the stroller's handlebar.

"He's not against other races; he's just against everyone. A nondiscriminatory hater." Lloyd was trying to tell a joke, Mas figured, but it wasn't registering with either Mas or Mari.

They turned the corner and walked down Flatbush Avenue, past coffee shops smelling of bacon grease and syrup, laundries with stacks of thin brown-paper packages in the window, and bakeries offering pastry cones filled with light-pink cream. Mas could feel Mari's anger now redirecting from the neighbor to her father, and could almost hear his daughter's thoughts. *Why did I ask him to come? I didn't want him over here in the first place, and now see what has happened.*

Once they were back in the underground apartment, Mari and Lloyd took Takeo into the bedroom and closed the door behind them. Mas, meanwhile, folded up the futon and blanket and placed them in a wicker chair by the fireplace in the living room. As he fumbled to take his cigarettes out of his pocket, Mas noticed that his hands were shaking. Even though Kazzy had been a stranger, it had been a shock to see the dead man's face. That was the strange thing: both Mari and Lloyd had known the man well, and they didn't seem that sad at all.

Mari was hard to predict when it came to emotions. During Chizuko's funeral at a mortuary in Little Tokyo, Mari wore sunglasses that would occasionally slip down her small nose. At first Mas thought that her pride was taking hold, her reluctance to let people see her weak and vulnerable. But as mourners passed by Chizuko's casket, Mas got a good sideways glance at his daughter's profile. Her eyes were clear and dry, not a speck of any kind of weepiness. Mas realized then that the dark glasses were to hide her lack of emotion, not her excess of it.

Mas had wanted the funeral banquet to be at Far East Café, only about six blocks away from the mortuary, but Mari opted for the chop suey house in Monterey Park, a suburb east of downtown Los Angeles. "More people live out there," she announced. "And there's plenty of parking." End of discussion.

Mas and his daughter had been seated at one of the round tables next to each other, but most of the time Mari was out of her chair. During one particularly long absence, Mas got up to look for her and thought he saw her by the cash register, arguing with one of the waiters. He was then waylaid by some family friends who spent a full useless fifteen minutes telling him what a saint Chizuko had been, how strong she was during her radiation and chemotherapy treatments.

Mas finally found Mari outside in the parking lot, where she was leaning against the yellow brick wall, an unfiltered cigarette in her hands. Her dark glasses were off her face, and tears watered down her cheeks.

"What happen?"

"They ran out of the damn *pakkai*."

"Itsu *orai*." Who cared about missing out on a serving of sweet and sour pork after seven other courses?

"It was Mom's favorite," she said.

But Mom not here, Mas was about to say, then stopped himself.

"It was mine, too." Mari pushed up her dark glasses and went back into the restaurant.

Mas hadn't seen Mari many times since then. He had given her all of Chizuko's jewelry—the wedding ring, the string of pearls from Hiroshima, and even the cheap stuff she had received from customers when she began cleaning houses after Mari started school. Mari had taken all of that, as well as some old black-and-white photographs and Chizuko's Japanese hymnal from her days as a schoolgirl in Hiroshima. Mas didn't understand why she wanted the black hymnal, since Mari couldn't really read Japanese well and, as far as he knew, had quit going to church. But that was all part of the mystery called Mari Arai. Now Mari Jensen.

Lloyd came out of the bedroom first. "I'm going to get some Thai food," he announced, grabbing his keys from the kitchen table. His voice sounded funny, and Mas knew that both he and Mari had been talking about him.

"I go wiz you."

"No, it's okay, Mr. Arai. Really. I think Mari wants to talk to you." The son-in-law looked dog-tired. His hair was tied back in a ponytail, and both the sides of his face and chin showed a healthy crop of golden beard stubble.

"I pay, at least." Mas reached down for his wallet. Again, Lloyd shook his head.

"No, Mr. Arai, it's fine." He went to the door and stopped as if he wanted to say something more. But he pushed forward, locking the gate behind him. Through the small barred window, Mas watched Lloyd's work boots reach ground level and then disappear toward the street.

The living room became progressively darker, but instead of turning on the lamps, Mas folded his hands together and sat back on the couch. He left the cigarettes on the coffee table. No sense smoking in a sick baby's house.

After some time, fluorescent light washed over the room. Mari had opened the bedroom door. "He's finally asleep," she said. Mas was surprised that Takeo could rest with so much light. She closed the door softly and turned on the kitchen light. She brought down an old aluminum cookie tin from one of the shelves, and after she pried it open with her fingernails, Mas realized that it was an *okome* canister, which held their daily supply of rice. As Mari began measuring cupfuls of rice into a rice cooker, Mas finally said, "I dunno your baby's sick."

"Yeah, I should have told you. But it was too hard to explain over the phone." Mari closed the tin and returned it to a shelf.

Mas wondered where his daughter had wandered to last night. He knew that she had inherited his personality: flashes of explosive anger and fear, a need to escape for miles and miles. In Mas's case, he would drive away in his Ford pickup. Mari, on the other hand, had to rely on her legs and public transportation.

She took a deep breath, as if she were getting ready to go underwater. "I thought about all the things I would tell you when you got here. What's been going on with me over the past few years. How I've been working on myself. Trying to be happier, becoming less angry. But on the day you arrived, I realized that this whole thing was a mistake. Seeing you was too soon. I shouldn't have called you, asked you to come all the way over here from L.A."

There was a hush over the apartment. There would be no turning back from whatever would come next.

"I can't tell you how wonderful it's been since Takeo was born. It's like the whole world's a little bit brighter, better. I never knew what my girlfriends with kids were talking about. All I saw were the inconveniences, the messes. Runny noses, crying, wet pants. No vacations, no career, no money. But the sacrifices have been worth it. Really."

Baby changes everything, Mas wanted to say, but thought better of it.

"I've been rethinking everything. You, Mom. What it took to raise me. I understand how hard it is."

Mas blinked hard. What was his daughter trying to tell him?

Mari turned on the faucet to wash the rice. "Sometimes I feel like walking away. I do. From Lloyd and the garden. From New York. And sometimes even Takeo."

She swished the grains of rice in the pot. "I even blamed myself for overworking while I was pregnant. Maybe that's why he has so many health problems."

Or maybe it's me, thought Mas. The legacy of the Bomb pumping through his body, to Mari's, and now the grandson's.

"I don't want to pass on my problems to Takeo. Keep him from knowing you because I don't. But now with all of us together, I realize that it's too much."

Mas's heart began to drop, from the base of his throat down to his stomach.

"I thought that I could handle it. But I don't think I can, Dad." Mari placed the pot in the rice cooker.

"I go." Mas had heard enough.

"Maybe it's because too much is going on. And now with Kazzy—"

"I go," Mas repeated. He didn't want to hear her excuses.

Mari nodded. "I thought that you'd understand," she said. She put the lid on the pot, pressed a button on the rice cooker, and then disappeared back into the lighted bedroom.

✣ ✣ ✣

It wasn't hard to pack his things. He hadn't changed his clothes or even bothered to take a shower during his first twenty-four hours in New York. His yellow Samsonite, in fact, was in the same spot where he had left it. Mas couldn't stand being in that underground apartment for another minute, and went to take a walk around the neighborhood.

He went back to the first stranger he had spoken to in New York. The operator of the small grocery store across the street.

Ever since Mas had gotten all his rotted teeth pulled out to make room for his ill-fitting dentures, he never could properly get the hang of chewing gum again. Tonight he didn't care. He placed a large package of Wrigley's Juicy Fruit gum on the counter. He figured that he could at least suck the sugar out of three sticks at one time.

"Marlboro?" This time it was just the old man.

Mas shook his head. "Nah, just dis. Izu go back to Los Angeles." He didn't know why he was offering any personal information, but there was no one else—not Tug, not Haruo—to talk to.

"Short trip," the shopkeeper said. "*Mijikai sugiru.*"

Mas widened his eyes. He shouldn't have been surprised. The man was most likely Korean and old enough to have been there when the Japanese had forced their language on those they conquered.

"Yah, too short, but whatcha gonna do?" Mas shrugged his shoulders. In these situations, Mas felt awkward speaking Japanese and opted to use English instead. Here the Japanese language seemed bitter and sad, remnants of a weapon that had been once used to wipe out a people's identity.

The shopkeeper laughed. "Yah, what you gonna do?"

❖ ❖ ❖

The minute Mas reentered the apartment, he knew something was wrong. Takeo was wailing, and the door to the bedroom was wide open.

"They said they'll be here in five minutes," said Lloyd, placing the telephone back on its cradle on the kitchen wall. Two large bags, bursting with the smell of strong spices, had been left on the counter. Instead of whetting his appetite, they made Mas feel like throwing up.

Lloyd grabbed his leather jacket from a hook on the wall. "We're going to take Takeo to the hospital," he explained to Mas.

Mari brought out the baby from the bedroom. He was wearing a knit cap and blue jacket, and who knows how many layers of clothing underneath that. Takeo's jacket arms were so stuffed that they poked out from his body like the plastic legs of an overturned toy animal.

Lloyd noticed, too. "He's already burning up, Mari. Don't you think he's wearing too much?"

"It's cold out there. I don't want him to get worse."

They hurried back and forth, packing blankets, diapers, and bottles into nylon bags, when a car honked out front.

"The cab's here." Lloyd, who stayed back to lock the door and the gate, seemed surprised to see Mas follow Mari outside.

At the top of the stairs to the adjoining apartment stood a middle-aged *hakujin* woman wearing a long sweater decorated with leaping deer. "Is the baby all right?"

"He has a high fever; we're taking him to the hospital." Mari bounced Takeo in her arms.

"Call me if you need anything."

"You'll be the first one we call, Mrs. Knudsen."

The cabdriver jumped out of the taxi to open the door for Mari and the baby. Mas was also ready to get inside, but as he leaned into the car, he met Mari's icy stare.

"Let him come, Mari," Lloyd said.

She said nothing, and then moved far enough down the backseat to allow a place for Mas.

The hospital was all brick and about eight stories tall. It reminded Mas of an old-fashioned hotel, like the Biltmore back in downtown Los Angeles, more than any kind of medical facility. Even the admitting area resembled a hotel lobby, with shiny tile floors, an expansive counter, and a couple of plastic plants on both sides. The emergency room, however, was nothing unusual, aside from the fact that they had a special section for children. The nurses admitted Takeo in no time flat, but told Mari that she would have to go to the waiting room with Lloyd and Mas on the third floor.

In the elevator, Mari flinched when Lloyd tried to put his arm on her shoulder. Her bony arms were folded tightly across her chest—the upper half of her body looked like a human clothes hanger, ready to poke anyone, perhaps Mas especially, in the eye at any minute. Mas couldn't blame her. It had taken the nurse a few tries to pry Takeo away from her arms.

The third-floor waiting room also resembled a fancy hotel. Fake plants were everywhere, as if the real kind would cause deadly allergies and rashes. Mas understood the hospital's need for artificial plants. Real plants needed gardeners to take care of them, and here the priority was to make sure people, rather than ivy or ficus trees, stayed alive.

They made themselves comfortable on couches and easy chairs arranged in a square. Mas opted for one of the chairs, while Mari and Lloyd sat on different couches facing each other. Mas was grateful for his Juicy Fruit chewing gum. After offering some to Mari and Lloyd, he stuffed five pieces in his mouth at one time. In spite of the sugar intake, he dozed off for a few minutes before hearing Mari ask in a sharp tone, "What are you doing here?"

It was that detective again, Ghigo, wearing the same black jacket and badge. Pretty low class to come at a time like this, thought Mas.

"Your neighbor, Mrs. Knudsen, told me you'd be here." He took a seat on a couch next to Lloyd.

"Can't this wait, Detective? Our son's not doing so well." The more time Mas spent with the son-in-law, the more he had to admit he liked him. Lloyd was quiet for a *hakujin*, but he also knew when to speak up.

"No, Mr. Jensen, this can't wait. You see, we checked

your credit card activity, and the records show that a hotel stay was charged to your card, Mrs. Jensen. A hotel in Midtown, checkout at eight this morning. Curious that you could be in Midtown Manhattan when you told us that you all were in Park Slope."

"We had a family situation." Mari's arms remained crossed.

"Would you like to elaborate?"

"Not really. It's a private matter."

Mas sucked on his wad of gum, which now felt like a wet rag in his mouth.

"Well, I have to disagree, Mrs. Jensen. It's now a police matter."

Mari jutted out her chin. Mas knew that she was close to attack mode.

Ghigo turned his attention to Lloyd on the couch. "Hadn't you had an argument with the deceased just two days ago?"

Mari's eyebrows pinched together as she stared at Lloyd. "Who told you that?" she demanded of Ghigo.

"Never mind who told us. Is it true?"

"It was nothing out of the usual. I was just telling him that we needed to alter our business practices," said Lloyd. "We're changing into a nonprofit, and we can't operate like a private enterprise. I was just telling him we should diversify our vendors; look for different suppliers of plants, equipment, fertilizer."

"Did he want to end the project?"

"He was always saying that. But he really didn't mean it.

He just needed me to reassure him that everything was going to turn out all right."

"You really had a stake in this working out," said Ghigo.

"What the hell are you trying to say?" Mari interrupted.

"A garden that was paying for your family's health expenses."

The power of the detective's words seemed to catch Mari off guard. Her eyes misted over, and then Ghigo softened his approach.

"Listen, I got two kids myself. I know how all this can add up, a doctor's visit here, a procedure there. A person may feel like he doesn't have many choices."

"We didn't hurt Kazzy. We wouldn't want anything to happen to him," Lloyd said.

Mari took a less calm approach. "What are you suggesting? That we threw Kazzy into the pond ourselves?"

"Do you own a gun, Mrs. Jensen?"

Mari's face grew very still, and Mas knew that something was wrong.

Lloyd hesitated for a minute. "No, of course we don't own a gun." He stumbled over his words like he was walking in unknown territory when it was pitch dark.

"Well, that's good to know, because we found a gun in a trash can down the street. A nine millimeter. It's only a matter of time before ballistics matches that gun with the bullet in the victim's skull."

"Bullet? I thought that Kazzy was pushed into the pond by vandals," said Lloyd.

The missing part of his head, thought Mas.

Lloyd and Mari exchanged looks. Finally Mari swallowed and spoke. "Well, there is this one gun. It's just a prop from one of the silly slasher films I worked on as an assistant cinematographer. The propman wasn't too professional and never kept track of it.

"I just kept it as a joke. I knew that I needed to get rid of it eventually, but I stuck it in a shoe box and forgot about it. Until all this stuff was going on at the garden. I was working there, sometimes alone, at all hours. I needed to use the foundation's digital equipment, you see. We don't even have a decent television set at home."

Mas nodded. That definitely was true.

"I took the gun to work just as a precaution. It wasn't loaded, of course. I just kept it in a drawer in case I needed to scare off any vandals late at night."

"You never registered it?"

"I wasn't going to use it. Did you do a search of the edit suite inside of the house? It's on the second floor."

"No gun in there." Ghigo tapped his pen on his thigh. "Do you know what kind of gun it was?"

Mari's voice sounded as small as a mouse's squeak. "Nine millimeter, I think."

Mas spit out his gum into a flattened Juicy Fruit wrapper.

"So who else knew about the gun?"

"Well, just me, for a while. Lloyd found it about a week ago. Told me to get rid of it. But I was too busy."

"I'd like for us to go over to the precinct. To sort everything out." Ghigo stood up.

"My son," Mari said.

Ghigo studied Mari's face for a moment. "Oh, yes. How is he doing?"

Lloyd stood up, and Mas wasn't sure if he was going to challenge the detective to a fight. "Not sure yet."

"Listen, you can make it easier on both of us if you just come with me. Wouldn't want to cause a scene, you know."

An older couple sitting on a couch at the other side of the waiting room looked over. Mas didn't relish his daughter and son-in-law being taken away in handcuffs. When a family member was sick, the hospital became your new world. It would be hard enough for Mari to return to this world without everyone knowing that they were suspects in a murder investigation.

"I'll go, Mari. We have nothing to hide." Lloyd put on his jacket. "Just call me as soon as you hear something from the doctor."

Mari nodded.

"And you'd better find us a lawyer."

While Lloyd and Mari discussed more details about doctors, Mas went over to Ghigo.

"You hang on to that gardenia?"

Ghigo, a bit puzzled, peered down at Mas. "Oh, you mean that white flower. Yep, we bagged it. But then there were a lot of flowers in that garden."

"That flower not from the garden," Mas told him. "Take a look—some kind of hair in the middle."

Ghigo stared at Mas for a moment as if he didn't know

what to make of the old Japanese man. "I'll have the lab check it out," he said.

Mas nodded. Somehow he felt that the gardenia was important, but he couldn't put his finger on why.

After Lloyd gave Mari an awkward kiss on the lips, he and Detective Ghigo headed down the hallway toward the elevators. Both Mari and Mas stood and watched until the two men disappeared into the elevator going down.

"He wants me to get an attorney. How am I going to find a criminal attorney?" Mari began pushing buttons on her cell phone when a nurse passing by stopped her, pointing to a large sign showing a picture of a phone with a red diagonal line through it.

"Dammit, dammit. Nothing's going right today, Dad." Mari buried her forehead in her hands.

"No worry, Mari." Mas meant to take the phone from her, but instead felt his daughter's fingers, ice-cold and trembling. "I may knowsu someone who can help."

chapter four

G.I. Hasuike was an attorney in Los Angeles with long black and gray hair that reached down to his waist. His hair was usually tied back in a rubber band; that's why Mas hadn't noticed its length the first time he had met him.

Since that time, they had shared enough beers and sake for Mas to learn that G.I. was short for George Iwao. He was a Sansei, a third-generation Japanese American, who ran around with a pack of friends from Boyle Heights, next door to East L.A. G.I. had fought in the Vietnam War, not because of any sense of duty, but because his friends had run out of soy sauce the night before their Army physical. They had a square gallon container of Kikkoman *shoyu,* which they took turns gulping (in between swigs of rum and whiskey and puffs of who-knows-what). G.I. unfortunately had too much rum and whiskey and not enough salt from the *shoyu,* so his blood pressure test came out free and clear to go shoot some other yellow men an ocean away.

G.I. specialized in spill-and-fall cases, but he was no stranger to criminal cases, either. He told Mas that he had witnessed dozens of men killed in the jungle, so what was dealing with a few murders in the streets of L.A.?

"Where are you calling from, Mas?"

Mas, clutching Mari's cell phone, stood underneath a pine tree on the corner outside the hospital. A few pine needles fell on his shoulder as a lost bird moved on to a warmer location. "New York," he said.

"New York? Damn, Mas. You sure get around these days. What's goin' on?"

Mas tried to explain the whole scenario, from the discovery of the body to Detective Ghigo's questioning of Mari and Lloyd. "You knowzu any lawyers in New York?"

"Do they have any money? Criminal defense lawyers like to have their fee up front."

Mas blinked. He pictured the underground apartment and pitiful television set. "No, no money."

"May be hard," said G.I. "But I do have a friend connected with the Asian Legal Defense Alliance. Her name's Jeannie Yee. She's young, but can kick anybody's butt."

Mas took down the name and phone number on the visitor's sticker the hospital had given him.

After he got off the phone with G.I., Mas realized that he had forgotten to tell the lawyer that Lloyd was *hakujin*, not Asian. Either way, he still needed defense. And besides, wasn't he a member of the family?

When Mas returned to the waiting room, Mari was talking to a young dark-skinned woman in a white lab coat. She resembled Mr. Patel, one of Mas's customers in Arcadia who owned a small chain of teriyaki fast-food stands. "Thank you, Doctor, thank you," Mari said as the physician headed for a door to the hidden heart of the hospital. Mas pulled out his visitor's name tag, which had hairs of his wool sweater on the once-sticky side and the lawyer's name and phone number on the other. "Youzu call dis Jeannie girl," he told Mari. "She supposed to help you out. At least thatsu what my friend G. I. Hasuike says."

Mari accepted the name tag and her cell phone. "Takeo's fever has gone down. He's going to stay overnight for some more tests, and they're going to let me be with him." She then shifted her weight from one leg to the other. "I know Ghigo told you that you can't leave New York, and you know what, I think that it's good that you'll be around. I've been fighting off this postpartum depression, you know, feeling bad after having a baby. Sometimes I don't know what I'm saying or feeling anymore."

Mas couldn't remember if Chizuko had suffered from this postpartum sickness—it had been more than thirty years ago. But Mas was so relieved that his grandson was doing better that he began babbling promises, promises that later he wasn't sure he could keep.

The first promise was that he would check on Lloyd. But it was now getting dark, and he had no idea how to get to this Seventy-seventh Precinct. Just the number—seventy-seven—scared him, because it meant there were at least seventy-six other precincts and who knows how many dozens more. He stuffed his hands in his pockets and thought about his alternatives. He could try one of those underground trains; he saw the stations here and there marked with red and green signs. But everyone was *gasagasa;* they probably wouldn't have the time to hear the troubles of an old Kibei man. He thought about the neighbor, the middle-aged *hakujin* woman with the flowing sweater, but they had not formally met. And then there was the Korean shopkeeper, but Mas had already shared too much about himself in a short time. He couldn't impose more, or his debt would be too great. Japanese straight from Japan always said, "*Osewa ni natta*"—"I have been in your debt"—but that usually applied to little things like being bought a meal or borrowing a cordless power drill, not going to a police station to rescue a son-in-law. In cases like this, it was best to lean on someone familiar, and tonight that person had to be Tug Yamada.

Mas first went back to the underground apartment to make good on his second promise to Mari—that he get something to eat. He was practically running on empty, fueled only by bread and Nescafé. He must have looked as tired as he felt, because Mari had commented that his face seemed pale and dragged down. Mas replied that it was the weather: how could a California man survive in thirty-degree temperatures? At least Mas was hot-blooded, and not a *samugari* like Chizuko, who had always complained when the house dipped below fifty-nine degrees.

The apartment smelled of the richness of Thai food and steamed rice, which seemed to almost lift the rooms above their subterranean level. Mas first called Tug at his daughter Joy's house. No answer, but an answering machine with strange music and a female voice mewing like cat. Mas couldn't believe that Joy would have such a message (what happened to a plain "Hello and leave your name and number"?), so he hung up and called a second time. What the hell—he left a message and hoped that somehow the human cat would deliver the message to his friend.

In the meantime, Mas began his mission of getting food into his stomach. He was grateful for Mari's making of the rice. Their rice cooker wasn't one of those high-tech, streamlined kind decorated with pink flowers or tiny elephants. Instead, it was the standard of the sixties and seventies, a white one with black handles that stuck out like ears. Mas put two scoops of rice on a plate and then foraged through the paper bags of take-out food. A strange stew of vegetables covered in a sweet-smelling sauce that was the color of yellow chalk. Chicken on skewers that reminded Mas of *yakitori* barbecued on hibachis at Japanese bars. And finally, thick rice noodles that were folded like pillows in brown gravy. Mas had never had Thai food before, but tonight he ate as if there were no other.

As he was chewing on the last chicken skewer, the phone rang. It was Tug, apologizing and telling him that he was without his rental car. Mas told him everything that had transpired: from Kazzy's death to Takeo's medical setback to the appearance of Detective Ghigo at the hospital. "Needsu to get to Seventy-seven police station; check on Lloyd," Mas told Tug. They made plans to meet at the Atlantic Avenue subway station ticket booth in the northeast corner. Mas had no idea how he was going to get to the Atlantic Avenue station, much less any specific corner of it, at eight o'clock at night, no less. At this point, he would just have to go out there and try. "Snooze, you lose," his former friend Wishbone Tanaka once told him regarding an opportunity to buy a nursery. At that time, Mas lost a business deal; but this time, he could lose much more.

Mas had put his old long underwear from his fishing and camping days on underneath his wool sweater and nylon jacket, but the blast of cold air still seemed to soak through the layers of clothing into his bones. He adjusted his Dodgers cap, but that was hardly any help in retaining warmth. At least it would disguise his age; he figured looking seventy years old would attract lazy thieves seeking an easy target.

On his subway map he had already traced the route of

the green line with the edge of his dirty index finger. Unfortunately, the Atlantic Avenue stop was a good seven blocks away from the underground apartment. Seven blocks during a winter day in L.A. would be nothing, but this was New York City at night. Luckily the path was a straight one along Flatbush Avenue, so Mas figured that at least there was no danger of getting lost if he went in the right direction.

He traveled alongside the moving wall of cars until he came to a gated area next to a sporting goods store. The gate was open, and an overhead light from the side of the building shone on a man digging around a small pond. The Teddy Bear Garden that Tug had talked about, Mas remembered. Mas couldn't help but walk a few steps into the dirt.

"Well, hello—" A balding *hakujin* man turned from his shoveling job. Mas noticed a flat of daffodils in square plastic planters. The man didn't seem afraid that a stranger had invaded his space, and Mas wondered if the night gardener might be a little *kuru-kuru-pa*. "Got kind of behind from the rain last weekend," the man said. "Wanted to at least get the daffodils going."

From what Mas could tell, the garden would look pretty good in late spring. But right now, the bare trees and planted seedlings only held a promise of what could be.

"Are you interested in gardening?" the man asked.

Mas didn't know how to answer. He had been doing it for more than forty years, but he honestly didn't know how interested he was in it. "Izu a gardener," he chose to respond. "In California."

"Wonderful, that's just wonderful." The man went to a folding chair and pulled a piece of paper from a stack that was held in place by a round polished rock. "We're having a barbecue here in a couple of weeks for anyone who wants to join us. We would love to have you."

"Izu be out of here by then." Mas glanced at the colored flyer, which was printed in English on one side and Spanish on the other.

The bald man looked sincerely disappointed. "That's too bad," he said. "But if you're around, please come."

As Mas left the gated garden, he just had to shake his head. He had had contact with plenty of strange *hakujin* in California, but the ones in Park Slope might even top them. He almost stopped by a wire garbage can to toss the flyer, but had second thoughts and stuffed it in his jeans pocket instead.

✣ ✣ ✣

Mas should have been warned about the size of the Atlantic Avenue station by the long line of letters and numbers encased in circles and diamonds on the sign in front of the station's stairs. There was an M, N, two Qs, R, W, 2, 5, and 4, their desired train line, in a green circle. As Mas descended the steps, he hung on to the metal railing, his left shoulder and elbow banging into passersby, plastic bags, and briefcases. The railing was cold and sticky, yet the last thing he wanted was to tumble down, break his neck, and be squashed by commuters.

When he got to the bottom of the cement stairs, Mas

was hit with the sour and acidic smell of *shikko* and attempted to breathe out of his mouth. It was the same in every big city: secret corners always attracted secret behavior. He stumbled toward the open lobby, where men and women swiped cards alongside long machines and rushed in and out of turnstiles. How was Mas going to find Tug in the chaos?

Then Mas remembered the mention of the ticket booth. Sure enough, against the wall was a box the size of two phone booths. Inside was a black man dressed in a blue uniform. Mas shuddered to think about being trapped under the street in such a small space.

"Mas, old man." A familiar voice called out to him. Tug walked through a revolving door made of metal posts like those found at the exit of Disneyland. "Thank God I found you. You're kind of easy to miss."

Tug, on the other hand, was not. His hair, which had a wave to it, was frizzier than usual. His white beard glowed underneath the fluorescent lights. Upon seeing his friend, Mas felt the knot in his stomach loosen. Tug was a few years older than Mas, but his mind was still sharp. Sometimes he forgot trivial details—the name of an old high school classmate, for example—but as an ex–government worker, Tug fully understood how to work the system. When their daughters were still young, the two families occasionally vacationed together. Those were the only times the Arais stayed at hotels fancier than Motel 6 or Travelodge. From Tug, Mas learned about AAA and the automobile club's hotel rating system. Tug and Lil never laid their heads on a bed in a room ranked less than two diamonds, while Mas and Chizuko couldn't even find their regular discount spots in the AAA book at all.

Tug was not a New York man, but he could navigate the city a hell of a lot better than Mas. "We've got to get you a MetroCard." Tug headed for the ticket booth, pulling out his wallet from his front pocket. "This will last you the whole week."

Before Mas could protest, Tug was at the window, placing a twenty-dollar bill through a hole in what looked like bulletproof glass. Why was everyone trying to make Mas commit to staying in the city longer?

Tug gave Mas a plastic ticket and gestured toward the fast-moving line of people going through turnstiles. "You place the ticket here," said Tug, swiping the ticket in an opening like those for credit cards at grocery stores. He pushed his way forward through a turnstile. "You go now, Mas."

Someone pushed Mas from behind, cursed, and then quickly moved to the next line. Mas felt his head grow hot as he carefully nudged the ticket through the slot and then awkwardly stepped forward, the metal post of the turnstile pressing against his lower ribs.

"You can use this card on all the other lines, Mas. You'll find it quite handy." Tug pushed Mas toward another section of the terminal, and Mas found himself descending stairs again.

Mas had seen images of modern subway stations on Japanese soap operas broadcast on Sunday nights in L.A., but he had never stepped foot in one. The trains back in

Hiroshima, before the Bomb, were powered the old-fashioned way: with coal. L.A. had its own so-called train system, but no gardener would have any use for that. As for Mas, he had his beloved 1956 Ford truck, which was a lot lighter these days after having been ravaged by a thief and a looter. But it still managed to get the job done, which was more than he could say for some modern-day vans and pickup trucks.

The train platform was plain concrete, stained by layers of spilled food. Down below, on the tracks, were remnants of people's lives. Dividing the "Manhattan-bound" passengers from the "Brooklyn-bound" were a few benches and advertisements about preventing disease. More people seemed to be on Tug and Mas's side, and Mas figured out that the ride to the Seventy-seventh Precinct would not be a pleasant one. The train car going in the opposite direction came and went, and then finally one on their side rumbled through the connecting tunnel and screeched to a stop in front of the platform. The car was a magnet for the waiting passengers, who all moved to the edge of a yellow-painted line toward one of the series of doors. Tug guided him, and as the doors whooshed open, Mas felt the uncomfortable closeness of people on all sides of him. Travelers spilled out of the train car as if they had been released from a dam. Mas and Tug's crowd, on the other hand, pushed forward, moving against the tide.

Once inside, Mas noticed that all the seats facing the center were occupied. Tug reached up for a metal bar parallel to the length of the car's ceiling, while Mas had to grasp on to the only stationary thing that he could reach—a vertical pole like those in fire stations. The doors slid shut, the train jerked forward, and Mas felt his body sway back and forth like a dead perch on a fishing line.

As the doors opened and closed at the next station, the crowd changed slightly with the subtraction of some passengers and the addition of others. A teenager in a basketball jersey, with a boom box blasting rhythms, came and went, replaced by another young man in a black hat, short, scraggly beard, and a set of two long ringlets—Mari used to wear her hair in similar curlicues when she was young. A group of black women, all friends, stood in one corner, their voices dipping up and down in a cadence that Mas was unfamiliar with. Many of the passengers, from the boy in the knit cap to the old lady in loose panty hose, sat reading books. Chizuko would have been impressed with this, thought Mas, who was a little impressed himself.

At the next stop, a muffled voice came on over the intercom. Mas couldn't make out any of it, but Tug nudged Mas and they were released into a station with a sign that read Crown Heights—Utica Avenue. They made their way from the belly of the station to street level. As Mas was met by the cutting coldness, he almost missed the pressing fever from the people of the train.

They walked north along a busy boulevard crowded with music shops, grocery stores, and restaurants smelling of burnt pineapple and other tropical fruits. At each intersection, Tug and Mas waited for the Walk sign while all the other pedestrians charged ahead. Even Tug got tired of them being the odd men out, and after looking both ways, they ran across the street against the red light with the rest of the crowd.

Finally they came to a two-story rectangular building that reminded Mas of the tight and simple structures in L.A.'s Toy District, near Little Tokyo. It was made of bricks the hue of the yellow tiles in Mas's bathroom back home. And like the bathroom, black dirt had accumulated in corners, proof of pollution, hard times, and neglect.

"C'mon, Mas," said Tug. "That's the police station."

They went through the black metal doors and approached the counter, where a curly-haired woman stood behind a computer screen. Tug didn't waste any time and made his plea. "I'm Tug Yamada, and this is my friend Mas Arai. Mas's son-in-law is here, and we'd like to speak with him."

"Name?"

"Lloyd Jensen."

The woman left her post and then returned after a few minutes. "There's no Lloyd Jensen here."

Tug glanced over at Mas, who handed over Detective Ghigo's business card. "How about Detective John Ghigo?"

The woman went to speak to someone else again. "Detective Ghigo is busy right now."

Mas bit down on his dentures as Tug continued to prod in his steady, respectful way. That way not going to work here, thought Mas. Like crossing against a red light, you needed to forget about the rules, and barrel ahead.

The clerk told them to have a seat on some hard plastic chairs, but Mas opted to pace the linoleum floor instead.

Displayed on the wall in a glass case were mug shots of criminals at large. No place for Lloyd and Mari, Mas said to himself. No, that was *baka na hanashi*. Stupid talk.

As he tried not to think about his son-in-law in jail, the metal doors opened, bringing in cold air and a heavy Latino man, who Mas overheard was a pickpocket victim. One after another they came, telling stories of missing Toyotas and broken noses. They were all given papers to fill out and sign. "Then come back here again," instructed the clerk.

The pickpocket and car robbery victims had finished first; then a young Asian woman breezed in. Her hair was cut bluntly past her shoulders, as if it had been shorn by a pair of hedge clippers. She clutched a leather briefcase. "Excuse me, excuse me," she called out to the clerk. "I'm here to see Lloyd Jensen. I'm his legal counsel."

Her voice was deep and throaty like that of a woman who drank and smoked too much.

"Miss, I'm going to have to have you wait in line." The rest of the victims nodded and hooted in agreement.

"No, I will not wait in line." The girl then began to speak faster and faster, using words that Mas had never heard of. Her voice became even more guttural; she seemed to be transforming into an *oni*, one of those red demons with knobby horns in Japanese fairy tales.

Finally the clerk sighed. Apparently the attorney's incantations had worked. "I'll be right with you," she said, leaving her post once again.

The attorney then turned around, and her black eyes met Mas's. Her face immediately softened and looked nothing like a red *oni* that Mas imagined. Her skin was as smooth as *mochi*, pounded rice, and her eyes, although not that big, were bright. When she held out her hand to shake his, Mas couldn't help but take a step back. "You must be G.I.'s friend," she said. "I'm Jeannie Yee."

❖ ❖ ❖

Jeannie Yee was originally from Torrance, California, a suburb thirty miles south of downtown L.A. That's where the well-to-do Japanese moved to in the 1970s after exhausting the charms of Gardena, the working-class town next door.

She was a *hapa*, too, half-Japanese and half-Chinese. Later she would joke that her Sansei mother had mixed sticky and long rice together, half and half, to appease both sides of the family. She had gone to UCLA for her BA, and then gone on to Columbia, Mari's alma mater, for her law degree. Mas couldn't imagine this young high-tone girl being connected with G. I. Hasuike in any way, but she explained that she had received a scholarship from his professional group, the Japanese American Bar Association, years ago. And although she had lived in New York City for seven years, her heart was still in L.A.

"Damn, I've got to get back. Can't take this weather." Jeannie had taken off her black overcoat, revealing a lavender suit the color of jacaranda blossoms. She tossed her coat over one of the chairs beside her.

Tug was the one to make most of the small talk with the girl lawyer. Her father was an engineer with the city of Los Angeles; Tug had been a county health inspector. They shared a world outside of Mas's. The most Mas could do was pull her overcoat higher up on the chair so the bottom did not drag on the linoleum floor.

"So, your son-in-law, is he a *hapa*?" Jeannie finally asked Mas.

Mas shook his head. "Hunnerd percent *hakujin*. Dat mean you won't help him?"

"Well, we don't discriminate," said Jeannie, "although we can't take every case. But since you know G.I., I'll take him on. We charge a sliding scale based on income."

"Next-to-nuttin' income, I think."

"Well, then," said Jeannie. "You've probably come to the right place."

Finally, the clerk called Jeannie's name and the lawyer was allowed through a door beside the counter.

"Cute girl," Tug said after Jeannie had left. "Said she was named after that TV show in the sixties, remember, the one with the blond genie in the bottle."

Mas, whose television tastes tended toward Westerns and detective stories, merely shrugged his shoulders and made himself comfortable in the seat Jeannie had abandoned. He folded his arms and closed his eyes. He couldn't block out the noises and murmurs of crime and tragedy, but at least he could escape seeing it for a few moments.

Finally, Tug nudged his elbow. "They're back," he said.

Lloyd had been the first to appear from the door next to the counter. Remnants of a frown still remained on his forehead. He seemed so happy to see Mas that he almost bent down to hug him; he caught himself, however, and placed his hand on Mas's shoulder instead. "Didn't know you had connections with defense lawyers," he said.

Mas bit down on his lower lip. This was one connection that he preferred not to have. But his need for criminal defense lawyers only seemed to deepen, as if he had stepped into a secret sinkhole that had no bottom.

The door banged open again. "Ghigo, I really expected better of you," said the girl lawyer, whose overcoat was now folded over her arm.

Detective Ghigo was right behind her. "Jeannie, I'm telling you, we were just having a conversation."

"Give me a break," Jeannie snapped back. "You were trying to intimidate him. He has a right to representation."

Even after he had stopped talking, the detective's mouth was still open halfway. In Mas's line of work, he had seen his share of stray dogs go after penned ones day after day. It was obvious that this stray, Detective Ghigo, had sniffed Jeannie before and wanted something more.

Mas stood next to Jeannie. "We gotsu to go," he said. Tug nodded behind them in agreement.

"Mr. Arai." Ghigo put on a fake smile. "Good to see you again."

Mas grunted. He waited until Lloyd, Tug, and Jeannie were safely out the door before he turned to leave himself.

"Oh, Mr. Arai," Ghigo called out, "about that flower—"

Mas stopped midstep and waited.

"Just got that lab result. The hair wasn't human. Animal hair, most likely a deer's. Don't figure a deer shot a bullet through Mr. Ouchi's head, do you?"

chapter five

Mas never understood why people wanted to make a fool out of him. In Japanese, there were two types of fools: *bakatare* and *aho*. You called someone a *bakatare* if he forgot to turn off the stove so that the teakettle became bone-dry and its bottom burnt black. The same went for using an edger much too close to the sidewalk and dulling the blade.

But *aho* was different. You were an *aho* when a gas blower salesman told you a fancy upgrade was quiet as a mouse, and you believed him, only to find out the expensive upgrade was not only loud but a piece of junk, too. Sometimes you couldn't help being *bakatare*, but there was no excuse for being an *aho*.

Detective Ghigo's announcement about the deer hair was supposed to make Mas feel like an *aho*. In that sense, the detective had succeeded. Mas didn't know why he had told the detective to take a second look. It had probably wasted some valuable time in finding clues to Kazzy's real killer.

"That Detective Ghigo probably thinkin' I makin' him run around for no reason," Mas said to Haruo on the phone that night.

"No worry, Mas. You always gotsu good hunches."

"I tellin' you, Haruo, that gardenia a giant one. Neva saw nutin' so big."

For once, Haruo didn't interrupt, and let his friend go on until he ran out of gas.

While Mas slept in the underground apartment that night, he dreamt of deer grazing in a lush green valley and then the valley on fire, the deer ablaze.

Both Mari and Lloyd were staying at the hospital, so Mas found himself on his own again the following morning. He planned to check on the cherry blossom trees after eating a bowlful of dry shredded wheat. There was no real milk in the refrigerator except for a carton of the soy kind. Mas liked tofu in his miso soup, but stopped short of putting milked soybeans in his breakfast cereal.

The phone rang, and Mas picked it up, expecting to hear either Haruo's or Mari's voice. But instead it was a *hakujin* man with a nasal accent. "Hello, is this the Jensen residence? I'd like to talk with Lloyd Jensen."

"Heezu not here."

"How about Mari Jensen?"

"Sheezu not here." Mas waited for the caller to identify himself and leave a message.

"This is Jerome Kroner with the *New York Post*. I really need to speak with one of them for a follow-up story I'm writing on the death of Kazzy Ouchi."

"They not here, *orai*? They can't talk to nobody," said Mas, slamming the phone. Mas never thought much of reporters. He was used to scaring them away from his TV star customer's property in Pasadena. These journalists were the type to lie, beg, and cheat to snap a photograph of an actor getting into his hot tub or picking up his mail. One time a reporter even offered Mas some cash to tell him who was staying overnight at his customer's house. "Is it a woman? Or a man?"

About ten minutes later, the phone began ringing again. Mas had the good sense not to answer, but listened as the machine recorded the message. This time it was a woman with the *New York Times*. Why was every *baka na* reporter calling now? What had that Jerome Kroner said, some kind of follow-up? That meant there was something to follow up from.

No. It couldn't be. But maybe. Mas got dressed and hurried across the street to the newsstand next to the greengrocer. *Post*, *Post*. Mas looked among the newspapers, but only saw the *New York Times*, *Wall Street Journal*. "You gotta *Post*?" he asked a heavyset black man in an apron.

"Right here." The newsstand man pressed his dirty fingernail against a tabloid right in front of Mas's face on the counter.

This a newspaper? Mas wondered. But he laid down a few coins anyway. Resting against a wall, Mas pulled at the pages as if he were shucking corn in the fields. Nothing, nothing. And then on page eight, a grainy photo of the empty pond, and then a story taking up a quarter of a page. SILK TYCOON KILLED IN GARDEN, the headline read with a smaller headline underneath, JAPANESE COMMUNITY FEARS HATE CRIME.

Hate crime? Mas thought. Of course, the killer must have hated Kazzy, but it might not have anything to do with him being half-Japanese.

The article reported the facts: Kazuhiko "Kazzy" Ouchi dead at age eighty. Believed to have suffered a gunshot wound. There was no mention of the gun found in the trash can; the police must still be figuring if it was linked to the shooting.

Then some background on Kazzy: he was born in the Waxley House, the only son of a Japanese gardener and an Irish maid. It went on to say that he was a self-made millionaire, having learned the rag trade in the Garment District as a young teenager. Founder and president of Ouchi Silk, Inc. Survived by a son, Phillip Hirokazu Ouchi, senior vice president of Ouchi Silk, and a daughter, Rebecca Emiko Ouchi, secretary of the Ouchi Foundation.

Mas read slowly, tracing each sentence with the tip of his index finger. Then came the paragraph:

> The Waxley House's director of landscaping, Lloyd Jensen, was unavailable for comment and, according to a source, was being questioned by police.

Sonafugun, thought Mas. The news was out. No wonder all these reporters were calling the underground apartment.

The article didn't end there. It mentioned that a homeowners' group had organized against the planned Waxley House Garden and Museum, led by a man named Howard Foster. Must be the neighbor, Mas figured.

> Members of New York City's Japanese community expressed concern that the killing could be linked to a recent spate of vandalism to the garden. "There's been animosity toward the Japanese for decades," stated Eddie "Elk" Mamiya, at the New York Japanese American Social Service Center. "It wouldn't surprise me if Mr. Ouchi's death was indeed a hate crime."

Mas tore out the story and smashed the rest of the paper in a trash can. He needed, more than ever, to get back to trees and plants. As he approached the Waxley House, Mas noticed that the sycamore tree out front seemed diseased, its distinctive patchwork bark funny-looking in some places. Mas was partial to sycamores, since many of the tall, giraffelike trees graced his neighbor's yard in Altadena. Every winter, the sycamores would shed their huge leaves shaped like giant outstretched hands. Mari had loved those leaves and collected them in scrapbooks and even played in piles of them, L.A.'s version of snowdrifts. Even though they were a hassle to rake, Mas couldn't bear to curse them.

Mas walked over to a branch, touching an area that seemed to sink in. Piece by piece, like shedding different shades of old green and brown paint, he peeled away the layers of bark. Sure enough, the wood beneath was bluish black, a bruise that signaled serious sickness. The limb would have to come off for the tree to survive.

So now it wasn't only the cherry blossom trees, but also the sycamore. The whole garden was in trouble.

Mas went straight to the front door and knocked. He didn't want to let himself in if he didn't have to; he, Mari, and Lloyd were in enough hot water as it was.

The door opened, revealing the full figure of Becca Ouchi. She was dressed in a tight brown turtleneck sweater and a pair of pants that ended just below her knees. Mas could see that she had a good set of *daikon ashi*, Japanese white radish legs that bulged out unapologetically. That must have come from the part of her that was Japanese. "Mr. Arai," she said, "oh, hello."

Becca's earlobes were clear of any jewelry today. Circles hung from underneath her eyes like cocoons; the woman looked as sick as the sycamore outside. "Are you here for the meeting?"

Mas didn't know of any meetings, and didn't care to. Meetings were for wasting time, created by and for high-tone people to justify their existence. Mas instead got right to the point. "You knowsu your tree gonna die?"

"Which one?" Like a mama bear hearing her cub's cry, Becca snapped out of her personal despair.

"Sycamore out front."

"Sylvester? What's wrong with him?" Becca's ample breasts shook in all directions as she rushed down the steps to the ailing tree. She gingerly traced the black bruise that Mas had uncovered. "Shit," she said. "The canker's come back."

Mas tried to ignore the fact that the woman had named the tree and was referring to it as a real person. Mas had run into some of these *kuru-kuru-pa* customers during his forty-year career who acted as though blood, instead of sap, were pumping through an oak or elm. And, of course, there were those activists who chained themselves to tree trunks or lived in tall branches like the Swiss Family Robinson to make a point that nature needed to be saved.

All nuts, Mas thought, and now he had one more to contend with.

"That branch gotta be cut, or itsu gonna spread all ova."

"Lloyd had that tree on antibiotics all summer." In response to Mas's frown, Becca added, "You know, antibiotics. Medicine to fight off the infection."

"No kind of medicine gonna save that tree. Gotta saw it off." Luckily, the branch was still young and stood only about three feet high from where it was connected to the tree. If Mas had a ladder, he could handle it on his own.

As they discussed various options, a man dressed in a black suit appeared from the house and stood at the top of the front steps. His face was as matte as the surface of a new frying pan. He had black thinning hair and a charcoal smudge of a moustache. "Is everything all right, Miss Ouchi? It's five to ten; everyone should be coming soon."

Becca nodded. "The foundation's lawyer," she whispered. Mas pursed his lips. New York City seemed full of attorneys.

"Just have to take care of some garden business; I'll be right in," she called out.

Mas wished that he had his own tree pruner and saw, one that he had inherited from an old Issei gardener who had learned his trade from an Uptown boardinghouse. Uptown was now present-day Koreatown in Los Angeles, full of indoor golfing ranges and restaurants. At one time, Uptown had been the gathering place for Japanese immigrants, many of whom had picked up the gardening trade. Even the Japanese church in the area had a stained-glass window with the image of a push lawn mower, a nod to the profession that had kept parishioners and the church well fed and clothed.

But the pruner and saw, as well as a dozen other tools, including his beloved Trimmer lawn mower, had all been stolen from his truck last year. He learned to make do, as he would today.

Mas followed Becca through the back gate. The yellow police tape was still around the dry pond, but it looked like most of their investigative work had been completed. "They got most of it done yesterday," Becca said. "Guess they were afraid it was going to rain."

They walked over to the wooden toolshed in the corner. Becca pressed down on a metal latch to open the door. As with most other toolsheds, the wooden shack was dark and damp. But while the ones in L.A. were ripe with the scent of mold and other growth, the Waxley toolshed was devoid of anything living, a freezer for dead equipment.

"Wait a minute," said Becca, taking hold of a flashlight on the top shelf. "Something doesn't look right." She slid forward a switch on the flashlight and circled the light around the shed's confines. "What the—"

"Sumptin' wrong?" asked Mas, who knew well enough that something was indeed amiss.

"What happened to our new equipment?" Other than a bright-yellow plastic ladder, all the tools looked like they predated World War II. Old, toothless rakes, hedge clippers, and yes, a tree trimmer. The trimmer would have worked for small branches, but not for the large infected sycamore outside. The shovels that Mas had used a day earlier were propped against the wall, scoops up. Aiming at one of the shovels with the beam of the flashlight, Mas noted that its face was dented. What kind of force had caused that deformity? The old gardener whom Mas had met at a boardinghouse in L.A. had once told him that tools reflected the character of the gardener. It was no wonder that Mas's tools over the years had been scratched and worn down, in some cases only held together with wire and duct tape.

"No, no, something is wrong here. I mean, the tools were in here yesterday. The day . . ."

The day we found your daddy's dead body, Mas silently finished Becca's sentence.

"Did Lloyd take some of the tools?"

"Lloyd too busy to take anytin'," Mas said a little too angrily. Was Becca now accusing Lloyd, too?

"This is all we need. Those tools cost us two thousand dollars. Dammit. Just another thing to report back to the police. Can you see if you can make do with anything else in there?" Becca handed the flashlight to Mas and left to attend to her lawyer.

Shelves lined the shed, but toolboxes and small tools were haphazardly arranged on the dirt floor. Mas got on all fours and pulled out the toolboxes to look for a saw. His old, battered knees cut into the cold packed dirt, and Mas was ready to give up when his flashlight caught the sharp teeth of a handsaw left sideways by the door. As Mas got hold of the wooden handle, something rolled toward him like a marble. Again he guided the flashlight to get a better look. The tiny ball was no children's toy but a dirt-covered bullet.

Mas didn't know what to do. Should he tell Becca and the grim lawyer inside? And what did it mean in terms of Lloyd and Mari's case?

Mas tried to slow his thoughts. What had Detective Ghigo said at the police station? That a bullet had gone straight through Kazzy's head. But then earlier, at the hospital, he spoke about matching the bullet to the discarded gun. Had he been bluffing? There was no mention of a bullet or even a specific gun in the *New York Post* story. So up to now, the police might not have had a bullet. Which means they had no way to directly link Mari's prop gun to Kazzy's death.

The shed door must have been open, but hadn't it in fact been closed when Mas had arrived at the garden that morning? Had the killer closed it? Or maybe someone else?

The whole thing didn't make any sense. The neighbor said that he heard the gun go off and reported the gunshot to police. The killer must have fled right away. He wouldn't have bothered to close the shed door.

Mas turned over different scenarios in his mind like he was throwing down dice and landing various combinations. He studied the dented shovel again. The wooden handle was especially long, maybe five feet tall. It certainly looked like the bullet had hit the face of the shovel and then ricocheted into the dirt floor.

He left the freezing-cold shed and began pacing around the pond, ignoring the yellow police tape flapping in the wind. The pond was completely empty now, so Mas could see some writing—Japanese *kanji* characters—carved into the cement bottom of the pond. If he'd been in a better frame of mind, he would have put on his reading glasses to make out the words. But they meant nothing to him now.

Kazzy had been around five foot eight. Since the back of his head had been shot off, the bullet would have landed up higher, maybe in the next-door neighbor's tree trunk. The killer could have been much taller, that was for sure. Or else Kazzy could have been on the bridge, squatting down on his knees. The shooter could have aimed the gun from the side, by the edge of the pond a few feet from the back stairs.

Mas went back into the shed and dropped the bullet into his half-empty pack of Marlboros. Since the back door was locked, he made his way around to the front of the house. A mailman was walking down the stairs and Becca was at the open door, leafing through a stack of envelopes. Then she stopped at one piece of mail, letting the rest scatter at her feet like dry leaves. She hurriedly tore open the white envelope and unfolded a letter. Mas was now only a few feet away from Becca, but she didn't seem to notice. Her eyes were open so wide that Mas could see her chestnut brown irises moving back and forth, absorbing the words on the page. Then she put the letter up to her forehead and began to scream.

Phillip was the first to respond. He came to the door, but didn't bother to console his sister. Instead, he glared at Mas like a dog waiting to take a bite out of a person's leg. "What the hell did you do to her?"

"No." Becca shook her head. "It's not him. It's this. A letter from Kazzy."

Phillip's face fell. He was much skinnier than Becca and looked like the type of person who had spent his childhood sick in bed rather than making trouble with other boys outside. While Becca reminded Mas of a solid wooden post, Phillip was like a piece of flimsy carbon paper, leaving irritating marks whenever he felt pressure from the outside.

Phillip pulled the letter from his sister's hands and went into the dining room. Mas couldn't help but to follow. "I have Kazzy's suicide note," he said, handing the letter to the attorney. The attorney took out a handkerchief and grasped the edges of the paper, laying it flat on the dining room table.

Around the table were the same people who had been at the house the day before. The sea urchin, this time in a lime green shirt and blue suit. The sumo wrestler, dressed again in black. The sixty-something-year-old woman, who smelled like she was dipped in perfume. She was the driver's boss—Miss Waxley, wasn't it?

Mas stood behind the attorney as he read the brief letter. Looking over the attorney's shoulder through his drugstore reading glasses, he could make out the words, all in capital letters:

DEAR BECCA AND PHILLIP,
I KNOW YOU MUST BE IN SHOCK. I'M SORRY, BUT IT'S FOR THE BEST.
K-SAN

"It's a lie. K-*san* didn't write this. He would never commit suicide. He had no reason to take his life." Becca folded her arms over her ample *chichi*s and sat in a chair in the corner.

"I have to admit it's kind of strange," the sea urchin chimed in. "I mean, Kazzy has seemed pretty agitated these days, with the vandalism and all, but he's not a quitter."

"But look, it's typed all in caps, the way he always issued his memos. Military style," said Phillip.

The others all began murmuring their theories on why Kazzy could have killed himself. Finally, the old woman spoke. Her voice wavered like a forlorn melody from a koto, a Japanese string instrument that Haruo's ex-wife, Yoshiko, played. "It could have had to do with his health, with his recent diagnosis and all."

"Diagnosis? What are you talking about?" Becca stood up from the chair she had been resting in.

"Lou Gehrig's disease. He was diagnosed last month. Didn't you know?"

Lou Gehrig. Mas remembered that New York Yankee baseball player—hadn't he even played in an exhibition game in Japan? Gehrig had died of a terrible disease that had weakened his legs, arms, and then the rest of his body, ending his career and life back in the late thirties.

Even Phillip looked out of sorts with the news. "Is that why Kazzy was so irritable?"

"Why wouldn't he mention anything to his own children? And why would he tell you, Miss Waxley?" Becca asked.

"Well, you know, we had business concerns."

"Then he would have told me," said Phillip. "That just doesn't make sense."

"Perhaps he didn't want to burden you all. Since my

own mother had struggled with multiple sclerosis, he thought that I might understand something of what he'd be going through," said Miss Waxley in the same singsong voice. "You know how proud your father was. He couldn't bear to admit that he would never be the same. He was devastated."

"That's true," added Phillip. "He wouldn't have wanted any one of us to take care of him. He was so stubborn—what's that Japanese word for it? *Ganko*?"

That Mas could understand. Any independent Nisei man—whether he be a gardener or a silk tycoon—wouldn't want his child to help him *shikko* into a metal bowl or change his diapers.

"Answer me this, then," Becca interjected. "If he killed himself, why did that gun end up in a trash can half a block away?"

Phillip's face turned red, and the room grew quiet. Nobody had an answer for Becca. The fry-pan–faced attorney then excused himself to contact the police.

The rest of them circled the letter as if it had been written by a dead president. Only Becca sat back. Finally, Detective Ghigo appeared with the same badge dangling off his black jacket. "So what do we have here?"

"Suicide letter," said Phillip.

"Did anyone touch this letter?"

Both Becca and Phillip nodded. Ghigo took out a small black notebook and clicked the end of his ballpoint pen. "Did Mr. Ouchi seem suicidal?"

"No," Becca said. "Absolutely not. He didn't have that type of personality."

"But we just found out that Kazzy had just been diagnosed with Lou Gehrig's disease," Phillip reported.

"Yes, we heard that from Mr. Ouchi's doctor. Would that be a reasonable motive for Mr. Ouchi to kill himself?"

A few people nodded, but Becca obviously wasn't going to give up. "It couldn't have been suicide. We found him buried under trash." Mas cringed when Becca mentioned "we." He wanted no part of the investigation, but it would be too obvious if he left the room now.

"Well," said Ghigo, "it could be that Mr. Ouchi's death and the vandalism are unrelated. I'm also following up on one of Mr. Ouchi's girlfriends."

"Which one?" Phillip made a face as if he were sucking on an especially tart pickled plum.

"Anna Grady. In Fort Lee."

"Anna? K-*san* dropped her weeks ago." Becca frowned. It was obvious that Becca was no fan of this Anna woman. But a lady friend—there could be some connection to the gardenia, thought Mas.

"Do you know if she took it hard?"

"She may have," said Phillip. "I think there might have been a problem with her background."

All of the others stared at Phillip. His talk about "background" reminded Mas of *omiai*, the Japanese-style arranged marriage in which one's past was examined with a fine-tooth comb. Mas's marriage to Chizuko, in fact, had been *omiai*, but Chizuko's family must have used a comb with missing teeth in looking into Mas's past.

"I don't know too much about it, but Becca knows, right?" Phillip said.

"I really don't have many details," mumbled Becca, but somehow Mas knew that she was lying.

"How did they meet?" Ghigo asked.

"Wasn't she living with some woman that Kazzy knew from a long time ago?" said Phillip.

"Her roommate's mother used to be a maid here in the Waxley House with our grandmother," explained Becca.

"That's right. They all hooked up after K-*san* started these renovations," said Phillip.

"Detective, I really don't think this woman had anything to do with Kazzy's death," Miss Waxley said. "Kazzy had a lot of woman friends. A bit of a ladies' man, I hate to say."

Becca lowered her eyes.

"Well, we'll check her out, just in case." Detective Ghigo's gaze then fell on Mas. "Mr. Arai, what a surprise to see you here again. Didn't know that you had any business with the Ouchi Foundation board."

"He was here to look after the trees," explained Becca. "But his family now plays a role on the board."

The sea urchin began to cough; it was obvious to Mas that he wanted Becca to stop. She caught on and looked awkwardly at Ghigo and the attorney. As if receiving a baton in a relay race, the attorney turned to Mas, then cleared his throat and continued Becca's train of thought. "In the event of Mr. Ouchi's death, he named a successor to the board," he said to Mas.

"Yah, yah, so?"

"That person is Takeo Frederick Jensen."

Nanda? Had Mas heard correctly?

Ghigo was also surprised. "You mean the baby?"

"Now, we haven't verified if this is legal," said the sea urchin, pulling at his orange spiky hair.

"Are you saying that the Ouchi Foundation contests the will?" asked Ghigo.

"No, it's just that we only heard it earlier this morning. How can a baby be a member of the board?" continued the sea urchin.

"Well, K-*san*'s will instructed that Lloyd would assume the position until Takeo became of age," said Becca.

The sumo wrestler sucked in more air into his immense lungs. Sitting down, he seemed taller than Mas standing up. "It's craziness. Utter craziness. I want our attorneys at Waxley Enterprises to take a look at that will before we do anything."

"Excuse me if I sound uncultured," interjected Ghigo. "But why do you care who's on the board? How much money do you get?" Mas listened intently. He was wondering the exact same question.

Miss Waxley laughed, covering her mouth with a hand dotted with age spots. "Quite the contrary, Detective Ghigo," she said. "You are usually expected to give money when you're named on a board."

"So who cares who's in and who's not?"

"The board decides the future of the garden and museum," explained Becca. "If the board votes to shoot the project down, it'll eventually die."

After forty-five minutes of this incessant talking, Mas had to leave. He felt bad abandoning the sycamore, but he figured a few more days of being attached to its infected limb would do no extra damage.

The route back to the underground apartment was remembered by Mas's legs, which automatically carried him past street signs, bus stops, bakeries. He turned on Carlton and unlocked the gate and door of the apartment, and was greeted by the friendly smell of cooked green onions, fried bacon, and soy sauce. Fried rice, the way Lil Yamada had taught Chizuko to make it when she first arrived in America. It had become Chizuko's specialty dish, now reprised in Brooklyn.

Mari had returned without Lloyd or Takeo, but with two other guests—Tug and his daughter, Joy.

"Mas, old man, we were wondering where you were," said Tug, getting up from his chair at the kitchen table, which had been moved into the living room. Mari smiled and scooped a serving of fried rice from a wok onto a plate in front of an empty chair. Her hair was wet, freshly washed. In fact, her whole spirit seemed freshly watered. She told him what he had already sensed: Takeo was doing much, much better, and would be released from the hospital after undergoing a few more tests.

Before he took his seat, Joy acknowledged him. "Mr. Arai, I haven't seen you in ages. Maybe even ten years." Joy didn't mention Chizuko's funeral, but that had been the last time, they all knew. Joy had the same moon face, and wore a dark-blue kerchief over her head. Her hair lay in two long braids, like those women in Hong Kong kung fu movies, except the right one was dyed bright pink and the other electric blue. When Mari was a teenager, she often said that Joy had "tight eyes," claiming that she herself found that kind of thin eyes attractive.

"Yah, long time," Mas replied. He couldn't believe that this two-tone-braided girl had been close to becoming a full-fledged doctor after completing her residency in South Carolina. He had once viewed her as being quiet and bland, like a boiled egg, but it was quite obvious that her shell was now broken.

"Well, Dad," said Mari, pulling out a chair for Mas, "tell us where you've been."

Mas took off his jacket and started from the beginning. He mentioned the sycamore, but quickly went on to the suicide letter and conversation at the Waxley House. Mari kept interjecting, filling in Mas's blanks. The sea urchin, Penn Anderson, worked with Phillip at Ouchi Silk, Inc., while the sumo wrestler, Larry Pauley, was a senior vice president of Waxley Enterprises, which donated money to the Ouchi Foundation. And Miss Waxley was the only child of Mr. Waxley, and chairman emeritus of the company.

"Who is this Waxley fellow?" asked Tug.

"The late, great Henry Waxley?" Mari said. "He started

Waxley Enterprises, a shipping company, before World War Two."

"Oh, yeah, wasn't there a biography that came out recently?" recollected Joy. "Sounds like he was a real SOB. A control freak, right?"

"Joy." Tug frowned and wiped his beard of any stray grains of fried rice. "He was a successful businessman."

"No, Mr. Yamada, Joy's right," said Mari. "I heard Waxley was a hard man to deal with. Actually, Kazzy was no better."

Mas didn't know why these daughters had to *warukuchi* so much. *Warukuchi* literally meant bad-mouth, and they were freely talking bad about men two and three times their age.

"Kazzy was lecherous, Dad," Mari maintained. "A *sukebe*. He even propositioned me when I was four months pregnant with Takeo."

"What an asshole." Joy tossed her blue braid behind her shoulder while Tug took a big swig of water.

"Maybe youzu get it wrong," Mas countered.

"No, Dad, I didn't misinterpret that. It was pretty clear what he wanted."

The four of them became quiet. Mas didn't know whether to be happy that Kazzy was dead or to view his daughter as being *shinkeikabin*, too sensitive. He watched Mari circle the table, collecting dirty dishes, until she stopped at his side. "Oh, I forgot to tell you," she then recalled. "Haruo left a message on the answering machine. Wasn't quite sure what he was talking about."

After she took the dishes to the sink, Mari turned the dial counterclockwise on the aged answering machine.

"Mari, don't you think it's time to go digital?" said Joy. "Damn, girl, you guys live like you're just out of the eighties."

"What can I say? Lloyd and I are old-school."

"More like prehistoric."

Mas waved the girls to be quiet as he positioned his ear toward the machine's speaker.

It was indeed Haruo, first breathing hard like he had run up a bunch of steps to make this call.

"I gotchu Mystery Gardenia, Mas. Call me as soon youzu getsu dis message."

Mas looked at Tug and didn't waste any time. Since Haruo had been up for his graveyard shift, he was probably already in bed, wiped out from the day's activities. But Haruo wasn't the type to mind if anybody interrupted his slumber, especially if it meant that someone out there needed him.

Haruo answered after the sixth ring. He had indeed been sleeping, but Haruo being Haruo, it didn't take him long to start talking, his words dribbling out like a steady rain.

"You be proud of me, Mas. Izu found your Mystery Gardenia."

Haruo's search actually began in the Flower Market, where he now worked part-time, a concrete refuge in downtown Los Angeles amid wandering transvestites, fenced factories protected by coils of barbed wire, and refrigerator box after box (apartments for the homeless). Inside, on the first floor, however, were rows and rows of blossoms—either grown locally in Southern California or imported from Latin America and Asia. Haruo always spoke about how he loved the scent of flowers. Like Mas, he had survived the Bomb, but unlike Mas, he always talked about sweet smells, whether they came from a garden or a woman's kitchen. The Bomb might have destroyed Haruo's face, but his nose was as strong as ever.

Haruo worked for his friend Taxie, an old-time chrysanthemum grower. They had an established routine. From two o'clock in the morning, Taxie was the front man, greeting the customers and showing them their flowers soaking in water. Haruo, on the other hand, worked in back, toward the cash register. He was the one who wrapped the dripping bunches in sheets of old newspaper and carried the flowers onto their customers' metal carts.

Mas thought it was well and good that Haruo was making some extra cash at the Market, but he had some concerns as well. The Market was rampant with gamblers. The game of choice was liar's poker, in which men brought out dollar bills from their pockets and wallets and gambled off of the bills' serial numbers. This wasn't the best environment for a recovering ex-gambler like Haruo, and Mas sometimes wondered when his friend would succumb to the temptation. But today was no day to go into a man's addiction.

"So whatsu the Mystery Gardenia?" asked Mas, hoping for a short explanation.

"You knowsu Kanda Nursery? Only gardenia grower

in Market. Roses, carnation, they all come from Latin America, *yo*, but gardenia plants, they have *mushi*, whatcha-callit, worms in soil. No out-of-country gardenia allowed. So Kanda doin' good."

Mas knew about the nematodes, wormlike parasites that could burrow near the roots of gardenia plants. The greenhouses of Kanda Nursery must be either north in Ventura County or south in Orange County, he thought.

"Well, anyways, I go ova to Kanda's stall and talk to the son. Good thing I brought ova donuts one day at the Market. He rememba and then make time for me. I tell themsu they gotsu the biggest gardenias I ever seen. He tell me about their special Mystery Gardenia. Thatsu whatchu call dat type, you knowsu, Mystery Gardenia. Ship all ova the country, I think. I tellsu them about the gardenia you lookin' for. 'No way,' he say. 'No way you can find who grow dat flower.' But I tellsu him how big and beautiful you say it was. So I guess heezu gotsu some *hokori*."

Mas knew that if you complimented a man on what he grew or made with his hands, you had a friend for life. Although Haruo didn't have a lot of common sense, unlike Mas, he had smarts on how to get along with people.

"Then he tellsu me, 'You go with my dad to ranch.' The father turns out to be Kibei, Mas, just like us. Name Danjo. Skinny guy, as skinny as a broom. But mouth, *okii*, so big thatsu you could sweep a whole day's worth of leaves in there. Born in Riverside, but spent time in Tottori."

"Yah, yah," Mas said impatiently. He didn't have time to hear Danjo Kanda's life story.

"Anyhowsu, the nursery in San Juan Capistrano. You knowsu, the place where the birds come." Mas had heard that swallows were supposed to visit the quaint town every spring. He didn't know if the story was fact or fiction, but he wasn't surprised to hear that Haruo had been charmed with the idea of a cloud of swallows descending on the town's old mission every March.

"I tellsu you, datsu a nice place. Cool. Not far from ocean. I'm thinkin', when I retire, I should move to dis place," said Haruo, knowing full well that retirement would never be in the cards for either him or Mas.

"So I get out of truck and see greenhouse, four of them, plastic, all lined up. I tellsu you, Mas, smellsu so good, like a ladies' cologne. Then when I go in, smell like wax. Danjo's wife doing hand tailorin', you knowsu, put flower in wax, then cold water.

"I go ova, take a closer look. I rememba whatchu say about flower, hair in the middle. Then I checksu what she doin', and then I shout out, 'Thatsu it, thatsu it.' I solve Mas's mystery."

Haruo took a deep breath and then spoke so loud that even Tug and the two girls could hear. "They use *shuji* brush for the wax. Hand tailorin'. Those brushes gotsu animal hair, Mas. You get me?"

Mas nodded. He was familiar with hand tailoring, as he had some friends up in Mountain View, not far from San Francisco, who were in the flower nursery business. Apparently the pollen from the gardenia flowers got on ladies' fancy dresses, so they dipped the half-open flowers in warm wax to seal the pollen. But Mas remembered seeing it done by hand, no brushes.

"And they gotsu New York customers," said Haruo, who proceeded to read off a list of five flower shops in Manhattan and Brooklyn. The effort Haruo expended to recite his story had taken its toll. Afterward, he seemed to deflate like a punctured balloon, and weakly excused himself to finish out his sleep.

"What's *shuji*?" Mari asked after Mas hung up the phone.

"You know, Japanese calligraphy. Didn't you take it in Japanese school?" Joy took the end of her pink braid and mimicked a brushstroke on the kitchen counter.

"Must have missed that session."

As a teenager, Mari regularly ditched her Saturday language classes, opting instead to smoke cigarettes three blocks away on a corner of Koreatown. Mas had seen her one Saturday on his way to a customer in Hancock Park.

"What's this about the animal hair?" asked Tug.

Mas explained Detective Ghigo's identification of the deer hair on the gardenia flower.

"Makes sense," agreed Joy. "Those Japanese calligraphy brushes are usually made of deer hair. Some use goat, horse, or even raccoon. But your regular Western brush is either synthetic or made of hog or sable hair."

Mari laughed. "Wow, you belong on *Jeopardy!*, girl."

"Well, brushes, they're my tools of the trade now.

Anyway, you're the one who went to Japanese school for thirteen years. You should know all that cultural stuff and at least a thousand *kanji*, right? In my measly two-year experience, I barely got through *katakana* and *hiragana*."

In Japanese, there are three levels of writing: two phonetic versions, *katakana* and *hiragana*, and then the highest level, *kanji*, modern-day hieroglyphics. All three types could be traced back to the Chinese.

Mas had no trouble remembering *katakana* and *hiragana*—there were only about forty symbols in each—but *kanji*, numbering in the tens of thousands, was another matter altogether. Over the years, Japan had simplified *kanji*, but Mas was actually more at home with the complicated versions issued during the Meiji Era in the late 1800s. *Kanji* after *kanji* had been drilled into Mas's head by a fierce junior high schoolteacher until school was eventually canceled during World War II. Mas sometimes felt that he belonged more to the era of Meiji, "Enlightened Rule," than today's era, Heisei, or "Peace Everywhere."

Joy, the daughter of two Nisei, had probably felt like a fish out of water during her two years of Japanese school. Most of the students during Mari and Joy's time had at least one parent direct from Japan. To hear words built from the sounds a, i, u, e, o would be as natural as drinking water to them. But there apparently was a price to be paid for knowing Japanese so well. To be American, Mari told Mas one time, meant that you knew only one language: English.

"I was jealous of you," Mari said to Joy. "Lucky girl, that's what I was thinking. You could go to sleepovers and watch Saturday-morning cartoons like the rest of the kids. No one would think of you as an FOB." FOB, Mari had used that term a lot in high school, Mas remembered. Now, what did it mean? Fresh Off the Boat, Asian immigrants like Chizuko and other so-called newcomers.

"But now, see," Joy argued. " 'Made in Japan' is cool. Video games, *manga*, everyone is getting into it."

"That's what Lloyd says, too. But he doesn't understand that it wasn't cool when we were growing up."

"Well, he's a white guy. What do you expect? They can go crazy for geisha and samurai, but it ain't gonna change the color of their skin."

"Joy—" Tug called out sternly.

Mari sat frozen, her mouth partially open, her tea mug steaming in her hands. Even Mas was surprised by Joy's harsh tone.

"I'm sorry," Joy said. "You know I'm just teasing you."

A friendship that went back to preschool obviously counted for something, because Mari shrugged her shoulders. "Just wait until you get serious with someone, Joy," Mari said. "I'm going to give you such a hard time."

Joy exchanged a look with her father and retreated like a hermit crab into its shell at low tide. Mas didn't understand what was going on with Tug, Joy, or Lil, for that matter. Tug had explained that Lil couldn't come to New York City because she had to babysit their son Joe's children. But the grandchildren had never stopped Tug and Lil from traveling together to Mount Rushmore and Branson, Missouri. Why, all of a sudden, would it prevent Lil from coming to the East Coast?

Tug slipped the end of his pipe into his mouth. Mas knew that Tug had no intention of lighting his pipe; it just felt good to bite down on something at times like these. Tug seemed deep in thought for ten minutes straight. When Joy pulled on her coat to leave, Tug finally spoke. "Heard of some of those flower shops Haruo was talking about, Mas. Have a friend who's a florist. I saw him at church last Sunday. I'll make sure he's going tomorrow. So, how about it, Mas—you game to go with me?"

Mas dislodged a piece of bacon from underneath his lower denture. The last place he wanted to spend his Sunday morning was cooped inside a Christian church or even a Buddhist temple. But if that's where the answers were, that's where they had to go.

"You guys aren't playing detective, are you?" asked Joy. "You better just leave that to the cops. No telling what kind of trouble you can get into. This is not Pasadena. It's not even L.A."

Normally Mas would have agreed with Joy. But things had changed for Mas recently. He had been running away from life, from the Bomb, for more than fifty years, but finally he'd had to face his past; in the same way, he had to find out who had killed Kazzy Ouchi, or else the future sequence of events would ball up into a boulder, sending them all off the edge.

With that the Yamadas left, soon followed by Mari, who

went to relieve Lloyd at the hospital. Mas was drying off a glass when Lloyd returned. As Lloyd sat drinking one of his dark foreign beers, Mas quietly told him that Takeo had been named the new member of the Ouchi Foundation board. Lloyd was not surprised. "I knew that," he said. "Kazzy did mention to me that when he died, Takeo would be next in line. We can help guide the future of the garden and the museum. Not be just hired hands anymore."

Mas pursed his lips. What would Detective Ghigo call this? A damn good motive.

"No matter what Kazzy thought of Mari and maybe even me," explained Lloyd, "he really adored Takeo. I don't know why. Maybe he saw himself in Takeo. He was always worried about Takeo's health, especially lately. All that stuff about Lou Gehrig's makes sense. Maybe he knew that he wasn't going to be around that long, and wanted to make some sort of amends."

Mas pulled out the newspaper article that he had torn from the *Post*. "You see newspapa?"

Lloyd nodded, taking another swig from his beer. "I'm still trying to figure out where that reporter got his information. I wanted to return his call, but Jeannie advised me not to. It's so frustrating; I want to defend myself, but I can't. So far, I've been able to keep this article away from Mari—not to worry her, you know. And I erased the phone messages from those reporters. But I'm sure she'll hear about it, sooner or later."

As Mas listened, he tried to figure out if his son-in-law was hiding anything. This was his grandson's father, his daughter's husband. That counted for something. After half an hour of watching the news with Lloyd, Mas went for his jacket, hung over a chair, and took out his pack of Marlboros. He then gently tipped the cigarette pack onto the surface of the coffee table and watched as the bullet rolled and finally stopped in front of where his son-in-law sat.

chapter six

Mas stuffed his hands into his coat pockets on the corner of Twenty-fifth Street and Seventh Avenue in Manhattan. He had made it to church an hour early, proof that he was getting used to the underground train. He had been so relaxed, in fact, that he had managed to doze through most of the commute, dragging himself out at Penn Station. He bought a hot dog from a cart for breakfast and walked to the intersection across the street from the church, waiting for Tug to arrive.

Other than a worn-out cross next to the glass door, the church looked like any four-story office building in a neighborhood of discount clothing outlets and tropical juice bars. A homeless man slept outside the industrial metal gates, which had been unlocked and pushed open by a Nisei man at about nine-fifteen. They even seemed to know each other, since the Nisei gingerly walked over the homeless man's body so as not to wake him.

Mas didn't understand the concept of church. He figured religion ran in someone's family like diabetes and thinning hair. So he was surprised when he learned that Tug was actually the first and only one among his brothers and sisters to become a Christian. His conversion had happened at the hands of a Christian Nisei soldier from Hawaii who had apparently saved Tug's life on the war front in Italy. The soldier was wounded badly and later died, so it only made sense that Tug would pick up the Hawaiian man's religion. That kind of gratitude Mas could appreciate.

Tug told Mas that converting to Christianity had not won him any popularity contests in the extended Yamada family. As the *chonan,* the oldest son, he was responsible for inheriting and taking care of the family *Butsudan,* the Buddhist altar. Any good son knew that every morning he must burn a stick of incense, put out a tangerine or a bowl of rice, and say a few chants in memory of the dead parents, whose framed portraits were usually placed on the arms of the altar. But Tug refused, saying that he wouldn't participate in ancestor worship. His first allegiance was to his *Kamisama,* his God, Jesus. Tug's brothers and sisters were aghast, calling him ungrateful and disrespectful behind his back. His younger sister took charge of the *Butsudan,* usually lighting two sticks of incense—the extra one to make up for the *chonan*'s obvious deficiencies. Soon after Tug shared that story, Mas noticed how Tug's parents' photos were prominently displayed on a polished *tansu*, a Japanese chest of drawers, in the Yamada living room. More often than not, a bowl next to the photos was filled with fresh oranges or apples. Although Tug had sworn off ancestor worship, it was obvious that he had created an altar of his own, Nisei Christian style.

As Mas opened and closed his hands to better circulate his blood in the cold, Tug rounded the corner on the other side of the street. Tug was wearing a suit and tie, and Mas suddenly felt self-conscious about his appearance. The homeless man, in turn, was shuffling away in a pile of torn blankets. It was indeed time for church.

Mas followed Tug through the glass doors, down a dim corridor, and finally to a set of open double doors. The same Nisei man who had unlocked the metal gates earlier stood smiling, offering both Tug and Mas sheets of paper, a program of the morning's events. It was too early for Mas to smile, so instead he bowed his head, surreptitiously brushing away a few grains of rice stuck to his sweater from the night before.

The main sanctuary was a narrow room with wooden pews, a stage, and a large cross in front. The unfamiliar room scared Mas. There were no windows—what would there be to look at, anyway? Most of the back pews were filled, black and gray heads everywhere. Most of them seemed to be Nisei old-timers like Tug, with a few younger Japanese foreign students, their hair misshapen from their pillows and sleep still in their eyes. Tug nodded to a few friends dressed in crisp suits and dresses, and Mas wondered which of them was the florist who might hold the key to the Mystery Gardenia.

Mas followed Tug in between a row of open pews. The hard seats were all set up to look forward and gaze at the cross. Mas imagined himself pinned down on that cross, his hands forced away from his body. He had only gone to church a couple of times with Chizuko, but that building was round with panels of windows. Mas didn't know if it was the gardener in him, but he felt that anything holy had to have at least a speck of green in it.

Attached to the back of the pew in front of them was a compartment for big, thick books. At their feet was some kind of folded-up board covered with a thin cushion.

Holding open these thick books, the Nisei sang in English, the young ones in Japanese. Somehow the sounds merged together, comforting Mas's ears, which hungered to hear the familiar rhythm of his two languages intertwined like crossed fishing lines. The rest of the service was downhill, with one suited speaker after another making announcements. At one point, Tug pulled down the cushioned contraption, which turned out to be a small padded bench. The whole line of worshipers then went down, kneeling on the bench. Mas didn't want to seem rude, so he followed along, too. Everyone closed their eyes and recited a prayer, and Mas couldn't help but think about Mari, Lloyd, and especially Takeo.

At the end of his speech, the Nisei minister, dressed in a heavy white gown, brought out a covered gold plate and a large cup. One by one, men and women, looking solemn and sad, went forward. They knelt down before the minister (your knees needed to be in good condition in Christianity, noted Mas), who picked up something from the now open plate and placed it in their mouths. They took turns sipping from the same cup—the minister wiped the rim each time with a white cloth. Mas doubted that was enough to kill the *baikin* that would make the whole lot of them sick. But Mas knew that it was important for them to share the same cup of germs and filth, because wasn't that the way it worked with people and life, anyway?

When Tug returned to his seat, Mas noticed he was brushing away tears from the corners of his eyes. What did Tug have to mourn about? His life was perfect. A war hero with medals. Two healthy grandchildren. A son who made enough money to live in a 1970s ranch-style house near the ocean. This religion was a strange thing, thought Mas. Even the saints seemed to have regrets.

After the last prayer, the white-gowned minister walked down the aisle, breaking the silence among the people in the pews. Everyone got up, smiled, and talked. The real work was now ready to begin.

Mas followed Tug closely down the stairs to the basement. Tug had come to church before, so he seemed to quickly understand its practices, both during and after the service.

A number of old veterans and their wives stopped Tug on the steps and asked about his family.

"Oh, Joy didn't make it again?" one person asked.

"Well, you know how it is."

Another Nisei inquired about Joe.

"Joe and his wife have two kids," Tug said, fiddling with the round "Go for Broke" pin attached to his tie. "He's the manager of his department now."

And then, to a question about why Lil wasn't with him, Tug answered, "She wasn't feeling well enough for this trip."

Mas was surprised by Tug's answers. Lil was supposed to be babysitting, right? And Tug himself had complained that Joe's aerospace company was downsizing, and as a result, Joe had suffered a fifteen percent pay cut. Tug usually played it straight, so Mas was surprised his friend was blurring lines. But they were the lines of his life. None of Mas's business.

Mas wandered to a table full of sweets and Styrofoam cups of steaming coffee and green tea. "Welcome, welcome. This is your first time here, right?" An old Nisei woman pressed down on the plastic top of a hot-water dispenser, releasing a stream of boiling water into a teakettle. She wore a bright pink and purple outfit, representing a young soul. But her skin, especially around her eyes and cheeks, was as flabby as the worn tread of a flat tire.

Ah, Mas thought, he was caught. Mas tried to ignore the

woman, picking up a quartered chocolate glazed donut with a napkin and balancing a cup of hot tea in his other hand.

"Naughty, naughty. You should have stood up when the minister called out for new visitors. This is no place to be shy, you know."

Mas bit into a donut. Even Tug knew well enough not to tell Mas to stand up in church, so he wasn't going to heed the nagging of strangers.

Tug then arrived to save him. "Sorry about that, old man," Tug said, grabbing a donut dusted in powdered sugar. Mas was happy that the basement was so crowded that he could take cover behind Tug's massive body as if he were getting shade from a redwood tree.

His tactic worked, because the woman turned her attention to Tug. "Hey, you look familiar. Weren't you at church on Sunday?"

"Yes, yes, I was."

"Yes, and you actually stood up," she said loudly, probably trying to make a point to the hidden Mas. "What's your name?"

"Tug, Tug Yamada."

"Yamada, Yamada."

Mas squeezed his Styrofoam cup. Both he and Tug knew what was going to happen next. The woman was going to go through a whole list of Yamadas throughout New York, the East Coast, and then all of the U.S. Didn't she realize that the Yamada name was pretty common, at least one of the top twenty back in Japan?

"No, no, no," Tug replied each time to a reference to a certain Yamada she knew.

"You in camp?"

"Heart Mountain, before I was drafted."

"Oh, Wyoming, huh? I was in Rohwer, Arkansas."

"My wife was in Arkansas," said Tug. Mas noticed that Tug's voice was becoming warmer, more interested. What was it about Nisei and camp? Sometimes it felt like an elite club to Mas, instead of a prison. But then, that was the way of the Nisei, especially the ones who had been able to reestablish their lives after World War II. In camp, they took discarded lumber and carved beautiful birds and assembled high-quality furniture. Now, years after camp, they made chrysanthemum flowers from clear plastic six-ring soda can holders. They had the knack of making beauty out of trash.

"Where were you before the war?" Tug asked.

"Montebello. Flower growers."

"Montebello? I'm from San Dimas, just a few miles away."

"We were neighbors, then. Haven't gone back in twenty years."

"You wouldn't recognize it now. No more flower fields in Montebello, just malls and tract homes," explained Tug.

"I need to get over there. I've been retired for a while now, and have been traveling throughout Europe. I do volunteer work at the New York Japanese American Social Service Center once a week."

The Japanese American Social Service Center had been mentioned in the *Post* article, Mas remembered. He appeared from his hiding place behind Tug. "Mamiya?"

"Huh?"

"Sumptin' Mamiya. Read it in the newspapa about Ouchi-*san*."

"Oh, Elk Mamiya. He's just an old coot. Don't listen to what he says. Got a lot of head problems. He just happened to be at the Service Center when the reporter came by. The reporter interviewed a bunch of us, but of course he quoted Elk." The woman poured the steeped tea into Styrofoam cups. "None of us said what we really thought of Kazzy's death. I mean, it was shocking, but then again—"

"You knew Kazzy Ouchi?" asked Tug.

"Of course, we all did. I mean, I didn't socialize with him. Different circles, you know. But I knew his first wife—you know that he was married three times?"

Three times? thought Mas. The man was an *aho*. What did he think he was, a Hollywood movie star?

"Yeah, the second's in Hawaii, and I think the third went back to Japan. But the first one was the sweetest. Harriet. Shimamoto was her maiden name. Was the mother to the two kids, Phillip and Rebecca. Went to church. My kids were in the same Sunday school. After the divorce, she moved to Brooklyn Heights with them. Didn't care to be in the middle of Manhattan anymore, I guess. Who could blame her? A few decades later, a couple of strokes did her in.

"That's what usually happens to the wife after a divorce. She stays single, while the ex-husband finds another woman right away. When I heard Kazzy was trying to restore that garden, people were saying that he was doing it on behalf of the community, to preserve our history. But I knew the truth. He was just feeding his male ego, making a monument to himself."

"But I thought he was doing it to honor his parents," said Tug.

"He just wanted to show how he was connected to one of the most powerful families in New York. The Waxleys. Just a big show-off. Wanted everyone to know that he was a Japanese Horatio Alger story, from rags to riches." The woman began to realize that she had said too much to complete strangers. "How come you want to know about Kazzy?"

To Mas's relief, Tug stepped in as their official spokesman. "His son-in-law," he said, gesturing to Mas, "works over at the Waxley House. We're looking into who killed Kazzy."

"Well, I wouldn't know much. But you should talk to Jinx Watanabe. They were friends from the war."

"I know Jinx," Tug said.

"Well, I'll find him for you." The woman disappeared into the crowd, and Mas excused himself to go to the bathroom. The men's room was underneath the stairs. The floor was made of tiny tiles, and the entire L-shaped bathroom was drafty like a meat locker. Mas could even feel the coldness of the tile floor through the thin soles of his shoes. In addition to a single urinal, there were two stalls. Mas went into the empty one, only to discover that the latch was broken. He had to resort to sitting on the edge of the toilet while he stretched out the tips of his fingers to keep the door closed.

The man in the neighboring stall flushed the toilet, and Mas could hear the jangle of the man's metal belt buckle as he got ready to go. Meanwhile, another person had stepped into the bathroom. When the man next to Mas opened the door of his stall to wash his hands, he addressed the newcomer. "Hey, Elk."

No reply, just the sound of water running in the sink. The door swung closed, but the running water continued. Mas looked through a crack by the hinges on the stall door. All he could see was the back of a balding man's head, which was shaped like a dinner roll.

Mas stood up, flushed the toilet, and zipped up his pants. He opened his stall door, keeping his eyes on the tile floor as he neared one of the two sinks.

Elk was washing his hands vigorously with a large bar of soap the color of green tea ice cream. As the bathroom had its own powdered soap dispenser, this must be special soap that Elk had brought in. Its smell was stronger than any kind of average cleanser. Mas recognized it as the same kind used by his friend, a linotypist who had worked at one of the Japanese American newspapers in Little Tokyo.

Mas pushed down the metal lever for the powdered

soap, trying to think of a clever line to start a conversation. Finally, all he could manage was "You Mamiya-*san*?"

"Huh, I dunno you." The man peered into Mas's face. His eyes were magnified by his thick glasses so they looked like giant black pearls in open oyster shells.

"Izu Mas Arai. From Los Angeles."

"Los Angeles? What you doin' here?"

"Gotsu a daughter. Sheezu connected with the Waxley House."

Elk's eyes snapped wide open.

"Waxley House? Where Ouchi died?"

"You knowsu anytin' about Ouchi-*san*?"

"Only that he was one of the top dogs among us Japanese. He was goin' make a museum for us. But then someone gets rid of him."

"Anyone wish sumptin' bad on Ouchi-*san*?"

"Well, they all do, don't you know? They don't want us to succeed, really. They'll give us a few crumbs, but that's all. Must've been that group, the ones who passed around that petition. That's who I would be lookin' at. I know their type. I lived in a hostel in Brooklyn during the end of the war. That sonafugun Mayor La Guardia didn't want us. Even though I'm from Seattle, I told myself that I was going to stay in New York just to spite them."

Them, Mas wondered. Was he talking about the mayor, the others who were against the Nisei, or perhaps someone else altogether?

Mas went to the paper dispenser, only to see that it was out of paper towels.

"You better watch yourself," Elk said. His glasses had slipped a little down his nose so Mas saw four eyes peering at him. "They'll do anything to get rid of us."

Mas left the bathroom in search of Tug, who was with a short, graying man with a wide-open forehead. "This is my friend Mas Arai," Tug said, introducing him to Jinx Watanabe. Mas didn't want to ask what "Jinx" stood for; it seemed better for everyone if that information stayed unknown.

"Hallo," he greeted Jinx.

"What camp were you in?" Jinx didn't waste any time trying to figure out where to place Mas.

"Mas wasn't in camp. He's Kibei. Was in Japan during the war."

"Oh, you one of those strandees." Jinx nodded, biting into a crumb cake. Mas didn't know if he had necessarily been stranded, since the only home he knew at the time was Japan. He'd had plenty of close friends, however, who'd been teenagers when they first set foot in Japan, and definitely felt more stranded there than in the States.

"Whereabouts were you? Wakayama? Kagoshima?"

"Hiroshima," Mas replied.

Jinx's cheeks colored, while his wide forehead remained pale. "Hiroshima. I went over there in 1947 during my leave. I was part of the Occupation in Tokyo, but I wanted to take a look-see at what happened down in Hiroshima and Nagasaki. Awful stuff."

"Mas was in the Hiroshima train station. Only a couple of miles from the epicenter, right?"

Mas swallowed some spit. The last thing he wanted to do was revisit Hiroshima. "So youzu in the Army?" he asked, trying to take the focus off himself.

"Yeah, actually, I was part of the Military Intelligence Service. You know, MIS?"

This MIS Mas had heard about at Tanaka's Lawnmower Shop back home. A bunch of Nisei—most of them pretty good in Japanese—had been trained to break codes and interrogate Japanese POWs in the Pacific. It had been top secret; a lot of the MIS-ers, in fact, had carried that secret to their early graves. But more than fifty years later, the government finally seemed to give them a green light to talk. No wonder *hakujin* people seemed to not know anything about the Nisei—not only were the Nisei not the kind to flap their mouths, but they had sometimes been explicitly barred from speaking the truth.

"Actually, that's how Jinx knows Kazzy Ouchi. They were at the language school together in Minnesota," Tug explained.

"Yeah, that's too bad about Kazzy. That's no way that a man like him should have died. Buried underneath a pile of garbage. Kind of strange, about the vandalism. Asians don't have that much trouble here. Must have been some kids. A prank that got out of hand."

"So you knew Kazzy well?" asked Tug.

"My wife had been close to his first wife. Kids used to come over all the time. I kind of lost touch with him myself after language school at Camp Savage. He was a big shot, after all. Didn't have time to go to church or hang out with us nobodies.

"He was actually my instructor at Camp Savage. If you excuse me saying this, he was a strict SOB. A real Mr. Chanto, you know, everything had to be just right."

Mas nodded. *Chanto* had been Chizuko's catchphrase. Everything had to be done according to the rules. They weren't written in stone, but floated around every Issei and Nisei's head.

"Kazzy was a stickler for grammar, proper usage of Japanese," explained Jinx. "Was really into honorifics, you know, how you address people, *kun, chan, san, sama,* all that stuff. Got mad as hell if we made a mistake and spoke as if we were higher in status than we were. It was all BS to most of us. We were Americans, after all. We were going to be questioning POWs, not the Emperor of Japan."

"Where heezu learn Japanese?"

"I guess his dad had been educated back in Japan. Although here the old man did mostly domestic work and gardening, he knew a lot of formal Japanese. Tutored Kazzy, I guess. Too bad the father died so suddenly when Kazzy was just a kid. Must've been rough to be orphaned like that, but that helped him later to be an independent sonafugun."

"What happened to the mother, anyway? She was Irish, right?"

"I heard that she died in childbirth. Second kid. The baby didn't make it, either. Kazzy's father died soon after. Probably from a broken heart."

Finishing up their conversation with Jinx, they searched for Tug's florist friend, Happy Ikeda. Happy Ikeda, as it turns out, looked nothing like his nickname. He had heavy lips, the lower one more swollen than the upper, giving him the appearance of a permanent pout.

"Yeah, I know Danjo Kanda's Mystery Gardenias," Happy said. "Order them all the time. But trying to find who sent that particular gardenia, that's a hard one, Tug. That's like looking for a needle in a haystack."

After Tug and Mas drained all the information they could from Happy, they left the church for the train station. "I guess you're wondering what's going on with Lil and Joy," said Tug in front of the stairs to the platform for trains en route to Brooklyn. Mas could tell something had been weighing on his friend's mind.

"I promised Lil that I wouldn't tell you, so I can't get into the details, Mas. But I'll just say that we're having a problem. A big one."

"Gotsu to do with Joy leavin' medicine?"

Tug laughed. "I wish it was just that. We could get through that." He smiled weakly, and Mas was afraid for his friend and himself. Tug and Lil had been Mas's rock. Life had enough uncertainty already; with the Yamadas teetering on the brink, Mas didn't know what he could actually count on.

"It's just like that childhood rhyme," said Tug. "The one

about Humpty-Dumpty sitting on the wall. Well, my daughter's fallen, and I don't know how to put her back together again."

❖ ❖ ❖

When Mas came home from church, there was a telephone message for him from Becca Ouchi. Kazzy's body had finally been released from the coroner's, so they were going to have a memorial service on Tuesday, with a reception at the Waxley House. Could Mas come over to clean up the garden and treat the sycamore on Monday? "Sylvester's looking bad," she said. Mas couldn't tell whether the warbling in her voice was from emotion or just the worn-out phone message tape.

"They don't want me going over there," said Lloyd later that afternoon. "Both Mari and I were told not to come to Kazzy's memorial service. I guess I'm still suspect number one. With Kazzy gone, I guess Phillip now is calling the shots."

Mas and Lloyd hadn't spoken about the bullet Mas had discovered on the dirt floor of the shed. Mas had left the bullet on the coffee table, only to have it disappear an hour later while he was taking a shower. It was now the son-in-law's responsibility, not Mas's.

"He fire youzu?" Mas asked, fearing that his grandson's medical coverage would dry up.

"Not yet. But I've been asking around for work, just in case. Everywhere seems to have a hiring freeze."

Mas wasn't quite familiar with the term "hiring freeze," but he could figure it out. It was a place that was cold and barren, a place where you had to stay outside. That night he dreamed of ice, Eskimos, and igloos. There was a hole in a frozen lake, where penguins, one after another, seemed to slip and fall right in.

chapter seven

Church seemed to have a strong effect on Mas, more powerful than even a six-pack of foreign beer, as it knocked him out until noon the next day. Lloyd had told Mas to sleep in his and Mari's bed, since both of them were going to stay at the hospital. Their bedroom was like a bear's cave, dark and insulated. Mas cursed his son-in-law's hospitality, and then Haruo's failure to call him at daybreak. He finally got out the door at one, the time he usually called it quits from work.

Already in a bad mood, Mas felt even more irritated to see another delivery truck parked outside the neighbor's house. The neighbor, the one who had reported the gunshot to the police, was pacing in the driveway, talking on his cell phone. When he saw Mas, he abruptly ended his call and walked down his driveway. "You're that Japanese man, the one who's helping with the garden, right?" he said to Mas.

Atarimae, of course I'm Japanese, Mas thought, making the mistake of making eye contact.

The man introduced himself as Howard Foster and gestured toward his open front door. "Come over here. I want to show you something."

"I gotsu work."

"It'll only take a few minutes."

Mas hesitated, but he remembered Elk Mamiya's theory. That people were out to destroy them. Did this neighbor hate people different from him so much that he had killed Kazzy Ouchi? The only way to know was to get close, and entering the man's house was one way to do it.

Mas didn't think Howard would risk his grand lifestyle by killing Mas in broad daylight. So whether it was pure stupidity or a good hunch, Mas climbed up the brick stairs and followed Howard into his wood-framed home.

It was different from the Waxley House—more light, more openness. The hardwood floors were pristine, and all the furniture looked as if it had been created for the space. Chinese vases and plates were on display on cherrywood tables and chests.

Howard went into the dining room area and pointed to a long, narrow screen on the wall. "My prize possession." It was a Japanese brush painting featuring a ball with bug eyes.

"*Daruma*," Mas said.

"Yes, this is a Zenga painting from the Edo Era. Beautiful, isn't it?"

Mas usually saw *daruma* figures in Japanese gift stores in Little Tokyo. Made of papier-mâché, the *daruma*'s round figure was all red, while his eyes were blank, missing. When Mari was a child, she asked him and Chizuko if he was a Japanese Santa Claus, but Chizuko explained that *Daruma* had been a Buddhist leader who looked at a blank wall for years and years. After a while, he lost use of his legs, thus turning into a ball. He also became blind, so when you bought a *daruma* figure, you were supposed to make a wish and color in one eye. Once the wish was granted, the other eye would be painted in.

"Nice." Mas never thought much of art, even though he had a torn screen in his home. But his was the generic kind, with an image of a couple of sparrows resting on a bare tree branch. The screen that this Howard Foster had was the real deal.

Mas circled the core of the house. Unlike the Waxley House, which had a staircase in the middle, a staircase appeared on the side of the building, across from the fireplace. "You here all by yourself?"

"Yes," Howard said, and then frowned. "Why do you ask?"

"No reason," Mas replied, but he was actually wondering about the neighbor's alibi. Sure, he had called in a report about hearing a gun going off at nine that night. But couldn't he have shot Kazzy first and then called the police when he got back to his house?

Howard stood in front of his prized Buddhist painting. "So, looking at this, would you say that I was a Japan hater? That I'm a racist?"

Mas didn't know what to say. It reminded him of one of his customers, who had decorated his house with moose heads and bear rugs. Did that mean he was an animal lover?

"Well, I'm not a racist," Howard answered his own question. "Just a man who takes pride in his house. Can you imagine if they make the Waxley House into a museum? There'll be visitors coming through there every day. I want peace and quiet, not crowds. That's all that I was doing with that petition. Now I'm getting crank calls, angry letters. Being harassed by the police. Somebody even threw eggs at my house a couple of days ago. So tell your people to back off."

What people? thought Mas. He had no people besides Mari, Lloyd, and Takeo. And they were too preoccupied to be thinking about throwing raw eggs at the neighbor's house.

"Youzu talk to Becca. Thatsu best way," Mas finally said.

"I can't talk to her. She's crazy. Unbalanced."

Mas headed for the door, attempting to make his escape.

"Tell them to back off," Howard repeated. "Stop telling lies, slandering me. I told the police that I'm going to file a grievance against the Ouchi Foundation, and I won't stop there, if you know what I mean."

❖ ❖ ❖

Once Mas arrived at the Waxley House, he decided to forgo seeing Becca at the front door and went straight for the garden. He'd been up for only two hours, and he'd had enough of people already.

Like all gardens, Lloyd's garden looked different in the early afternoon than in the morning. Mas preferred the early hours, when there was a hush over the trees and bushes, as if the insects hadn't fully awakened yet. He checked the tape on the wounded cherry trees and was happy to see that the tight blossoms, mini baby fists, were ready to break open at the first sign of sun. He raked a few dead leaves and clipped off the unruly sides of a pine. He even began moving the rocks from the pile by the shed to their proper places around the pond. Walking to the far north side of the pond, Mas noticed that Lloyd had installed a *tsukubai*, a stone washbasin. The stone was the size of a bowling ball, the top and middle hollowed out to hold water. A piece of bamboo served as the water spout, but of course everything was still dry, because the pumping system had not been fully installed. This kind of *tsukubai* was used by followers of the tea ceremony. Mas was no expert on the tea ceremony, but had a former customer, a *chado sensei*, who had a special tatami room beside her kitchen for her classes every Tuesday. She made her students cleanse their hands in a makeshift *tsukubai* outside her screen door. Mas was told it was for purification purposes, but he just enjoyed seeing the women, even the old ones, in brightly colored, stiff kimono once a week.

Mas walked from the *tsukubai* to the bridge over the pond. The yellow police tape was still haphazardly draped over the gourd-shaped concrete floor. Mas squatted down to get a better look at the inscription Becca had been trying to show him that first day. Carved on the side, probably with the end of a stick while the concrete was still fresh, were the *kanji* characters 子, *ko*, and 生, short for *ikiru*. "Child lives"? Strange. What had Kazzy's overeducated father been trying to say with this message? These artistic *erai* types had all kinds of sayings that made no sense to Mas.

Next was Sylvester the sycamore. Mas tentatively made his way to the toolshed. As he reached down for the handsaw, he couldn't help but feel for the small indentation that had once held the bullet. Armed with the saw, Mas set up the ladder by the sycamore and went straight to work. The handsaw was old, probably from the seventies. Years of rain had seeped into the wooden handle, so Mas should have seen it coming. But he didn't. With each push and pull of the saw, the wooden handle jiggled and the metal blade curved back and forth, instead of remaining straight. Seeing little result from his effort, Mas cursed under his breath and dragged the blade forward with all his might. The handle burst free, the blade sinking its rusty teeth into the soft tissue of his left hand, in between his index finger and thumb. A streak of blood immediately dripped down his hand. The wound burned so badly that Mas feared that he would do *shikko* in his pants. Mas was too stunned to even hear himself yell.

"Mr. Arai!" Becca poked her head from the upstairs window. "What have you done to yourself?"

Becca wrapped Mas's hand in a dish towel and guided him up the staircase to the second floor of the Waxley House. Once they reached the top of the stairs, Mas could see that there were two rooms at opposite ends of the hallway, perfectly symmetrical like a set of weights on a barbell. Both doors were wide open. A TV set and fancy electronic equipment were stored in the room on the right, while an old-fashioned desk and typewriter sat in the left. They headed to the bathroom that was right smack in the middle.

"I'm so sorry," said Becca. Mas sat on the closed lid of the toilet. "I should have told you not to bother with Sylvester without the proper tools." Becca made Mas keep his hand elevated. She opened up the medicine chest and took out a plastic bottle of antiseptic and a tube of Neosporin. From the cabinet at the bottom of the sink came a roll of gauze bandage and some white tape.

"I think I'd better take you to the hospital. You might need some stitches. And definitely a shot for tetanus."

Mas shook his head. He'd had enough of hospitals on both coasts. He had had his share of gardening war injuries over the decades; a sliced hand was as common to a gardener as a black eye to a boxer.

Becca must have realized that it was useless to argue with Mas. She soaked a cotton ball with the antiseptic and pressed hard against the cut, making sure that it hurt. While she was wrapping the gauze bandage, the phone rang. Becca went into the room with the TV equipment to take the call. She spoke about fruit platters, cheese, and other kinds of appetizers that Mas had never heard of. The bandage still dangling down his arm, Mas walked out of the bathroom, looked both ways, and headed for the unoccupied room—the one with the old-fashioned desk and typewriter. This had been Kazzy's office, Mas figured. A row of bookshelves lined one of the walls. A small circular table sat in the middle, while a wooden desk, looking like it belonged in the TV Western *Bonanza*, was against the wall by the window. The desk had a roll top, which had some sort of lock, but it was a Cracker Jack kind that could be jiggled open with a nail file. Above the desk on the wall was a framed black-and-white photograph of a *hakujin* woman with a broad face and laughing eyes. Mas saw a slight resemblance to Becca. Must be the grandmother, Kazzy's mother. On a small table was the ancient typewriter, labeled Remington. Mas remembered seeing that kind of typewriter at his janitor friend's workplace, the *Kashu Mainichi*, once the number two newspaper in Little Tokyo. Now it was number zero, because it went belly-up in the early nineties. Housed in an old factory on First Street, the newspaper staff worked amid pigeons resting on a beam near a skylight, while one of the staff members' cats prowled on the cement floor.

For old times' sake, Mas pressed down on one of the typewriter keys. Had to have strong fingers to type on these old machines, that's for sure. Not like those fancy computer keyboards they had now.

He heard the front door open and shut. He walked away from the typewriter, knowing he shouldn't have been in the room. He kept his hand elevated and waited for Becca to complete her phone call.

"Hello?" It wasn't Becca but the old lady, Miss Waxley. Miss Waxley was probably a little younger than Mas, but she seemed from another era. She smelled like the fragrance counter of a department store. She probably used a handkerchief to blow her nose and went to the hairdresser's once a week.

"Mr. Arai," she said, and Mas was surprised that the *hakujin* woman had remembered his name. "Where's Becca?"

"Telephone," he said, gesturing with his bandaged hand toward the other room.

"What happened?" She put her fancy pocketbook down on the circular table and took a closer look at Mas's wound.

Mas didn't want to get into the story, but allowed Miss Waxley to grab a pair of scissors from the desk and snip the loose gauze bandage. "Sank you," he managed to say.

They stared at each other for a good minute before Miss Waxley tried to make conversation. "Do you know that this was my parents' room?" Miss Waxley said.

"Oh, yah?"

"In fact, the typewriter and desk were originally theirs."

Tsumaranai. Boring as hell to hear an old lady talk. But

she had extended her friendship by helping Mas with his hand, so he at least owed her some listening time.

"My mother was housebound for years with her illness. She could putter around the house a little; even make some meals, I was told. I don't have any memories of this house, because we had moved to Manhattan, closer to my father's office, by the time I was one. It was a new start for our family, I guess.

"Now it's just me," Miss Waxley said with a weak smile.

Since everyone called the old lady "miss," she had probably never married, figured Mas. Even though she had money, she must be lonely, all by herself. Good thing she is involved in the garden project, he thought.

Becca then walked in, freeing Mas from Miss Waxley's stories. The conversation turned to food, so Mas excused himself, saying that he would be leaving after he put the remaining bandage roll back in the bathroom.

After closing the door of the medicine chest, Mas heard a couple of male voices through the open bathroom window. Underneath the diseased sycamore tree were Phillip and a young man, a teenager, wearing a blue knit beanie cap trimmed in gold.

"This is the last time. I'm telling you," Phillip said. Mas couldn't see his face, just the top of his thinning hair. He opened his wallet and stuffed some bills in the boy's hand. "If you say anything, it's not only my head, it's yours, too, remember?"

The boy said nothing. After getting his money, he walked away from the house, toward Flatbush Avenue.

As Mas quickly made his way down the stairs, he heard the jangling of a key at the front door. Slipping out the back, Mas hurried to the sidewalk in search of the teenager in the beanie cap.

There was no sign of him on Flatbush. He couldn't have walked that quickly, unless he had taken a taxi, Mas thought. Or the underground train, a block away. Mas headed for the hole of the train station, marked this time by the letter Q in a yellow circle. He had no idea what direction the boy would travel, so he did what any betting man did in cases like this—he took a wild guess. Train going to Manhattan.

The train had already arrived, and the doors were open. Entering the train, Mas scanned the crowd for the blue beanie cap. There was no time for hesitation. Before the doors screeched closed, Mas dashed in like a cockroach seeking shelter. This time there were plenty of empty seats. Jerking left and right, Mas walked the whole length of one car. No luck. Looking through the window in the door of the adjoining car, Mas learned that he had scored a home run. In the far corner sat the teenager, his eyes closed, oblivious that he was being watched.

After entering the teenager's car, Mas made himself comfortable in an empty seat down the same row. Phillip was obviously paying the boy off to keep a secret. But what kind of secret was Phillip keeping? Had he paid off the boy to kill his father? Mas shuddered. He hated to think that a son would go to such lengths to calculate his father's murder.

Hadn't that newspaper article said that Phillip was the

number two man at Kazzy's company? Mas knew many customers who had their sons working for them. More often than not, some kind of problem would come up, and eventually the son was not welcome at the parents' house anymore.

Mas looked down the row of passengers to the boy in the beanie cap again. He could pass for *hakujin*, but Mas wouldn't be surprised if the boy was part Asian, Latino, or even Jewish or Arabian. He had a strong nose, dark skin, and a healthy crop of black beard stubble, along with a pair of pork-chop sideburns. Mas could tell he was not *baka;* the kid had some smarts, based on the way he sat with his back straight, not hunched over, and his shoes flat on the ground.

Stop after stop, Mas waited for the boy to rouse out of his sleep. But even when the train emerged from below ground, the boy did not stir. They traveled over a bridge, its metal girders casting shadows over the windows of the train. Below was the gray slate of the river, which both comforted and saddened Mas. Some would say water was water, but Mas could feel the difference between the Atlantic and the Pacific. The Pacific had a greenish tinge, containing the promise of fish strong enough to withstand the power of sewage and other man-made pollution. The Atlantic, on the other hand, seemed to be covered with a cold, concretelike layer. Mas knew that there must be some kind of life underneath, but it was well hidden from those above sea level.

The train churned ahead to an island full of skyscrapers, a small pot full of overgrown plants. Mas glanced at his

Casio watch. Already four o'clock. It would be dark soon. He regretted that he had left his Dodgers cap on the couch back at the apartment.

After a muffled message over the intercom—Mas couldn't make out the street but heard "Times Square"—the boy finally rose. He pulled at his knit cap, as if he wanted more protection for the backs of his earlobes. As the boy scanned the rest of the people in the train car, Mas quickly lowered his eyes. No flicker of recognition. Mas, fortunately, was passed over again.

With the opening of the doors, out went the boy, Mas right behind. Tug had described this island of Manhattan as a river of people, and he wasn't just making up stories. Even starting in the train station, the crowd pushed and pulled Mas forward, as if he didn't need to take any steps of his own.

His hand still smarted, but *shikata ga nai*. There was nothing he could do about it, so there was no sense in crying about the pain.

As they were released outdoors, it was more of the same. A wall of cars and yellow taxicabs and then the moving force of the crowd. Mas followed the boy so closely that he almost stepped on the heels of his shoes. Normally Mas would have attracted attention, but here he was just like any other ant trying to make it up the anthill.

They walked west, below enormous neon signs and billboards; Mas felt as if he had stepped into an overbloated Disneyland that had gotten sick and thrown up on itself.

But after a few blocks, there were no neon signs or tourists with video cameras. The buildings were all red brick of different sizes. Some spanned blocks—most likely they had housed some kind of factory at one time. Others were long and narrow, with the familiar crisscross of fire escapes.

Even the smells became more pungent. They were a mix of smoke, grime, *shikko*, and peppery spices. The boy turned off into an alley in between two factory buildings, and Mas hesitated. Alleys in any city were dangerous places. Perfect locations for broken bottles and broken bodies. As far as Mas could tell from peeking from the corner, there were no bodies here. Just a few vegetable crates and a rubber trash can.

The boy knocked on a faded red door and was let inside. Mas thought about what he wanted to do next. A pigeon flew from one fire escape to another on a building facing the other side of the alley. Mas approached the building and put his ear to the red door. He heard the healthy pitch of young male voices. So the boy was now among his peers. What was Mas going to do next?

Mas felt like an *aho* again. Wasting time wandering around Manhattan when there was plenty to do at the garden. Then he noticed light coming from a lone window about ten feet from the ground. Couldn't hurt just to take a look.

Mas balanced one of the crates on the rubber trash can. Holding on to a pipe alongside the wall with his good hand, he lifted himself onto the trash can and then one more step up on the crate, blackened by mildew and other decay from the water and snow. The wood slats were starting to come loose from the frame; Mas knew that he would only be able to stay on his unstable perch for a few minutes.

Still hanging on to the pipe, Mas lifted his body so that his eyes were at least an inch above the window frame. There were five good-for-nothing boys drinking beer, some of them guzzling the foreign kind that Lloyd liked. They sat sunken in couches and stuffed chairs around a low table. On the table, besides the dozens of open beer bottles, were packages of pills. On one corner were stacks of money.

Throughout the years, Mas had seen his share of changes. Computers. Telephones that could float around without a cord. Cars that ran on electricity. But some things never changed, in particular a man's lust for drugs and sex. Back in Hiroshima right after the war, it had been *hiropon*. Heroin. Mas had watched one orphaned buddy after another fall to its temptation. If it wasn't *hiropon*, then it was alcohol that was actually meant for cars. Teenage drunkards—all *chinpira*, would-be gangsters—burned their insides drinking that stuff, but apparently in a strange way it also eased the pain in their heads.

Mas didn't know what *chinpira* of today had to be sorry for, but he had seen enough. The crate underneath him was ready to crack open, so he lowered himself onto the lid of the garbage can. As he jumped to the ground, he heard a slight sound, the crunch of gravel. An arm went around his neck and tightened against his throat.

Mas struggled to breathe. Feeling a surge of adrenaline, he instinctively bent forward and let his attacker flip over his back as easily as a sack of rice. Luckily it wasn't the pill-popping teenager in the beanie. Mas would have had no chance against that power. Instead, it was Phillip Ouchi, a weed of a man.

Phillip remained on the soiled concrete, shocked and maybe even dismayed that he had been overturned by a seventy-year-old man. Mas knew that he might try something again, so he grabbed a loose wooden slat and waved it, nail side down, in front of Phillip's face.

"What do you hope to achieve, Mr. Arai?" Phillip asked, breathless, but with the same nasty attitude he'd shown at the Waxley House.

Mas tightened his grip around the slat with his right hand, while his bandaged left hand pulsed with pain—probably all the extra blood and excitement churning through his body.

"Hey! Hey!" Phillip suddenly called out.

Now, what was the sonafugun trying to prove? Mas then heard the squeak of a hinge and the opening of the door behind him.

The five *chinpira*, including the one with the beanie cap, circled Mas and Phillip. The beanie cap boy had a gun in his hand, and the tallest guy of the bunch had brought out some long and skinny object—perhaps a lead pipe to beat Mas?

"What's going on here, Mr. O.?" the beanie cap boy, obviously the ringleader, asked Phillip, who was now struggling onto his feet.

"This man followed you from the Waxley House. I trailed him the whole way here."

"So what happened, you tripped?"

Phillip said nothing and looked down the length of the alley.

"Dang, I think the old man knocked him down," one of the teenagers spit out, and then all of them began laughing.

"He looks about a hundred years old."

"Seventy," murmured Mas.

"Excuse me?" The beanie cap boy raised his gun to Mas's chin. The nozzle felt cold and smelled smoky, as if it had been fired recently.

"Izu seventy." Mas felt his knees shake, but he still managed to stay standing.

"You hear that—he's seventy," the ringleader announced to his friends. He then looked at Phillip. "So, Mr. O., you got punked by a seventy-year-old."

All the young men began laughing.

Phillip brushed the seat of his pants as though the condition of his clothes were more important to him than the teenagers' jeers.

The ringleader turned his attention back to Mas. He had lowered the gun, and Mas managed to swallow. "So why were you following me?" the teenager asked.

"I see youzu get money. Tryin' to figure out why."

"He'll probably go straight to the police, Riley," Phillip said. So Riley, that was the kid's name.

Mas shook his head. "Die on drugs, I no care."

"Then what do you care about, old man?"

"Kazzy Ouchi. How he die."

Riley's face turned instantly darker, like clouds before a summer shower. "Had nothing to do with that. I told you," he said to Phillip.

"He doesn't know what he's talking about," Phillip said. "His daughter and son-in-law are suspects, so he's just trying to point the finger at anyone he can."

Riley took hold of Mas's right wrist. The wooden slat clattered to the ground. The teenager had taken note of Mas's injury, because he gestured for one of his other *chinpira* to grab Mas's bandaged left hand. This one knew what he was doing, because he pressed into the very softness of the wound. Water sprang to Mas's eyes, but he kept from dripping tears down his face. He wouldn't give any of these sonafuguns the satisfaction of seeing him cry.

"I don't want to hurt you, grandpa. Just forget you've seen anything, and you'll have no problems," Riley said.

Mas knew that the ringleader was talking about the drugs, so he nodded.

"And drop the whole thing with the dead man in the pond. It was suicide, you got it? The old guy shot his own brains out."

Mas nodded again, but he had no intention of going along with the boy's demands on that one. They released his hands, and Mas noticed that the bandage around his left palm was now bright red from a flow of fresh blood.

"And you," Riley said to Phillip, "get the hell out of here. I'll need an extra grand now with this complication."

Phillip looked like he was going to protest, but he must have realized that he was physically overmatched. He stumbled down the alley, a stain visible on the back of his pants.

One by one, the young men returned to the room behind the red door, the last one being the tall teenager with his long and skinny weapon. With the light above the door, Mas could finally see that it was not a lead pipe but actually a shiny new top-of-the-line Weedwacker.

Mas barely made it back to the underground apartment. His left hand had finally stopped bleeding, but both hands were still trembling. Those sonafuguns had stolen the equipment from the garden, Mas was convinced. The beanie cap boy had claimed that he had nothing to do with Kazzy's death, but he was a damn *usotsuki*, a liar of the worst kind.

He dropped his dentures into one of Mari and Lloyd's drinking glasses and gritted his gums together. This was too much for him, he finally had to admit. He collapsed onto the couch, hoping for even nightmares to take over his reality.

chapter eight

"I thinksu I needsu to go home now," Mas said to Haruo the next morning. He hated to admit defeat, but enough was enough.

"Mari still needsu you. Garden not finished. You can't leave sumptin' *chutohampa*."

Half-done, so what? No different from when I came, thought Mas. He poked at the soiled bandage around his left hand. More blood had seeped through during the night.

"And whaddabout Ouchi-*san*'s death?" Haruo continued. "You can't leave dat alone."

"Police, they figure it out. I'm dead, Haruo. Ole

man. Not cut out runnin' around in a place I have no business in."

"*Gambare*." Haruo tried to encourage Mas to carry on. "You tough, Mas. You the toughest guy Izu eva know."

"Dat a long time ago." Weren't most of their friends one step away from their graves? Back in L.A., Mas was going to a funeral every other week. You were expected to bring *koden*—maybe twenty, thirty dollars—each time. These dead people were making Mas go broke. The only good thing about dying was that at least families would be returning all the money you had paid out over the years. The bad thing was that you weren't alive to see it.

"Listen, Mas, us gardeners, we work when othas give up. Weezu the ones out there when itsu a hundred degree, *desho*? All otha people can't handle it. But weezu neva give up."

"Yah, yah," Mas said. Haruo could be one of those silly male cheerleaders at the UCLA football games. Or, better yet, a mascot in a bear costume, constantly waving to children even though his team was getting pummeled by its rival. Mas hadn't finished his *monku*, his list of complaints. "Tug wanna go to all these flowers shops. Look for dat Mystery Gardenia."

"Let him do most of it, Mas. In meantime, you rest. No sense in gettin' sick. Gotta lean on otha people sometime."

"Yah, yah," said Mas, attempting to cut the conversation short. Haruo sounded like he was going to launch into his counseling hocus-pocus. That would just make a bad mood go worse.

❖ ❖ ❖

When Tug called later that morning, Mas was in a better mood. He thought about what Haruo had said. *Gambare.* Never give up. Mas wasn't a quitter, and he wasn't the type to let others pinch-hit for him. The police had their case, and he and Tug had theirs. The Mystery Gardenia meant something; Mas was sure of it.

They met at Happy Ikeda's Midtown store. "Good thing I brought these tennis shoes, Mas." Tug pointed to a pair of all-white sneakers with inch-thick rubber soles. "Lil and I got these on sale from Barstow." Gamblers traveling to Vegas always stopped by Barstow, a desert city along Highway 15 with two sets of factory outlets. Only, in the case of the Yamadas, Barstow's factory outlets were their final destination, not the bright lights of Vegas.

Mas, on the other hand, had on the same pair of penny loafers that he had purchased from the now-defunct Asahi shoe store in Little Tokyo fifteen years ago. His feet were sore, his legs weak. When he walked, he cradled his injured left hand in his right. His lower back also had a kink, probably from throwing down Kazzy Ouchi's useless son.

Happy kept immaculate records, both computerized and by hand, all of which he made available to Tug. "Sometimes the computer makes mistakes," Happy said unsmilingly. On Thursday, there had been a delivery of fresh gardenias in a round glass bowl to a women's luncheon at a members-only club on the Upper East Side. Some gardenia corsages for a wedding anniversary in Chinatown. And a special gardenia bouquet for a performer at the Metropolitan Opera House.

They had no luck at Happy's and then struck out three more times at the other florists that Haruo had mentioned in his phone message. Some florists said the information was confidential, with all the executives and celebrities who were their customers. Others didn't keep detailed records, but just mentioned that gardenias were not hot sellers in the wintertime.

The only shop left was back in Brooklyn Heights. They should have started out with that one, but they wanted to meet with Happy first in Manhattan. A mistake, perhaps, but Tug was the one who had meticulously mapped out their whole path on his AAA map like he was leading a reconnaissance offensive. Chizuko had traveled the same way, so Mas was used to following. Besides, he wasn't thinking that straight today.

"So, Mas, you going to tell me what happened yesterday to get you so jittery?" Tug and Mas walked south alongside Central Park, its bare trees full of crows.

Mas had almost knocked down a fake plastic pillar at one shop and stepped in a planter full of peat moss in another. There was no doubt that he was shaken by the run-in with Phillip and the drug dealers. He had said nothing to Mari and Lloyd, but went over it with Haruo early this morning over the phone. Who was this hired gun, Riley? He and his gang had probably stolen the gardening equipment from the Waxley Garden, so did that mean they killed Kazzy as well? If not, why had Riley insisted it was suicide?

Mas spilled the beans once again to Tug, every single part of it, including his conversation with the neighbor who complained too much. "I don't think Foster do it," Mas said. "Just an *urusai* neighbor. A dime a dozen. Don't think he'd kill to get his way. Type to drive people *kuru-kuru-pa* and make them want to shoot him."

"Well, how about the son, Phillip?"

"Well, I think he hire the boy to do some kind of *itazura*. I just don't know what, exactly."

"Well, Lil always tells me to get a second opinion. Maybe I'll have a talk myself with this Phillip Ouchi." Tug walked over to a pay phone and lifted a New York phone book attached by a flexible cord. The pages were all curled up and shrunken from repeated soakings of rain, sleet, and snow. "Ouchi Silk, Inc., right?"

Mas didn't want to see Phillip Ouchi again, especially so soon after the incident at the factory building with the red door. He didn't know what Tug was hoping to prove. Phillip could have contacts with other *chinpira*, that was for sure.

Ouchi Silk, Inc., had an office in the Garment District and then on Broadway. Tug called both to find out where Phillip Ouchi's office was located. It was on Broadway, just south of Central Park.

Ouchi Silk, Inc., was in a modern steel building about ten stories tall. Each floor seemed a little narrower as you went higher; at least that's what it looked like to Mas from the sidewalk. Mas tried to talk Tug out of going inside the building, but it was no use. Mas knew that during World War II, Tug had been in charge of his squad's fifteen-pound

Browning automatic rifle because of his great size. Just like in Europe, Tug was on a mission in Manhattan, and there was no stopping him.

Mas opted to wait outside. Tug must have thought Mas was losing his nerve, but actually Mas desperately needed a cigarette. Resting his tired back against a parking meter, he pulled out his next-to-last Marlboro and clicked a flame on his Bic lighter. He remembered how he once delighted Mari with smoke rings. "More, more, Daddy," she'd beg from the dinner table. He'd let the smoke fill the cup of his closed mouth, round his lips, and then blow out perfect rings in descending size. The line of rings eventually distorted, broke down, and disappeared in a swirling tail of smoke.

Mari had also become a chain-smoker during her college years. But Mas saw no signs of tobacco in the apartment, so she must have broken the habit.

He also needed to quit someday, Mas knew. But this morning was not the day. Just for good measure, he walked the length of the block, blowing out a series of smoke rings, which seemed to hold their shape longer because of the cold air. He crossed the street. Parked against the curb in a no-parking zone was a Cadillac, the boy with the eel-like hair and red waffle-sole shoes leaning against the driver's-side door.

"Hallo," Mas said. What was the driver's name again, J-O? J-Y?

"Hey." The driver looked up. "I remember you from the Waxley House. I never got your name."

"Mas. Mas Arai."

"Hey, Mas, good to see you. J-E, remember?"

Mas nodded and, without J-E even asking, handed him a fresh cigarette. Mas would even use his last Marlboro to get in the driver's good favor. "So your boss ova here?"

"Yeah, she has some kind of meeting with Kazzy's son."

So now Phillip was working on Miss Waxley, was he? He had said himself that he wanted to stop the garden project before it bled more money. Becca, the sea urchin, and the sumo wrestler all seemed to be on the other side. Perhaps Phillip and Miss Waxley were conspiring to recruit one of the others to vote to get rid of the garden, once and for all.

"You goin' to Mr. Ouchi's memorial service? Right after lunch."

Mas shook his head. He had forgotten about the service.

J-E blew out some smoke from his cigarette and looked toward the Cadillac. "I wish I could quit this gig. But can't afford to go back to taxi driving. I have a kid and all."

"Oh, yah?"

"Ten months old." J-E was wearing gloves again with the fingertips cut off. He dug his right hand into his coat pocket and produced a photo of a fat baby, in an oversized football jersey, drooling on a toy football.

Mas grunted. A baby was a baby, unless it was your own. Or your daughter's, Mas added silently.

"You know who was over here, too? Howard Foster. And those other jerks, Penn and Larry. But they already took off."

"Oh, yah." Mas pretended not to care.

"Yeah, Waxley Enterprises's just across the street."

Sure enough, on the other side of Broadway stood a

tall coral-colored building with lettering in gold, Waxley Enterprises.

"Those two are assholes, man. Always telling me to take them places. They know that I'm hired by old lady Waxley. She's the ones who pays me, and they don't tip, neither."

Mas stared at the gold lettering on the building across from them. "You gonna be here for a while?"

"At least an hour."

"Do me favor," Mas asked. "If you see a Japanese ole man with white hair wandering around, tell him Izu ova there." Since Tug hadn't emerged from the building, he must have gotten a meeting with Phillip.

"Sure thing, Mas." J-E nodded, the cones on his head trembling.

✣ ✣ ✣

Mas walked across the street, trying remember the sumo wrestler's full name. Larry something. Larry Perry. Larry Ball. What the hell was it? Something with the letter P. Pauley, like UCLA's Pauley Pavilion basketball arena.

He entered the building's lobby, which reminded him of a deluxe funeral home's mausoleum. Everything was dead quiet and empty, other than a coffin-shaped desk in the middle. On one side of the granite wall was a list of departments and floors. Mas took out his reading glasses and looked at the directory in the lobby for a good ten minutes. Finally the receptionist, wearing a blue blazer and a floppy striped bow tied underneath the collar of a crisp white shirt, left her coffin desk and came to Mas's assistance. She told him that Larry Pauley was vice president of public relations on the eleventh floor. What was public relations, anyway? Well, Mas was part of the public, so perhaps Larry would make time for him.

Mas took an elevator to the eleventh floor, where another receptionist sat. Too many women sitting in comfortable chairs doing nothing, thought Mas. "Mr. Larry Pauley," he said.

"Do you have an appointment?" she asked.

Mas shook his head. "But very important."

The receptionist took down Mas's name (she asked for the spelling three times) and then relayed it to someone over the phone. Like a secret password, Mas's name opened a door. The receptionist told him to go through it to a hall to the left.

The whole office looked like a maze for rats, cubicles in the middle stuffed with people, papers, and computers. Mas knew that those in the center were the actual workers, while the ones in the outer offices were the queen bees. That's the way it was for insects and employees, Mas figured.

Larry Pauley had a corner office that overlooked Central Park. From eleven floors above, the trees looked like dried-out shrubs ripe for a bonfire.

"Mr. Arai, to what do I owe this pleasure?" Larry spoke easily, words dripping out like oil from a leaky engine. How was it that this big shot in New York City was talking to Mas like he was an old friend?

Larry wasn't wearing a jacket, and his shirtsleeves were

rolled up to his beefy biceps. Mas noticed the edge of a tattoo on his left arm. It was one thing for Lloyd, a miserable gardener, to have a wedding ring tattoo, but quite another for a vice president of a company with two sets of receptionists to be marked on his arm muscle. Mas could smell blue-collar, and that's where this Larry Pauley came from.

To see that Larry himself might not be as high-tone as his corner office gave Mas added strength. "Came about Takeo," Mas explained.

"Your grandson."

Mas nodded. "Izu afraid of all dis board thing. Don't want my grandson to be mixed up with dis mess."

Larry's eyes gleamed like charcoal briquets ready for a steak barbecue.

"Is that so, Mr. Arai?"

Before Mas could respond, a thin man knocked on his half-open door. "Mr. Pauley—" he said, and then noticed Mas. "Oh, I'm sorry. I didn't know you had a guest." He handed Larry a Styrofoam box—lunch?—and then at least a half dozen shiny gold strips of paper. Even though Mas hadn't seen them before in New York City, his gambling instincts kicked in. Lottery tickets.

Mas never played the lottery in California. The odds were too big. Sure, some fools told him, you'll never win if you don't try. But these guys tried every week and had nothing to show for it. Mas thought the poker tables were a safer bet, where you relied more on your wits to get ahead.

Larry quickly took the lottery tickets and slipped them into his top desk drawer as the male clerk left. It didn't look good for a big shot vice president to play a fool's game. "Please have a seat," Larry said, extending his huge palm toward a black leather chair held together by metal bars. Larry sat behind his mahogany desk, his Styrofoam box on the desk's top right side like a postage stamp on a letter.

Mas instead circled the office once around. He stopped at a framed oil painting of galloping horses and glanced at a collection of commemorative beer steins with various logos of racetracks from around the nation.

"Like horses?" Mas asked.

"Just a little hobby."

Mas pointed at a beer stein decorated with purple San Gabriel Mountains, horses, the smiling face of Laffit Pincay, Jr., and the words Santa Anita Racetrack. "Have dis one at home," he said. Mas was partial to Pincay; he had made at least five thousand dollars by betting on the jockey throughout the years.

"You're a track man, too, Mr. Arai?" Larry's voice went up an octave higher.

Mas nodded.

"Here, let me show this to you," Larry called Mas over to his desk. Mas edged behind Larry's chair and almost choked on his strong cologne. A man would only soak himself in fake scent to mask his natural bad skunk smell, Mas figured. With a clear view of Larry's wide forehead, Mas noticed a funny scar just below his receding hairline. A result of a childhood accident or a more recent incident? Mas didn't want to ask.

Larry took out a file from his top drawer and opened it

to the centerfold. A beautiful black racehorse, its coat and muscles taut and shimmering in the sun. It had a necklace of roses tossed over its neck and a jockey at its side.

"Good-lookin' horse," Mas managed.

"I'm buying her next week. Her name's Last Chance."

Last Chance. Not much of a name, thought Mas. But maybe it had some special meaning for Larry. Mas knew that some gamblers just went for the names of horses, whichever one gave them a tingle of hope and possibility.

Larry closed the folder and Mas finally sat down in the leather chair, safely escaping Larry's scent. "Anyway, you were talking about your grandson?" Larry said.

Mas swallowed and prepared to cast his line. In lake fishing, you waited to see ripples on the surface of the water. Mas thought he saw some movement in Larry's mind, and lowered the bait. "Yah, Waxley Garden. Don't think Takeo should be involve—too danger, you knowsu, with Mr. Ouchi's death and all."

"I understand, Mr. Arai. I completely understand."

"So I'm tellin' Lloyd and Mari, get Takeo outta there."

"I think it would be for the best." Larry smiled wide for the first time for Mas. His smile was a dazzling white, as if he had used a bottle of Clorox to bleach his teeth. The cologne, the white teeth, what was real about Larry Pauley? Mas thought that it might lie in that hint of a tattoo.

Larry went on to say that he would be more than happy to assist Mas in any way, because it was Takeo's welfare they were thinking about, yes? Mas nodded like a Tommy Lasorda bobble-head doll, a big grin pasted on his face. He was glad there were no mirrors in Larry's office, or else he would be making himself sick at this point. Larry didn't want Takeo and probably Lloyd to have anything to do with the garden. The question was, why? Larry finally said that he had another appointment to go to, so Mas rose from the chair.

"Youzu goin' ova to memorial service?" Mas asked.

"Unfortunately, I won't be able to make it," said Larry without a tinge of regret.

Before Mas left the office, he turned to Larry. "Mr. Ouchi not a track man," Mas stated more than questioned.

"Kazzy? Are you kidding me? His Highness would never rub elbows with commoners."

✥ ✥ ✥

Mas went back to the sidewalk, only to find the Cadillac gone. Tug was not around, either. A few minutes later, Tug appeared. "You didn't tell me that Mr. Ouchi's memorial service is today, Mas."

"Yah, I forget."

"So Phillip was in a rush to leave. He was pretty upset to hear that I was a friend of yours. I told him that I meant no harm, that I was sorry about his father's death. He didn't look too good."

Tug explained that Ouchi Silk was on the fifth floor of the metallic building. "I think they are downsizing, because half of the offices were vacant. They must be having economic troubles." Mas remembered how Tug's son, Joe, was going through the same thing at his job back in California. This downsizing was an epidemic.

"*Warukatta*. Sorry I putcha in a bad position."

"No problem, Mas. That's just part of the job."

What job? Mas wondered. Since retiring, Tug had devoted himself to fixing broken objects in his house and Mas's. It was obvious that he was now trying to fix broken people.

Even on the train ride back to Brooklyn Heights, Tug wasn't acting himself. A man entered the train car holding a carton of chocolates. Mas didn't give it a second thought. Everyone was selling something in New York, and subway passengers were a captive audience. Even the homeless stood up in the train car, sharing their woes and tribulations so eloquently that Mas was almost moved to place a buck in their empty hats. Almost moved, but not quite.

Now the chocolate seller was making his spiel. "My church is hoping to get your support. We are a small church, no building to speak of, but we have the spirit inside of us," he said, pacing the length of the car and holding up 100 Grand and Nestlé Crunch bars.

The man was selling a load of garbage, but Mas was surprised to see Tug taking two dollars out of his wallet and giving it to the man for two 100 Grand bars. Tug handed a candy bar to Mas.

"Could be poison, Tug," Mas warned.

"Let's live dangerously," Tug said, tearing off the wrapper.

"*Orai*," said Mas. He sensed that Tug, away from Lil for the first time in a long while, was transforming into a rebellious teenager. There was a Japanese term, *heso magari*, that mothers called such children. *Heso* meant belly button; *magari*, crooked. In New York City, Tug's belly button was moving away from the middle.

"Go for broke," Tug said before taking a large bite.

The 100 Grand bars didn't kill them, but gave Mas a mean stomachache. It was from not eating all day, Mas figured. And at least the stomachache somehow lessened the pain in his hand and lower back. Tug had purchased a fancy Brooklyn Heights map and had highlighted their path to the last flower shop, one with a fancy French name.

"This place reminds me of Paris," Tug said as they neared the corner storefront. Sometimes Mas took Tug for granted and thought of him as a simple man whose most worldly adventures went as far as discovering cockroach infestation in an all-you-can-eat buffet. But Tug had actually been to exotic places like Rome and Paris, Mas had to remind himself.

The shop was painted a golden yellow, with upside-down bouquets of dried flowers hanging from the ceiling like whisk brooms. On the floor sat cement angels and rabbits in between baskets of ribbon and vases of pink and lavender tulips. A fresh-faced girl stood behind the counter, her blond hair tied back in a high ponytail.

Tug licked his lips. "Let me take the lead on this," he said. Mas clutched his belly, happy to oblige.

"Hello, can I help you?" Even though it was past lunchtime, the girl was enthusiastic. Must be new at this, thought Mas.

"Ah, actually, I was referred to you by Happy Ikeda, you know, of Happy's Floral Design in Midtown?" Tug said.

The girl looked blankly at Tug. Mas guessed that Happy's name didn't have much weight in the fifty-and-under crowd.

"Anyway, I know that you order Mystery Gardenias from California. San Juan Capistrano, in fact."

"Oh, yeah." The girl became more animated. "They are so beautiful. Gigantic ones."

"Yes, well, I know that this is a strange request. But do you have records on who bought any of those gardenias on Wednesday, Thursday?"

"Why?"

"Well, you see"—Mas cowered to see what Tug was going to come up with next—"we're investigating a murder."

"Murder?" The girl looked him up and down. She seemed to take note of Tug's well-kept beard, his button-down shirt, the casual yet expensive designer jacket his kids had most likely purchased him for Christmas. Good thing she couldn't see Tug's bargain tennis shoes. Then her eyes moved to Mas.

Tug quickly displayed something from his wallet. "I'm an investigator," he said, and then pointed at Mas. "This is

Inspector Arai. From Japan. He doesn't speak much English."

Mas was ready to protest, but then thought better of it. Tug was pretty sly when he wanted to be. This way Mas didn't have to open his mouth and make fools out of both of them.

The girl waited.

"Kazzy Ouchi," Tug said. No reaction from the girl. "His death was in the paper."

Unfortunately, youngsters didn't read newspapers, much less the *Post* tabloid.

"Anyway, he has international connections. Both here and in Japan."

"Wow," the girl said, her mouth partially open, revealing chewed gum on her pink tongue.

"So, I'm sure that you would want to assist in the investigation."

"What does this have to do with gardenias?"

"One was left at the crime scene."

"How do you know that it was a gardenia from our shop?"

"Forensics," Tug said. "We have advanced research laboratories."

"Well." The girl played with the keys of her computer, which probably doubled as the cash register. "I'll have to check with my boss."

"There's no time for that," Tug said. His voice took on an official tone like workers at government offices. Even Mas jumped slightly, recalling the way he had been treated at the Department of Motor Vehicles and Social Security offices. After forty years of loyal work with Los Angeles County, Tug had fully adopted the required attitude.

The girl looked confused and bit the side of her lip.

"I wouldn't want to come here with a warrant. That would cause all sorts of problems for your boss."

"Well, I guess it wouldn't hurt to just look." The girl finally caved in.

"A delivery to Kazzy Ouchi," Tug said quickly, so as not to lose momentum. "Prospect Park."

The girl's nimble fingers tapped the keyboard.

"Yes, there was a delivery to Kazzy Ouchi on Thursday."

"From whom?"

"Somebody named Anna Grady."

Anna Grady, thought Mas. Kazzy's ex-girlfriend.

"Wait a minute. I remember this. I took the order over the phone." The girl continued staring at the computer screen.

"You have her address?" Tug asked

"Yes, Fort Lee, New Jersey."

Tug stepped behind the flower shop girl and noted the address in a small spiral notebook he kept in his shirt pocket.

"What's that?" he asked, pointing to something on the screen.

"Oh, she wanted a note with the gardenia. That's right. I remember now. She kept changing it. She finally came up with this."

" 'Meet me in the garden at eight tonight,' " Tug read out loud.

Mas forgot that he wasn't supposed to know English. "Thursday?" he reconfirmed.

The girl nodded her head. "Yes, last Thursday. Is that important?"

❖ ❖ ❖

"Thursday the day Kazzy shot dead," Mas said as they walked toward the underground apartment. "Girlfriend somehow connected." Tug's feet were swollen in his new tennis shoes, so he trudged behind Mas, a few steps back.

"Yes, I was thinking the same thing." Tug stopped at the corner and leaned his hand on a neighboring brownstone. "My feet are aching, Mas. How are you holding up?"

Miraculously, Mas's hand didn't smart anymore, and even his stomachache had gone away. Mas figured that he had extra-strong white blood cells, perhaps enhanced from the radiation of the Bomb.

He told Tug that he could soak his feet in Mari and Lloyd's bathtub, for which Tug seemed eternally grateful. "I'm getting tired of Joy's brown water," he explained.

As Mas opened the gate and door of the underground apartment, he remembered a moment at the flower shop.

"Whatsu dat ID you show the girl?" he asked Tug.

"Oh." Tug smiled. "It was my old health inspector badge. Just covered up the side that said Department of Health."

Mas laughed and let Tug into the underground apartment. He pointed through the bedroom to the bathroom and then checked the refrigerator. Empty, aside from a half-empty carton of soy milk and various bottles of mustards, sauces, and pickles. Luckily, in the freezer was a plastic bag of leftover rice. As he heard water running in the bathtub, he brewed some green tea and microwaved the rice. He poured the steaming tea over the rice in two rice bowls. He was delighted to find a small bottle of *umeboshi* on the refrigerator door shelf and floated a couple of the red pickled plums in his rice concoction.

Tug walked barefoot through the house, leaving traces of water on the hardwood floor. When he saw the rice bowls, his eyes crinkled in a smile. "*Ochazuke*," he said. "Just like home."

They slurped down the rice and bit into the pickled plums.

"You think you could live in a place that has no Little Tokyo, Japantown, or J-town?" Tug asked.

"I dunno," Mas said. "How about you?"

Tug shared that he had been in New York three times, the first time after he had been honorably discharged from the Army in 1946. Instead of heading straight back to what was left of the farm in San Dimas, California, he spent a good two weeks with his Army buddies near Spanish Harlem on Riverside Drive, where most of the Nisei had congregated during the war. Some were college students, and others became two-bit international traders dealing in cheap china figurines or silk. A group of them went dancing at the Ninety-second Street YMCA with Nisei girls wearing their hair rolled up on the sides (Tug, of course, never forgetting about Lil, who was back in Los Angeles with her folks).

"I tell you, Mas, I felt like a country boy."

"Well, where you from, pretty *inaka* back then. Nutin' there."

"That's true," Tug said. "Those New York Nisei, something else, I tell you. Risk takers. Big dreamers. But you know me, Mas. I'm not much of a gambler. All I wanted to see were green fields, foothills, and San Gabriel Mountains."

Mas spit the plum seed into his fingers.

"But they think we California Nisei are small-minded, boxed in," said Tug.

"Maybe."

"So what if we are a little stuck in our ways?"

Mas agreed with Tug. The West Coast Nisei had more to fight against; hadn't the Yamadas themselves had to reinvent themselves after they lost the chili pepper farm? They never regained their prewar success.

As Mas washed the *chawan* bowls, Tug sat on the couch and was rewriting Anna's name and address on another piece of paper when Mari entered the apartment.

"Lloyd told me that he would stay overnight at the hospital," she said. Looking over Tug's shoulder, she read, " 'Anna Grady.' Sounds familiar. Wasn't that Kazzy's ex-girlfriend?"

Mas nodded.

"I never met her, but Lloyd has. Kazzy even told Lloyd that he was thinking of marrying her. Why do you have her address?"

Mas let Tug tell the news. It had been his fake ID, after all, that had forced the hand of the flower shop girl. "It turns out she sent Ouchi a flower and a note that she wanted to meet with him at the garden the night he was killed," Tug announced, wiggling his toes.

"The gardenia," Mari murmured, and Tug nodded again. As Mari listened to the whole story, Mas saw a familiar look of determination on her face. "Lloyd will be with Takeo. I say that we go over there and talk to Anna Grady."

"I'm kind of worn-out, Mari," Tug said. "How about tomorrow?"

"This can't wait." Mari was driven to find the answer. "How about you, Dad? Ready for a bus ride?"

Mas had taken the bus a few times before in Los Angeles, but that was when it had been known as the RTD, not all the fancy names it was called today. Now in Southern California there were bright-red buses called Rapid; small buses, which just circled downtown L.A.; and sky-blue buses, which traveled all the way to Santa Monica, just blocks away from the Pacific Ocean. Even Pasadena had a free bus line, with vehicles elaborately painted with images of jazz singers to prove that the city had some culture. It was as if you needed to trick people to ride the bus.

Mari claimed that the New Jersey Transit was the fastest way to travel to Fort Lee, New Jersey, from Manhattan. Fort Lee sounded like an old military unit, a fortress made of wooden logs and manned by soldiers wearing moccasins and carrying rifles.

They took the underground train to the Port Authority

Terminal on Forty-second Street, and from there a bus. The bus looped south and then traveled north, passing the bare gray trees of Central Park and the tall, high-tone apartments on the west side of the avenue. The sun was going down, but instead of the spectacular sunsets of smog-tainted Los Angeles, the grayness just got darker, like a shade being pulled down.

Several blocks later, the scene changed to dilapidated houses and a starkness that stripped Mas's heart.

"Columbia's not far from here," Mari said.

Mas felt his mouth go dry. So they had spent thousands of dollars on a university in this neighborhood? "So youzu still like New York," Mas stated more than questioned.

"Can't go back to California. I know that the weather's so much better. But we've become New Yorkers. And besides, we couldn't afford any place in Los Angeles, either."

You could live with me, Mas impulsively thought, and then took back his silent offer. What kind of *baka* idea was that? He was fine by himself, letting dust settle on his furniture and bowling trophies. Keeping his refrigerator stocked with just necessities: Budweiser, jalapeño peppers, hot dogs, eggs, ketchup, and kimchee. With Mari's family there would be soy milk, tofu hot dogs, yogurt, cantaloupe, apples, strained spinach, and carrots. He would have to put away all his fishing hooks and lines, and smooth circular *go* game pieces, which could get lodged in a baby's throat.

The bus passed over a massive bridge, woven bars of the metal laced together to hold the weight of fifty-ton trucks. This was nothing like the wimpy two-lane "suicide" bridge in Pasadena, held up by delicate arches. The Pasadena bridge was a favorite in cheap movies and television shows, but had no other real purpose, except for once serving as the diving board of the brokenhearted beaten down by the Depression in the thirties.

Finally they were dropped off at an open plaza boasting a concrete monument, as big as a celebrity's headstone, with the message WELCOME TO FORT LEE.

Mari opened up her map. "Anna Grady's apartment is not far from here. You up for walking half a mile, Dad?" They passed a quaint business district with outdoor cafés, more streets, and then came upon a tall high-rise.

"This is it," Mari said.

While Waxley Enterprises had a receptionist with a striped bow, the high-rise had a full-fledged security guard wearing a uniform and even a holster fastened around his bloated belly.

Mari licked her lips and went to the counter with a sense of purpose. "Hello," she said. "We're here to visit Anna Grady."

The security guard had them sign a piece of paper fastened to a clipboard. He then picked up a phone and mumbled something into the receiver. "Who are you?" he asked, not bothering to consult his clipboard.

"Mari Jensen and Mas Arai," said Mari. "We're friends of Ms. Grady."

Mas held his hands awkwardly at his sides. He was ready to get kicked out, and instead the security guard nodded his head. "Take those elevators. Seventeenth floor."

Mas was amazed at how they could get clearance so easily. They didn't even know what Anna Grady looked like.

"Can't seem scared, Dad. Have to act like you belong." That was easy for Mari to say. She had a college degree worth thousands of dollars from a fancy university. Even though she was small, she walked like a person twice her size, as if she dared anyone to question her right to be anywhere.

The elevators opened to a long hallway and a line of doors. Which door? It was as bad as a game of roulette. Some guys claimed they had a system to win, but Mas knew it was just a guessing game. Before they had a chance to try their hand, a door opened on the right-hand side. A Japanese American woman of around seventy stood in jeans, sweatshirt, and slippers. Her graying hair was neatly arranged in a *chawan*-style cut, shaped as if the barber had put a giant rice bowl on top of her head. Mas thought that hairdo had gone out of style in the seventies. "So you are friends of Anna?" the woman asked.

"Yes, I'm Mari, and this is my father, Mas."

The two of them made quite a pair, Mas then realized. Both just a little above five feet tall, who would think that they were flat-out liars?

The *chawan*-cut woman, who introduced herself as Seiko Sumi, Anna's roommate, gestured for them to come in. The apartment was airy; a sliding-glass door in the living room opened out to a balcony crowded with ferns and other houseplants.

"Anna was resting, but she'll be out in a moment. She's

had a difficult day. A close friend of ours passed away, and we went to the memorial service this afternoon."

Mas stared at Mari, but she instead was focused entirely on Seiko.

"Sit down, sit down." She gestured to the couch. As Mas and Mari complied, Seiko began to ask, "Now, how do you—" Mas cringed as he prepared to hear the dreaded question.

"You have a lovely apartment," interrupted Mari, leaping to her feet.

Mas took a quick look at the living room. Reminded him of any other Nisei house. Some Japanese *sumi-e* paintings of jagged mountains. A Japanese doll wearing a bright kimono in a glass box. A couple of papier-mâché tigers. Somebody there was obviously born in the Year of the Tiger. Mas followed Mari as she examined a special glass case in the corner. It looked like some kind of mini historic display with an old nursing uniform, old books, and a badge that read Seabrook Farms. Mas faintly remembered a gardener mentioning that he had worked back East on Seabrook Farms during World War II.

"Seabrook Farms," Mari said. "I was the videographer for the fiftieth-anniversary reunion event."

"Oh, really? My mother was in Seabrook—she worked in the infirmary. She died some years ago, but I know that she would have loved to go to the reunion. Quite an event, I heard."

Mari nodded. "Five hundred people. They have a museum, you know."

"Oh, yes, I've even donated some of my mother's belongings to them." The *chawan*-cut woman paused, her eyes darting from Mas to Mari. "Well, you know Anna was there in Seabrook, right? My mother got to know her when Anna was in the infirmary, recuperating from chicken pox. Newcomers aren't exposed to the same diseases as we are."

"Ah, of course—" Mari stumbled on her words.

Seiko's eyes thinned. "How do you know Anna again?"

Mari seemed to know that they couldn't keep playing this game. "I really don't know Anna," she admitted. "I'm really sorry to have deceived you. My husband actually has met her. He worked on Kazzy's new garden."

Seiko's mind seemed to be percolating. "But you weren't at the memorial service."

"Our three-month-old son has been ill. We've had to be at the hospital."

"What is your name again?" Seiko asked.

"Mari Arai—well, Jensen now."

"Jensen." The tone of Seiko's voice was sharp, like a bird whistle. "Is your husband Lloyd Jensen?"

Mari nodded.

"I read about him."

Mas felt like folding his hands over his eyes. It was over.

"I don't know what you want with Anna, but I'm sure that she won't want to see you. She's gone through enough already."

The door to one of the back bedrooms opened. A *hakujin* woman who looked like an older version of actress Ingrid Bergman in the movie *Casablanca* stood in the doorway. A calico cat slithered through the woman's legs. "Tama," she called out. Mas was surprised. Tama was a Japanese name meaning "ball," the same meaning as the name Mari. The cat sniffed at Mas's right jean leg and then opted to go into the kitchen.

Anna took a step forward. "What's going on, Seiko?" Mas couldn't help but notice that she was shaped like an old-time Coca-Cola bottle. In spite of her being at least sixty, the woman's figure was good, especially her legs. She must have known that, since she was wearing a skirt cut above the knee.

"These people lied to get in here. I'm going to call the security guard downstairs." Seiko headed for the telephone in the kitchen.

Anna looked confused, afraid to move.

"Please, just a few minutes of your time, Ms. Grady," Mari implored. "We know that you sent Kazzy a note to meet him the evening he was killed."

"How did you—" Anna said, and then shifted gears. "I've already spoken to the police."

She spoke as if she was holding something in her mouth, and Mas detected a slight accent. Maybe this Anna Grady was not from America.

"But did you talk to the police about the gardenia?"

Anna's blue eyes desperately searched for her roommate.

"Security's coming," reported Seiko, appearing from the kitchen, not a strand in her *chawan* haircut out of place.

Mari placed her business card on the couch and pulled

at Mas's jacket sleeve. "We didn't mean to cause any problems," she said. "But call me if you change your mind." They quickly walked out the apartment into the hallway. Mari rushed to the elevator and furiously punched the Down button. Luckily there were two elevators, and the one that opened first only had a woman with a child in a stroller. They slipped in, and as the doors closed they heard the next elevator ring to announce that it was on its way.

They had effectively eluded the sole security guard and practically ran to the bus stop in the open plaza. Fort Lee looked nothing like its name, but Mas felt that they had dodged some serious bullets at the high-rise. He had no intention of coming to Fort Lee again.

The ride on the bus back to Manhattan was quiet. Mas dozed off as soon as he settled in a seat next to Mari. Transferring to the crowded subway at Port Authority, Mas and Mari had to grab on to a pole and stand. It was obvious that Mari had been thinking this whole time.

"I have a friend, a professor, who helps out at the Seabrook museum."

Mas tried to follow Mari's thinking. "You think this Seabrook has sumptin' to do with Kazzy?"

"Well, I'm going to e-mail him when we get back to the apartment and see if he knows anything about Anna Grady."

Mas was dead tired by the time they got home. He didn't bother to take a bath or change out of his jeans and sweater. He was, in fact, dreaming of cats, the Japanese kind with no tail, when he felt something pull on his shoulder. "Huh—" He looked up from the couch to see Mari in a flannel nightshirt. "Whatsamatta?"

"My friend already e-mailed me back."

Mas made two fists, one with his good right hand and the other with his bandaged left hand, and tried to rub the sleep from his eyes. "Sumptin' on Anna Grady?"

"Nothing on her, but listen to this: Kazzy went to the Seabrook museum six months ago, asking to see some documents on Asa Sumi."

"Who dat?"

"Seiko Sumi's mother."

"Huh?"

"Anna Grady's roommate."

Mas's mind couldn't catch up with Mari's words.

"I don't know what's going on with those two roommates, but it's worth looking into. Do you know if Tug still has his rental car?"

chapter nine

Mas sat in the back of Tug's rental car with a Triple A map spread out over his knees. He didn't bother to fasten his seat belt, although Tug had asked him to before they left the curb of Carlton Street at nine o'clock in the morning. But that was two bathroom stops ago, and Tug had apparently forgotten to reissue his gentle reminders.

Tug was in the driver's seat, and Mari was in the passenger's. She had her own map, but said she didn't need it, because she had been to Seabrook before, to film the reunion. "It was a few years ago," she said to Tug. "It was organized mostly by

Japanese Americans, all celebrating when they first came to work at Seabrook Farms in 1945."

Mas shook his head. The Nisei were always celebrating this, celebrating that. When Chizuko was alive, she and Mas were invited to their share of twenty-five-year wedding anniversaries. Usually they took place in the back of a Japanese restaurant, where they were served limp tempura and rolled sushi with rice a little hard from being left out too long. In front of each place setting was usually an origami crane or a dollar bill folded up like a stiff *kaeru*, frog, the symbol of luck among the luckless Nisei and Sansei.

But it didn't stop with wedding anniversaries. There were *yakudoshi* celebrations, so-called bad-year birthdays (thirty-three for girls, forty-two for boys), and then those events when sixty-year-old fools dressed up in bright-red caps and vests to prove that they were born again.

And then there were those camp reunions. Why did they want to remember being locked up together during World War II? Mas had wondered. Tug explained to him that most of the organizers for these reunions had been young, teenagers in camp. Their memories were much sweeter than those of their parents, who were now gone.

"So, whatsu dis Seabrook, anyways?" Mas asked. He could barely find it on the map. New Jersey was shaped like a flattened boxing glove, and Seabrook was located on the bottom tip, right underneath PHILADELPHIA, a city in all capitals.

"There's nothing much there anymore," explained Mari, who pushed her sunglasses up on her nose. "But it once was one of the centers of the vegetable canning industry. They called this Charles Seabrook the Spinach King." Mari went on to describe Mr. Seabrook's grand scheme of workers on the run from the Great Depression, Stalin, communists, and, of course, American internment camps.

"Knew some guys in the service who had family over in Seabrook," commented Tug. "Mr. Seabrook and his staff recruited them right out of camp. Even if they worked long hours, it was better than being behind barbed wire, I guess."

Mas knew what kind of deal that was. Work like a dog for nothing. He looked out the window and saw great empty spaces, tilled land ready to give birth to green vegetables. Accumulated water stayed still in the furrows, and now and then Mas saw a lone creek or marsh. The gray skyline was held up by lines of trees, their bare branches resembling a witch's gnarled hair. Now that they were away from the hubbub of New York, Mas thought that he would be relieved. But instead his stomach felt on edge, as if there would be no place to go in case of trouble.

They continued on the New Jersey Turnpike until they hit a smaller highway and then eventually transferred to Route 77. More trees and then a lone white building, looking prim and proper like something from America's pioneering days. Mas noticed a Japanese motif on the front of the building.

It was as if Mari had read his mind. "Yup, that's the Buddhist temple," she said. "A lot of the members are non-Japanese, I think. Even had a *hakujin* woman minister once."

Mas pursed his lips. Everything took on another angle here on the East Coast.

"The church must have been established around World War Two, when all the Japanese came," Tug said.

Mari nodded. "A lot of the Japanese have moved out to New York and other places," she explained. "But they do have a JACL chapter here. Their annual chow mein dinner sells out every year." Japanese Americans and Chinese food, the traditional combination. Funny remnants, here and there, thought Mas. One big shot recruits workers, and look what happens. Buddhist temples and chow mein fund-raisers. People and cultural practices that were being trans-planted like weeds stuck on the blades of a lawn mower.

Mari then gave Tug more directions—"Turn right, then left"—and finally they parked in an open lot next to a brick building with a yellow steeple. The steeple was boxed in by a fancy fence and topped with a weather vane.

Before Mas could ask, his daughter said, "This is the city township building, you know, like their city hall. And also the location of the Seabrook museum."

This was what they had driven more than two hours for? Mas asked himself.

They piled out of the rental car. Like a roll-away bed, Mas hunched over to get out of the two-door sedan and then straightened up in the parking lot, pounding his sore back with the back of his right hand.

"It's down here." Mari pointed to the side of the build-ing, where stairs led down to a yellow door. One by one, they entered: first Mari, then Mas, and finally Tug.

❖ ❖ ❖

They went down a hallway and then entered a brightly lit, airy room. A banner reading Seabrook USA hung from the ceiling. Familiar Seabrook Farms labels had been framed and placed on the walls. Mas headed straight for a diorama of the entire operation, which included a water tower and a factory marked by a long chimney. This Seabrook had once been quite an operation. Mas had seen his share of rice paddies in Hiroshima, lettuce fields in Watsonville, and rows of tomato plants in various towns in Texas. This Seabrook made all of those farms look like someone's backyard vegetable garden.

"Hey, Mari," said a young Sansei man in a plaid flannel shirt and jeans. His hair was all shaved off like an *obosan* at a Buddhist temple. The rest of him looked strong and healthy, the type to be hiking in the hills, not hiding in the basement in a small town called Seabrook. He walked around a counter and gave Mari a quick hug. "Haven't seen you in ages."

"About five years." Mari's face seemed flushed, as if she had been in an *onsen,* a hot-spring bath. "This is Tug Yamada, and my dad, Mas Arai. Kevin Tachibana."

Kevin had a firm grip, and Mas was surprised to feel that his hand was callused.

"You a farmer?" Mas couldn't help but blurt out.

"Dad!" Mari said. "He's a professor."

"No, it's quite all right. I've bought an old house outside of Philly. Been renovating it myself. I guess I have some home-improvement battle scars." He grinned, and Mas took a liking to him instantly. A Sansei, smart, and even worked with his hands on his own house. Why couldn't Mari have fallen for a man like this?

"So you're the boss today," Mari said.

"Well, it's my spring break. I'm just filling in while the director's on vacation." Kevin looked at Mari's left hand. "Well, how are you? Married, I see."

Mari, thankfully, did not have a matching tattoo ring, but a simple silver one instead.

"Yeah," Mari said. "And one baby."

"You're kidding."

"Three months old." Mari's eyes grew watery.

"Wow. I guess you'll want to get back to your baby ASAP. So, let's see—you're doing research on Kazzy Ouchi, right?"

Mari nodded. "You mentioned that Kazzy had contacted you about six months ago."

"Well, since I'm doing my research on prewar Nisei in New York and New Jersey, he wanted to meet with me. He specifically wanted to know about this Asa Sumi."

"Yes, the mother of Seiko Sumi, right?"

"Yeah, Seiko lives up in Fort Lee. Really nice woman. Have you met her?"

Mari nodded.

Mas noticed small beads of perspiration on his daughter's nose. Whenever she was caught in a lie or a tight situation, her nose would begin to sweat.

"Well, anyway, apparently Seiko's mother had worked as a housekeeper over in the Waxley House back in the thirties. I guess she worked under Kazzy's mother, Emily, and even filled in when Emily was pregnant. During the war, Asa was over here, in Seabrook, so I guess he wondered if we had any information."

"Did you?"

"Well, Seiko had showed us a journal."

"Yes," Mari murmured. Mas also remembered some sort of diary on display in the high-rise apartment.

"She didn't give to us, of course, but did leave some sample pages. She wanted to know if we could translate it for her or at least find someone who could. Unfortunately, I can't read *kanji*, only some *katakana* and *hiragana*, you know? My Japanese is terrible; I took Italian for my PhD. For a while I was introducing myself as Tachibana-*san* to visiting scholars, until I found out that no Japanese puts '*san*' after their own name."

Mas wasn't surprised about the young man's inability to speak Japanese. He was third-generation, after all. Even a Nisei like Tug didn't know much. The World War II camps and racism in general had made the Japanese lose their language. Why try to retain it if it was just one more thing that the government and people would hold against them?

Mari apparently felt that way. "But we're not Japanese. We're American," she said.

"That's true." Kevin laughed. "Maybe it was my subconscious, attempting to assert its Americanness, huh? Anyway, I couldn't read the thing. Neither could most of the staff. But we are planning to apply for a grant to do the translation. Seiko couldn't afford it otherwise; she's a retired nurse and also a perfectionist. Her Japanese is limited to a few phrases she learned from her parents. Simple stuff that I also remember hearing from my grandparents. But no writing or reading of *kanji*. Seiko wanted it professionally done. She told us that she would keep the original for now, but that we could have access to the journal anytime we wanted."

"Do you have the sample pages?"

"Oh, yeah, I dug them out for you. I have it in the back. Hold on a second." He disappeared through a door to a storage area.

Meanwhile, Tug had wandered to a photo exhibit of Seabrook, and Mas joined him. One photo had a line of women, their heads covered with white caps like the ones nurses used to wear, sorting vegetables on a conveyor belt. Men and teenagers picking beans. Nisei singles dancing, twists of crepe paper overhead.

Tug pointed to a black-and-white photo of girls, both Nisei and *hakujin,* standing together in Girl Scout uniforms. "Kind of like a mini United Nations. Jamaicans. *Hakujin* escaping the Dust Bowl."

Mas stared at an image of a line of *hakujin* women wearing headbands and long, flowing dresses with geometric patterns. "Theysu Americans?" Mas asked.

Tug examined the photo in front of Mas. "Oh, no. There were a lot of Estonians who were here. Their country was over by Russia. The Soviets occupied them, then the Germans, then the Soviets again. Some escaped to come here in fishing boats."

"*Hakujin* boat people?" Mas was surprised. People were running away from their troubles any way they could. It didn't matter if you were black, Asian, Latino, or even *hakujin*. "Dat Anna Grady not American. Sheezu come from somewhere else."

"Maybe she's Estonian."

Mas nodded, and Tug took out his notebook from his pocket and jotted some notes. Health inspector turned detective, Tug took on his new role with relish.

Kevin finally returned to the counter with some papers in hand. Tug and Mas could overhear him and Mari struggle with the Japanese.

"Let's see, hmm, well, this is the date, right? Damn, the year's written by era. What are they again?" asked Mari.

"Meiji, Taisho, Showa," Kevin recited. "Showa is during Emperor Hirohito's reign. Starts around 1926, I think."

Mari held a page close to her face. "These are the characters for Showa. How does it work again? The year in which the era begins minus one plus the number that follows the era?"

"Confusing."

"I know," said Mari. "It's just like when babies are born in Japan; they come out a year old already. We had a heck of a time figuring out what year my grandmother was born after she died."

"Dad"—Mari finally called over Mas—"can you help us with this?"

Mas got out his reading glasses, not that eager to serve as

a linguist. He looked at Tug, Mari, and then Kevin. If Mas was the most literate one of them all, they were in deep trouble.

The pages were written in a woman's fine script. She must have had some kind of education, because the strokes from her pen were definite and crisp. Each sentence ran straight from the top to the bottom without the aid of lined paper.

"Youzu start off here," Mas told Mari and Kevin, pointing to the far right side.

"Dad, that much we know. What does it say?"

"Novemba sixteen, letsu see, 1930. *Kumori*, gray day. *Ame*, rain. Go buysu beef from whatchacallit—"

"Butcher?" offered Tug.

"Yah, butcha. So dis person—girl, right?—went to buysu beef for some kind of dinner. Stew. For, letsu see. Wakusuri."

"The Waxleys!" Mari exclaimed.

"Yah, Waxley family, I guess."

Mas flipped through more pages. All notes about preparing meals and rooms to clean. The writer was obviously some sort of housekeeper, like Chizuko, because all she wrote about was making the Waxley family more comfortable in the Prospect Park house.

Mas dragged his dirt-lined fingernail up and down the lines. This woman was wired to be *chanto*, to take her work seriously.

"Pretty *tsumaranai*" was Mas's final analysis.

"What?" Kevin asked.

"Boring," Mari translated.

"Well, it's her day-to-day activities." Kevin shrugged his shoulders.

"Do you have more pages?" Mari asked.

"No, those are the only ones."

"Can we make a copy?"

"Well, normally, we need to get permission from the donor. But since I know you—"

"Thanks, Kevin." Mari followed Kevin to the photocopy machine. Kevin flicked a button on the machine. The photocopier purred and hummed as it warmed up.

"When I showed this to Kazzy, he got pretty excited," said Kevin. A flash of bright light leaked from the edges of the photocopier's glass cover. Why would these daily accounts have been of interest to Kazzy? wondered Mas. Maybe it was like the young professor said—Kazzy had known that he was going to die soon, so he wanted to piece together as much of his past as possible.

"Is there any mention of Kazzy in there?" Mari asked.

"I think some cursory stuff. He said that he could probably do the translation himself in exchange for getting access to the whole journal."

"He didn't have time to do a translation job. He was busy with the garden," said Mari.

"Well, he was pretty adamant. He was on a mission to reclaim his childhood. Once you hit seventy, eighty, you're dealing with your own mortality." Kevin then realized that he was in the company of two seventy-something-year-olds and covered his face with his right callused hand.

Tug laughed, his eyes dissolving into thin sideways crescents. "Mas and I know our days are numbered."

Mas grunted. Everybody's days were numbered, he thought, both old and young. The thing was, you didn't know what number you were dealt until it was too late.

"Well, anyway"—Kevin recovered from his embarrassment—"I provided him with Seiko's phone number and address, but I think that she was pretty resistant."

"Really? But she was willing to deal with you."

"Yeah, but we're a nonprofit institution. I think Seiko was a little taken aback by Kazzy's aggressiveness. I mean, here's this silk mogul who keeps bothering her about her mother's diary. Even knowing that he and his family are mentioned in there, she was reluctant to help him."

"So do you know what ended up happening?"

"I'm not sure, actually. Like I said, I met with Kazzy about six months ago, and Seiko was complaining to me about Kazzy's constant calls soon after. But about four months ago, it all stopped. Hadn't heard much of anything, until the reports of Kazzy's death came in and you got in touch." Kevin handed pages of the photocopied journal to Mari. "So, what's the deal with Kazzy's death?"

"What do you mean?"

"Was he bumped off, like people are saying? Some *hakujin* neighbor, or his *hakujin* gardener, right?"

After seeing the fields and furrows, Mas felt a little more open to the landscape of Seabrook, but the ground still seemed foreign. California had sandy loam, loose soil that allowed for the best strawberries and flowers in the nation, but everything here seemed dense, immovable. Sticky adobe soil. A farmer's nightmare.

Even as the sun was starting to set, the open space didn't seem right. Usually dusk brought a hush, a fuzzy hopefulness that with the end of this day, the next would be better. All Mas felt right now, however, was dread. That somehow crows and nocturnal pests would crowd into the fields to take them over.

They stopped by a small roadside diner that Kevin had recommended. Mari stayed outside for a while to call the hospital and check on Takeo. When she joined Mas and Tug in a red leather booth, her face looked relaxed. "Takeo's doing well," she said, slipping in beside Tug. "He'll be coming home tomorrow."

"Thank God," Tug said, grabbing her hand. She rested her small head on Tug's shoulder. With her short hair, she looked like a sparrow digging into her nest. "Thanks, Uncle Tug."

Mas felt awkward. Shouldn't he be the one comforting his daughter? He should be happy with the news about Takeo, yet, at the same time, he felt painfully inadequate. "Yah, good news, good news," he finally said.

The simple menus—a single page laminated in plastic—came with hot coffee in heavy white ceramic cups.

"Dad, you should order the Philly cheesesteak. That's the specialty here."

"Oh, yah," Mas said, grateful that his daughter was thinking about what he might enjoy.

He was surprised, however, when the waitress placed a long sandwich, instead of a slab of red meat, on a plate in front of him. *Nanda*, sandwich? I could have a sandwich any day, he thought. But today should not end with *monku*, a litany of complaints. Saying nothing, Mas stuffed his mouth with one end of the sandwich.

Mas was pleasantly surprised. "*Oishii*," he declared. The bread was soft, just as he liked it. And the steak, tender, like slices of sukiyaki meat. And plenty of fried onions, lettuce, tomatoes, and cheese to bring the flavors together.

"See, Dad, I told you," said Mari, chewing on her sandwich. "I wouldn't steer you wrong."

Tug had remained uncharacteristically quiet throughout the whole meal. He excused himself and left the table for a long time, long enough for Mas to worry that the cheesesteak had upset Tug's stomach. If that was the case, it was only a matter of time before Mas and Mari were its next victims.

Had it been worth it to come all this way? Mas wondered. "Find out whatcha need to find out ova at the museum?" he asked Mari.

"Well, at least we know that this journal is important in some way. But how is the question."

Father and daughter discussed various options. Had Anna and Seiko discovered some damaging information about Kazzy's background? And if they had, what had they done with that information? Mas didn't understand Kazzy's relationship with Anna, either. Why had he broken up with her?

Tug finally returned to the table. "Let's go," he stated more than asked. He didn't even put up a fight when Mas went to the cashier and paid the bill, grabbing some toothpicks to get at any stray pieces of meat.

After they loaded into the car, Tug guided them back on the road, checking his rearview mirror every ten seconds.

"Sumptin' wrong, Tug?" Mas finally asked.

"Do you have your seat belt on?"

"Yah," Mas lied.

"Good. I didn't want to mention anything earlier, but I think we're being followed."

"What?" Both Mas and Mari looked behind them and saw a dark car, one of those new, roundish Impalas, nothing like the classic ones of the sixties.

"I noticed him in the parking lot of the Seabrook museum. He followed us to the restaurant, and now he's right behind us."

Mas fumbled to slip on his seat belt.

"Thought maybe it was just some kind of coincidence, you know. I mean, the restaurant seems kind of popular. But he just stayed in his car, waiting. I saw him from the bathroom window."

No wonder Tug was in the *benjo* for so long, thought Mas.

"Speed up—" Mari ordered from the passenger seat.

"I'm going over the speed limit as it is, Mari."

"Uncle Tug, I'm serious. Put your foot on the gas."

Tug had no choice. He followed Mari's instructions, only to have the Impala follow right behind and practically hug their bumper.

The driver was no longer hiding in the back of parking lots. It was no secret. He was after them.

"Turn," ordered Mari, motioning to a dirt road, a break in the fields, on the right.

Tug swerved the car, and Mas was then happy for the muddy, sticky ground, which kept the car from jackknifing. Yet the same soil also kept the Impala on track.

"Maybe we should talk to him," Tug said.

"Uncle Tug, forgive me for doing this." Mari unfastened her seat belt and then Tug's, climbing over his massive lap. "But move over."

With Mari at the wheel, the rental car first lost a little speed. The seat was too far back for her, so she held herself forward with the steering wheel and then pushed her foot as far as she could on the gas pedal. The car revved and then suddenly pitched forward, causing Tug to hit his head against the car visor. "Hang on!" Mari cried. She turned the steering wheel sharply to the left, and Mas felt his body lurch to the side, papers from the Seabrook museum flying in every direction.

As the car straightened out, both Mas and Tug realized what Mari was doing. She had made a U-turn, and now the Impala was heading straight for them.

"Mari—" Tug had fastened his seat belt long ago and was shielding his neck with his hands.

"I dare him. I dare him," she muttered, along with a

string of expletives whose meaning Mas wouldn't even dare to imagine.

Mas wasn't about to die with his eyes closed, shivering in the back of the car. No, if his only child was going to look death straight in the eye, he was going to, too.

The Impala continued forward. Just when it looked like their front bumpers would crash into each other, the Impala swerved to the right. The side of the Impala brushed past the rental car, snapping the side mirror forward on its hinge. Mas looked out the side window. The car bounced into the sleeping fields of young spinach. The engine stalled and then revved up—the Impala was on the move again.

"He's going to expect us to take the Turnpike. I'll just go through Philadelphia," said Mari, pushing the car seat forward and then adjusting the side mirror back in position.

Tug lifted his head, and Mas knew that he had been praying to his *Kamisama*. Whatever had saved them, Mari's guts or God's grace, Mas wasn't going to bother to figure it out. At this point, he would accept anything they could get.

They moved from the country to mansions with neatly kept lawns to finally the middle of the city. They rode on a massive bridge, a crisscross of metal over a dark, overwhelming river lined by factories and steam pipes. Mas felt as if Philadelphia were going to swallow them alive.

Mari's idea apparently worked, because there was no sign of the Impala anymore.

"Didja get a good look at him?" Mas asked Tug.

"Little bit. *Hakujin*. Young. Wore a beanie cap."

"I've knowsu dat guy."

Mari almost swerved the car into the next lane. "What?"

Tug also seemed surprised.

"Riley," Mas sputtered out.

Tug took out his notebook, his pen stuck in the spiral. "You sure, Mas?"

"Who the hell is Riley?" Mari demanded.

Mas knew that he couldn't keep things from Mari any longer. He told her about following Riley to the factory with the red door, the gun, and the boy's threats.

"Phillip's behind this," Mari announced. "He thinks we know something that we obviously don't, or at least don't realize it. But one damn thing is for sure"—both Tug and Mas cringed as Mari let loose a string of foul words—"he picked the wrong people to tangle with."

❖ ❖ ❖

When they finally got into Brooklyn Heights, Mari stopped the car in the hospital parking lot. Leaving the engine on, she got out. Both Tug and Mas got out as well to stretch their aging limbs, change seats, and say good night to Mari.

Mari hugged Tug first, her small body swallowed up in Tug's grizzly bear one, and then surprisingly went to Mas and hugged him, too. "Thanks, Dad," she whispered in his ear. "You did good."

As he watched his daughter enter the hospital, Mas was amazed by her resilience. Her husband a suspect in a murder, her son hospitalized, and her life even on the line, yet she still had the presence to give two broken-down old men an embrace.

"I did nutin'," he said out loud.

"What, Mas?" Tug waited in the driver's seat.

"Nutin'," Mas said. "Nutin' at all."

chapter ten

The next day the sun was out, causing the daffodils in Mari and Lloyd's pitiful backyard to stand as straight as chopsticks. It was as if Tug's *Kamisama* knew that today Takeo was coming home. Mas took an extralong shower, even dragged a disposable razor across his chin and the sides of his face. After getting dressed in a fresh shirt and jeans, Mas cracked open a new plastic container of Three Flowers oil. A fingerful of grease, two swipes of a comb, and he was ready.

At the hospital, he, Lloyd, and Mari met with the East Indian doctor again. She spoke as if Mari and she were old friends—for all the time Mari spent in the hospital, they might as well have been short-term sisters. Mas was continually amazed at how much the world had changed. Now so many girls Mari's age or even younger (attorney Jeannie Yee, for example) seemed to be vital members of the working world. He supposed that the *hakujin* men were still on top and would always be, but now the number two man could be black, Latino, or even a woman.

"It's such a beautiful day; you should take a short walk in the sun on your way home," said Dr. Bhalla.

"Won't that be too much for him?" Mari clutched at Takeo, cocooned in a pure-white blanket.

"He's been cooped up long enough in here. Isn't there a park or something where you can go for half an hour?"

Lloyd unhinged the collapsed stroller and expanded it like an accordion. "I know exactly where we can take him."

The Brooklyn Botanic Garden felt comfortable to Mas even though he had never been there before. The bare wisteria trees twisted around the wood-framed archways like frayed rope, their branches bent like arthritic fingers. But they held the promise of what was to come in a few months. L.A., on the other hand, barely showed any signs of seasons. Sure, every spring the lavender blooms of the jacaranda trees popped open, spreading sap and petals on luxury cars, to their owners' dismay. Around the same time, the flowers of the long-stemmed agapanthus plants exploded like white and purple *hanabi*, fireworks, in freeze-frame. But perhaps the biggest seasonal rite of passage was the summer forest fires eating dried-up hills surrounding Los Angeles. Mas remembered one time a fellow gardener's truck came close to becoming molten metal when flames jumped the Glendale Freeway in search of more dead brush. That summer, flakes of ash like crushed dried seaweed covered Mas's driveway and got stuck in the dandelion heads on his lawn. And everywhere, there was the scent of smoke.

No fragrance, either good or bad, was coming out of the Brooklyn Botanic Garden this early in spring here. They passed the herb garden, and Mas noticed a cement planter with a sign, MUGWORT. Mugwort was used to make moxa, cigar-shaped sticks that Japanese used to burn against their skin to relieve their aches and pains. But instead of the leafy plant, there was only a blanket of brown pine needles and weeds underneath the plant's name.

Down the path was the familiar construction of a Japanese-style fence, simple planks of wood assembled without any signs of nails. And then, as if the fence slid across to make way for the view, Mas walked into the world of Takeo Shiota. Beyond the seven-foot stone lantern and an open wooden house along the *kokoro*-shaped pond was the *torii* gate, bright persimmon orange and wading in the green water. Of course, it wasn't as grand as the gateway Mas remembered at Miyajima. The New York version looked like an oversized toy, yet it still made its impact. Mas stood still, his hands balled up inside his pockets. He remembered going to Miyajima on a train and then a boat with his mother and his two oldest brothers one time when he was seven.

The fog had first hidden the tree trunk posts of the *torii*, and then, like a curtain, the mist lifted. Had a giant placed the *torii* there in the water? he had asked his mother. "*Bakatare, baka*," his brothers spit out, spinning their black school caps on the ends of their fingers. His mother said nothing, but Mas could feel her hand faintly squeezing his shoulder.

"Not bad, huh, Arai-*san*?" Lloyd said. He then pointed to the rectangular sign at the top of the gate and read the Japanese characters. "*DAI-MYO-JIN*. Great bright God. Enlightenment, right?"

Mas shrugged his shoulders. Here again, the sign, like the message left by Kazzy's father on the bottom of the concrete pond, was hard to understand. But what Mas could appreciate was the sweeping arch of the top crossbar and the straight line of the bottom bar right underneath it. The arch seemed to lift the whole gate out of the water, clearly transporting people to another place and time.

"What happen to this Shiota?" Mas had never heard of the landscaper before he stepped foot in New York.

"Died in an internment camp. Actually, I haven't been able to verify his exact year of death. Some say 1943, but his relatives back in Japan think it's 1946. But either way, he didn't spend his last days in New York."

"No camp ova here, *desho*?"

"Yeah, the Nisei in New York were safe, but some of the Issei pioneers, even diplomats, were taken away. There were these State Department internment hotels, I guess you can call them. One was in North Carolina, where I think Shiota might have been."

Mas frowned. A man who created this would be viewed as a threat? Didn't make sense.

"He even had a *hakujin* wife. But no kids. That's probably why no one knows anything about him. She sent her in-laws care packages after the war, but we don't really know what happened to her later in life, either."

As Mari bent over the stroller, Mas and Lloyd made their way to the wooden house by the pond. It reminded Mas of a similar structure in a botanical garden not far from his house in Altadena. They sat on a bench, their faces shaded by the extended roof. Next to them were a couple of *hakujin* women in nuns' habits who spoke softly in a language Mas couldn't make out.

There had been one thing that Mas had wanted to ask of Lloyd. "Whyzu you a gardener in the first place?" he finally asked.

"Probably the same reason why you are. I love plants, being outdoors."

Yeah, yeah, thought Mas. That's what the *hakujin* always thought. "But youzu write, *desho*? A type of poet, datsu what Mari said one time."

Lloyd laughed. "That was a long time ago. I was an English major at Columbia. I considered teaching English, but got hooked on horticulture instead. My PhD is on hold right now, but I hope to go back to it."

It was easy to lose sight of your first love, your first passion. Mas had wanted to become an engineer in Hiroshima, but over time he'd had to successively scale back his dreams. "I planned on buyin' nursery," he told Lloyd, "by the beach. Deal fell through, and besides, Mari and Chizuko make a big, big fuss. Don't wanna move away from friends."

"So you sacrificed for your family?"

Mas never thought about it quite that way. "Maybe," he said. "Maybe."

Lloyd jutted out his jaw and ran his fingers through his oily, thin hair. "Do you think the man in the Impala was really out to get you? I mean, maybe Tug got into his lane accidentally, you know. A type of road rage."

"Hard to say," Mas said. But Tug was convinced that they had been followed. And something else was *kusai*, stinky. "Youzu ever meet dis Anna Grady?" Mas asked.

"Yes, an attractive woman. But then, Kazzy always went for the pretty ones."

It made sense to Mas that Kazzy would have been consumed by beauty. Based on the last outfit he wore alive, the shoes and the suit, he seemed like a man who needed to be surrounded or touched by pretty things. Mas was hardly tempted by good-looking packages. It was like the Japanese folktale of the Tongue-Cut Sparrow: A greedy old lady, who had savagely clipped off the tongue of a wayward sparrow, forced her way into the Sparrow World. Her kind husband, a former traveler to the Sparrow World, had brought home a great treasure in a small box. Like her husband, the old woman was offered a choice between a small or a large gift. The woman chose the larger, only to discover that the box was full of demons. In Mas's experience, the same could hold true for beautiful women.

"Why he callsu it quits wiz her?"

"You know, that's a good question." Lloyd balanced his right ankle on his left knee. "It could be because he found out he was sick. Did you get a chance to read the other pages in the journal?"

Mas shook his head. After all the excitement from yesterday, reading about buying meat and cleaning house was the last thing that Mas wanted to do.

As they sat in front of the green pond, *koi* splattered with bright-orange, white, and black markings whipped their fins and tails toward the water's surface. Kissing the air with the circles of their mouths, they begged for food. But Mas wasn't about to stick a nickel in a machine that offered brown food pellets instead of gum balls. He'd leave that for lovers and children, people who thought nothing of wasting money for a bit of happiness.

After ten more minutes, it was time to leave the garden. Mas and Lloyd passed through the turnstile while Mari rolled Takeo's stroller through an adjoining gate. They had reached the ticket booth when they saw Detective Ghigo, the flaps of his overcoat blowing back from the wind: a black crow bringing bad news. He was with another man, short and bald. "Mari Jensen," Ghigo said. "We have a warrant for your arrest."

In the time it took Mas to blink, a pair of metal handcuffs was fastened on Mari's skinny wrists.

"Whatthe—" Mas felt like someone was peeling away at his heart.

"Get the hell away from my wife!" Lloyd went for the bald detective, but Ghigo stopped him.

Mari's eyes widened like those of a squid waiting for its head to be lopped off. Her skinny legs were planted next to the stroller. No set of handcuffs was going to keep her away from her son.

"Itsu suicide," Mas blurted out, even though he didn't believe it. "Ouchi-*san* killsu himself."

Ignoring Mas, Ghigo recited some police language in Mari's ear, including something about murder and a lawyer.

"We callsu Jeannie," Mas declared.

Mari nodded. "And get Takeo right home."

The attorney, Jeannie Yee, didn't waste any time. She was at the front door of the underground apartment soon after she had stopped to see Mari at the police station. "It's all circumstantial evidence," she said after she settled herself on a chair in the kitchen.

Mas looked blankly at Jeannie. Instead of a suit, she was wearing a plain white shirt. A plastic headband kept her thick hair away from her face.

Jeannie tried again. "I mean, they have the gun—which, by the way, they did trace to the half-rate production house that Mari had worked for—and they have the bullet—"

"Bullet," Mas couldn't help but murmur.

"Yes, the bullet. Aren't you the one who found it, Mr. Arai?"

Lowering his head, Lloyd squeezed his wedding ring tattoo. "I had to turn it in, Mr. Arai," he finally said. "They would have found out sooner or later."

Inu. Dog. Cheat. How could he sell out Mari like that? Mas felt his whole world turn. Had he misjudged Lloyd that badly? He had given that bullet to Lloyd because the son-in-law was the main man in his daughter's life. It was his responsibility to keep his family safe.

He wasn't supposed to give it to the authorities. Perhaps Lloyd was tired of Mari, had a woman on the side. Did he want Takeo to himself? If that was his plan, it wouldn't happen without a fight from Mas.

"Look, guys, we have to focus here." Jeannie spread her fingers on the surface of the table. "Apparently an anonymous source has been feeding Ghigo information. First someone called about Lloyd having an argument with Mr. Ouchi, and then made mention that Mari had filed a complaint with her independent filmmakers' union that Kazzy had been sexually harassing her."

"Who told Ghigo that?"

"That's the thing," Jeannie explained to Lloyd, "it's a-non-y-mous. Ghigo doesn't even know. They used a voice-altering device, so we don't even know if it's a man or a woman."

Mas was surprised that Jeannie had so much inside information. So was the son-in-law. "Ghigo told you that himself?"

Two pink marks like those atop baked rice cakes appeared underneath Jeannie's eyes. "Yes," she said, and then attempted to change the subject. "Is there anyone who would be out to get you or Mari?"

"Who are we? Nobodies. We have nothing," said Lloyd.

Mas grunted in support.

Lloyd raised his head. "Why would anyone think that we would be any kind of threat?"

Mas pushed his tongue against a space in between the roof of his mouth and his dentures. "Phillip, the son, he no good." Didn't want the garden in the first place, wasn't that what he had said?

"Yup, Ghigo's looking into that." Again, the girl lawyer seemed one step ahead. "These charges against Mari won't stand up. No judge wants to waste the taxpayers' money going through with this. This won't go past a preliminary hearing." Jeannie shot words like machine-gun fire throughout the room. "They just need someone to hang the crime on, since it's gotten so much media attention."

"Media? You meansu *Post*?"

"The *Post* started it, but now it's beginning to get some national news coverage. You have to admit that it has a sexy angle: business tycoon killed in a Japanese garden in New York."

Mas saw nothing sexy in that, especially since he was the one who had seen the dead body.

"They are playing it as a hate crime, and that's the last thing the NYPD or the tourist industry wants. They need to arrest someone, quick and fast. With Mari's connection to the gun, she's a logical suspect."

Mas was getting angrier by the minute. So Mari was a convenient scapegoat, is that what the attorney was saying?

Jeannie picked up a pen and began scribbling on papers

in a manila folder. "Oh, yeah, there's also the matter of the bail."

"Will they give her bail?" Lloyd asked.

"Well, I figure that with her clean record, good reputation, and, of course, being the mother of a sick baby, the judge will be lenient."

"How much?"

"I think that we have to be prepared for fifty thousand dollars."

Mas gulped.

"You'd need something worth at least fifty thousand for collateral. And then ten percent of that in cash. Could you come up with that?" Jeannie pushed back her headband, and Mas noticed that her hairline was shaped like a vampire's. An American ghoul who sucked blood.

"Look around, Jeannie. Does it look like we have that kind of money?"

"How about relatives? Friends?"

Mas shifted in his seat. "Izu put my house up." To hear himself say it even shocked Mas, not to mention probably Lloyd.

"No, no, Mr. Arai. We can't have you do that. There's got to be a better way."

"Anybody else?" asked Jeannie.

"My parents," said Lloyd. "I can ask my parents."

Why not? thought Mas. Go to the husband's side.

"Good. We'll get Mari out of there right after the arraignment."

After Jeannie left, Mas felt his belly get cold and hard. The last thing he wanted was to be alone with Lloyd, the traitor.

"Mr. Arai, this will just blow over, I know it," said Lloyd, oblivious to Mas's aloofness.

That night Takeo cried continuously. In Lloyd's gangly arms, Takeo looked as compact as a football. Lying on the couch, father rested son on his shoulder, then his chest, and finally his belly. Mas couldn't take the noise anymore and reached for the baby.

Takeo's face was as red as the ripest tomato. He had little bumps on his body—Mari said that he had problems with dry, itchy skin. He slept with mittens on his hands so that he didn't scratch himself.

"*Nen nen kororiyo okororiyo,*" Mas sang, then paused. He couldn't remember the rest of the old lullaby. So he kept repeating it. *Nen nen.* Sleep. *Kororiyo okororiyo.* Rock, rock. Yet Takeo didn't sleep. He kept crying, hungry for only one person, his mother.

The next day, Lloyd left with a driver in a Lincoln Town Car for the arraignment. No babies allowed in the courthouse, so Mas was the one who would have to stay behind with Takeo. It was just as well, because Mas couldn't stand to see his handcuffed daughter in an oversized jumpsuit, standing in front of a judge.

Mas had slept maybe three hours, if you combined the little snatches of sleep here and there. His sweater, in fact, was damp with tears, sweat, and *hanakuso* from Takeo's eyes, overheated body, and nose. The grandson was finally sleeping in his crib, although every half an hour his legs and arms would jerk as if he was having a bad dream. That he inherited from the Arai side, thought Mas, wondering what kind of nightmares a baby could have.

At about eleven-thirty, the phone rang, and Mas felt his heart lurch. What had happened with Mari? As he expected, Lloyd was on the other line. "There's a snag here on the bail situation, Mr. Arai," he said.

"Whatcha talkin' about?" Mas felt his head and fingers go *piri-piri* with a bad tingling sensation.

"Bail's set higher than Jeannie expected. A hundred thousand dollars. My parents don't want to provide any money for bail. We're flat broke. In fact, we're in the hole. We're almost maxed out on our credit cards."

"Youzu take my house," Mas said. He had bought it back in the sixties for three grand, but with the rising L.A. housing prices, the house had now far exceeded the three-hundred-thousand-dollar mark in value.

"You wouldn't have to give it to us. Just put it up for collateral. But we would need probably ten thousand dollars in cash. We'd pay you back, every penny."

Mas squeezed the phone receiver so hard that sweat was dripping down his arms. He listened carefully as Lloyd told him to take Takeo up to Mrs. Knudsen, the neighbor, then go to an office in Brooklyn. "Worm's Bailbonds," Lloyd said. "He'll be expecting you."

Worm Lewis was like a human snowman—everything about him was perfectly round—his belly, head, and green eyes. Even the silver buttons on his vest were round balls. But instead of a coal smile and pipe, he wore a frown, which held an unlit cigar.

"So you're the father?" Worm looked through round-framed glasses at Mas. They sat on opposite sides of Worm's metal desk, surrounded by stacks of white papers, manila folders, and brown accordion file holders.

Although it had cooled to fifty degrees outside, the one-room office was hot and suffocating. The walls were covered in wood paneling; the floors, linoleum. A space heater two feet away glowed with coils of bright orange.

Mas felt sweat drip into his ears. He had already taken off his jacket and wanted to do the same with his sweater. He wouldn't dare to get half-naked in front of Worm Lewis, however.

"Yah, Izu Mas Arai."

"Where you from?"

"California," said Mas. "Altadena. Whatsu dis gotta—"

"Listen, you want to post bail, I need information." The unlit cigar remained in Worm's thick lips.

Mas smoothed out a piece of paper that he had folded up into his pocket. "Dis all information I have."

Worm began typing on a keyboard connected to a computer that seemed to have seen better days. Red duct tape held together its rectangular hard-drive case.

"Hmm, first-degree murder, this is a bad one. So what happened?"

Why do I have to give play-by-play? Mas wondered. He was too afraid to question the bail bondsman. This was Worm's world, not his, and Worm had the key to set Mari free.

"Dis guy Kazzy Ouchi shot dead. Last Thursday."

"Kazzy, what kind of name is that?"

Well, what was Worm? thought Mas, practically biting his tongue. "Kazuhiko heezu full name, I think. Anyhowsu, American. Born here." Like me, Mas added silently.

"So what connection did he have with your daughter?"

"My son-in-law's boss."

Worm shifted his cigar to the other side of his mouth. The cigar was half-chewed, and Mas wondered if he had had it in his mouth all day. "Some kind of love connection?"

Mas felt his mouth go dry. "Heezu old man. Older than me."

"Happens all the time. I've seen it all, you know." Worm typed Mas's residence into his computer. "How much equity do you have in the house?"

"Paid off," Mas said.

Worm printed out some paper and pointed to sections where Mas had to sign. "Now, you realize if your daughter hightails it out of here, you'll have to forfeit the house, right? We'll take a hundred thousand from the sale."

Mas closed his eyes. The McNally house, the small ranch-style home. Two bedrooms. One bath. Porch with a Japanese pine and rocks in the front. The only house he had ever owned.

Mas opened his eyes and stared into Worm's round face

and noticed a large wart on the side of his left nostril. "Yah, I understand."

"So, I'm going to need ten percent. That's our fee."

Even though Lloyd had told him to be prepared, it was still a shock to hear it. Worm stapled a set of papers together. "Ten thousand dollars," he said. "Cash, credit card, or some kind of loan agreement through us."

Mas looked at stickers of different credit card companies stuck to the side of the desk. Visa, MasterCard, American Express. Even a credit card from Japan.

Mas pulled out his new credit card, never been used. How was it that he had come to New York City with a fifteen-thousand-dollar line of credit and a paid-off house and a few days later was ten thousand dollars in the hole and in danger of losing his home? This is a sacrifice for Mari, he told himself. This is for my daughter.

Mas was making salami sandwiches when Lloyd and Mari finally came home. He had picked Takeo up from the neighbor's place, and the baby was fast asleep. Before peppering them with questions, he gave them a chance to see Takeo and change out of their dirty clothes.

Mari was the first to emerge from the bedroom. "Thanks for putting up the house," said Mari.

"Jail pretty bad?" Mas had gone to visit someone at a jail in L.A. for the first time last year and hadn't relished the experience.

"We don't need to talk about it right now." She picked

up one of the salami sandwiches and ate it *musha-musha*, as if it were the best thing next to pickled mackerel sushi.

The phone rang and Mari answered, with a ball of salami sandwich bunched up in her left cheek. She stopped chewing and asked a few questions. Her dark eyebrows furrowed like a wire spring pressed together too tight.

"That was Anna Grady," she said, getting off the phone. "Seiko is dead."

chapter eleven

Mas had been truly afraid only three times. The first time was, of course, when he stood in the black rain of the Bomb; the second, watching Chizuko being eaten by the cancer; and the third, when the Bomb returned from its hiding place in his memory. In those instances, fear slapped him square in the face and kept his legs from moving. The tangle of Kazzy's murder was different. Here now fear slowly seeped in, causing him to run faster and faster. *Hayaku, hayaku,* just like the pace of the city.

He was now in Fort Lee on the thoroughfare by

the bus stop in the plaza, passing familiar cafés with lit candles on the tables.

Anna Grady said that she wanted to talk to Mari, face-to-face, but there was no way Mari could risk bail by leaving New York City. Lloyd was ready to go. News of Seiko Sumi's death had altered his thinking. Lloyd had said he thought that the run-in with the Impala in Seabrook was more a case of road rage than anything else. Apparently Mari had gotten in her share of shouting matches and short-term chases when she was behind the wheel of a vehicle. But now, with another dead Nisei, you couldn't help but make certain connections.

But Mas told Lloyd to stay home. If Anna had taken a fancy to Kazzy, a half-Japanese man, maybe she would open up to Mas.

It was no problem locating the exact high-rise building. Three police cars, lights flashing, were parked at the loading zone, radios squawking out numbers and addresses over the crackle of static. In spite of the late hour—nine, ten?—there was a small crowd of men and women surrounding the parking lot, cordoned off by familiar yellow police tape. Huge lights had been propped up, as if it were a location for a movie shoot. Mas knew about these things because he had driven past his share of production sites in L.A.; hell, one director had paid him one hundred dollars to park his Ford gardening truck in the background of a scene.

The figure of a body was outlined on the concrete ground. The coroner's department must have carted away the body, but had left behind a puddle of blood. Under the bright lights, the blood glistened, still wet with floating chunks of body parts—was that part of a brain? Mas felt his dinner come to his throat, but he pushed it down.

He couldn't believe that only this remained of the *chawan*-haired woman so prim and precise.

The same security guard was outside with the crowd, so in spite of the high-rise being the scene of a bloody death, Mas found it easier to get to the elevator, and then to Anna Grady's floor. The apartment door was open, more radio voices. A long, colorful ribbon decorated the knocker. Mas hadn't noticed that before.

Police officers, men in suits and ties, and women in sweaters and slacks walked into and out of rooms, talking among themselves and taking notes. Again, no one seemed to pay attention to Mas.

The sliding-glass door was ajar, letting a cool breeze in. Mas could smell the sourness of an overworked river. A wind chime shaped like a Buddhist bell tinkled from the top of the balcony. Most of the plants had been overturned, soil dumped out, roots exposed.

"Mr. Arai, you came."

Mas turned. Anna Grady was wearing a tight black dress with part of her *chichi*s showing. At her age, her breasts should have drooped down to her *heso*, belly button, so either she had on one amazing piece of underwear or else her body was still in tip-top shape. "Please, over here—" She gestured to a small dining room table in the corner.

Mas sat with Anna in silence for a few minutes. The display case was busted open, glass shards everywhere, and the journal and clothing were gone. They watched as police officers went from place to place—door, light switch, telephone—collecting evidence.

"That's all they took," Anna finally said, gesturing to the display case. "Seiko's mother's things. They left my jewelry. Seiko's money—she had at least a thousand dollars in cash in her closet. All of that, untouched."

"Book." Mas kept staring at the destroyed display case.

"Yes, the journal's gone. Do you think that's what they were after?"

Mas recalled the detailed questioning by the bail bondsman. "What happen, exactly?"

Anna crossed her legs. "I was out with a friend. We went out to a concert in the city. When I came back, the police were already here, and Seiko's body—" Anna covered her face with her hands. Her fingernails were filed and painted a funny tan shade the color of garden snails.

"Sorry, so sorry." Mas wished that he could leave. He could barely stand it when any woman cried. He didn't know what was worse—when it was a stranger or your wife.

"They say that she was thrown off the balcony. Why would anyone do that to Seiko?" She dabbed the corner of her eyes with her fingers and took a deep breath, making the top of her dress move up and down. "I asked for you and your daughter to come, because she had asked me about the note I sent Kazzy."

She then leaned over to Mas, so close that he could feel the softness of her *chichis*. "I'll tell you what happened as long as you tell no one," she whispered. "Especially Becca."

Becca? What did she have to do with Anna Grady?

She placed a folded-up note in Mas's hand. "Read this later," she whispered. "Kazzy wrote me back. He messengered it to me the same day. Thursday. The day he died."

Mas stuffed the note in his jacket pocket.

"With Kazzy dead and now Seiko, what am I going to do?" She leaned her head against Mas's arm, and Mas could feel her soft hair on his chin.

"Mr. Arai, what the hell are you doing here?" Mas pulled away from Anna to see Detective Ghigo standing in the middle of the noisy living room.

Mas felt the blood drain from his face. Was Ghigo, the crow, ever present?

"We can ask you the same question, Detective," Anna said. Kazzy's ex-girlfriend knew Ghigo? "Aren't you out of your jurisdiction?"

"Like I told you before, Mrs. Grady, the New Jersey police is working with us on the murder investigation of Kazzy Ouchi. Since we were just here interviewing you, we were called in. Just to see if there's some kind of connection."

"Well, there's no connection; I can tell you that."

"We'll see." Ghigo turned his attention back to Mas. "So how do you know Mr. Arai?"

"He's a friend. Old friend." Anna put her hand on Mas's shoulder, snail-colored fingernails in full view.

"That's interesting," said Ghigo, "especially since he just arrived in New York last week."

Before the detective could say more, his bald-headed

partner called him over to the balcony. "Don't go anywhere, Mrs. Grady," he said.

While Ghigo's back was turned to them, Mas rose. "I betta go."

Anna followed Mas to the hallway, picking up her cat, Tama, on the way. "Oh, Tama-*san*," she cooed in the cat's ear. "You must be so afraid."

"Tama, thatsu Japanese," said Mas, who was feeling a pang of jealousy. *Baka*, he told himself, who would be jealous of a cat?

"Yes, I like the Japanese people. They were my first friends in this country. I trust the Japanese."

"You 'Stonian?" Mas asked without thinking.

"Yes, I'm from Estonia. My family moved to New Jersey after World War Two. Why do you ask?"

Estonia had been taken over by a couple countries, by one twice over, isn't that what Tug had said at the Seabrook museum? Anyone who had gone through that would be suspicious of people in power, especially those in uniform. It would make sense that Anna Grady would feel more comfortable with the people who had befriended her first. There were plenty of untrustworthy Japanese people, Mas knew that firsthand, but Anna didn't need to know that right now.

Mas remembered the question that had brought him and Mari to Anna Grady's apartment in the first place. "So whyzu you send him a gardenia dat night?"

"He had been coming over here regularly, wanting to

talk with Seiko. She just didn't like him at first. She said he was—what was the word she had used?—too high-tone. But we ended up getting to know each other better each time he came around. And then one day in January, it was snowing so hard, he just appeared at the apartment, his felt hat in his hands. I told him that Seiko was gone to see a friend, but he told me that he was actually here to see me.

"Then he brought out this gardenia. It was so beautiful—huge, with a wonderful smell. I told him that it looked like hope in the middle of winter. That was our first night together."

Mas averted his eyes, as if he was watching an intimacy that he had no part of.

"I even saved the gardenia," said Anna. "All brown and shriveled up, but I don't care." She went on to describe how wonderful Kazzy had been on all their dates. Mas didn't have the stomach for such nonsense, but he knew that he had to hang in there like a dentist wiggling a rotten tooth. "We had gotten so close in a short amount of time. Kazzy even talked about marriage."

Mas didn't doubt it. If Kazzy had married three times, what was one more?

"But then that terrible daughter of his—"

Mas became more alert. What was that? She was talking about Becca.

"She was the one who poisoned Kazzy's mind. She was so jealous; she couldn't stand for another woman to be involved in her father's life."

Becca had just seemed like a silly female to Mas, not

someone capable of any kind of poisoning, whether physical or emotional.

"You don't believe me, do you? Well, she threatened me. Yes, she did. She even hired a private investigator to look into my past. Not only in New Jersey, but even in Estonia."

Mas waited to see if Anna would divulge the private investigator's findings.

"I told her that I didn't care what she found, I wouldn't break it off. But then Kazzy calls me. Tells me that he cares about me, but he has to end it." Her mouth had become small and puckered. "So I sent him a gardenia last Thursday. I wanted him to remember the sweetness of our first time. But now I'm thinking that he probably used me."

Mas pulled at one of his earlobes.

"He just wanted to see that damn journal so much." Anna's voice was powerful, an uppercut punch. "If he couldn't get it through Seiko, he was going to get it through me. I was the one who Xeroxed it for him, a few pages at a time. I had to go behind Seiko's back to do it. I felt awful, but she had already sent off a whole copy to the Japanese American Museum in Los Angeles. But if they could see it, why couldn't Kazzy? I didn't understand."

"You knowsu whatsu in it?"

Anna shook her head. "That journal's cursed. You don't want to know what's in it."

When Mas got home, Lloyd was still awake, his stocking feet on the coffee table. He had the television on, but he wasn't watching it. He had been doing some heavy thinking, and wanted to hear what Mas had learned in Fort Lee.

Mas told him the whole story and then pulled out the note, folded into a small square. Lloyd unfolded the paper and read the typed message aloud:

DEAR ANNA,
UNFORTUNATELY I CANNOT MEET YOU TONIGHT.
I THINK IT'S BEST IF WE DO NOT KEEP IN TOUCH.
K-SAN

"So businesslike," commented Lloyd. "I mean, that's the way Kazzy was, but even this seems too cold for him."

"Maybe because Kazzy knowsu already he gonna die."

"That's true," Lloyd said. "But why didn't Anna just hand this over to the police?"

Mas couldn't answer that for Lloyd. He wouldn't understand. He probably grew up learning to trust the people in power. Anna Grady and Mas knew different. That sometimes people in uniform were to be feared.

Mas silently read the note again. One thing had been nagging at him on the bus ride back to New York City. "K-*san*, that was on the suicide note, too. Kazzy's MIS buddy, dis Jinx Watanabe, he tellsu us Kazzy was *chanto* man."

"*Chanto*, that means proper, right? Yeah, that was Kazzy, all right," Lloyd said.

"But no *chanto* Japanese put '*san*' on his own name." That was an honorific reserved for other people or, in the case of Anna Grady, for cats.

Lloyd waited a beat. "That's true. I never thought of it. Wait a minute, I have some notes from Kazzy." Lloyd shuffled through papers on his overburdened desk and found at least six old memos. Every single one of them was typed in capital letters; every single one of them ended with one letter, a single K. No *san* added.

"If Kazzy so *chanto*, he *chanto* till the end," said Mas.

"You think someone else wrote this note to Anna Grady?"

"And *jisatsu* note."

"Suicide letter," Lloyd repeated in English.

Phillip was the first person who came to Mas's mind. And then the teenager behind the red door. Mas shared his thoughts with Lloyd.

"You think this Riley may have been the one who followed you and Mari in Seabrook?"

Mas nodded. The physical description fit, and based on the gun he'd shoved in Mas's face, he had the temperament.

"Tomorrow," said Lloyd, "we'll go pay this Riley a little visit. You and I, Mr. Arai."

The next morning, even before Takeo had a chance to cry from behind the bedroom door, Mas called Haruo.

"Mas, I just getsu home. Whatsu goin' on with the dead man?"

"Two dead people now. Ouchi-*san* and a woman."

"Woman? *Toshiyori* or a young one?"

"*Toshiyori*. Nisei. Sheezu about our age."

"Thatsu *nasakenai*. How she die?"

"Thrown over her balcony. Seventeen stories high."

"Catch the guy?"

"*Mada*. But soon." Mas could at least hope. "Anyhowsu, I needsu your help, Haruo."

"Anytin', Mas, anytin'."

One thing about Haruo, he knew a lot of people. To describe someone like him, the Japanese said *Kao ga hiroi*, "Your face is wide," and Haruo's face was one of the widest among Mas's friends. "You gotsu any contact wiz museum?"

"Which museum, the one in Little Tokyo?"

"Yah."

"Come to think of it, my counselor, her sista work ova at the museum. Why, Mas?"

"There's sumptin' I wantchu to take a look at."

Mas was eating breakfast when the rest of the family came out of the bear's lair and settled in the living room.

"You'll need to stay home with Takeo today," Lloyd told Mari, who was giving the baby his morning bottle.

"Was planning on it anyway. And I'm expecting that call back from Dr. Bhalla. What's up?"

"Your father and I have some things to do. Then I'm going to go to the Ouchi Foundation board meeting."

"They're not going to let you in."

"They'll have to. I'm now officially on the board. That's why Becca had to legally inform me of the meeting."

"But they think we killed Kazzy."

"Charged, but not convicted. Anyhow, that's you, not me."

Mari gave her husband a shocked look as if she were a trout pulled straight out of the water.

"That didn't come out quite right," Lloyd corrected himself. "You know what I mean."

"Why does my dad have to come with you?"

Mas looked up from his bowl of dry shredded wheat, curious about how Lloyd would answer.

"I need him," Lloyd said, "for moral support."

More than a physical place, New York City was a feeling. Mas was learning that to get around in the city, he couldn't get too stuck on maps and street names. The best way for him was to depend on his intuition.

In L.A., this approach would never work, namely because you could start driving in one direction on a hunch and suddenly be in either Nevada or Mexico. If you took a wrong turn in New York City, you eventually hit the water, so you then just backtracked in the opposite direction. Mas relied on his inner compass to get to the red door. They got out at Times Square Station and then walked west. Mas knew that they were going in the right direction when the buildings became grimier.

"This area's called Hell's Kitchen," said Lloyd after they had traveled for several blocks.

"Get hot ova here?"

"It's not that. Actually, I'm not sure why it got its name.

It used to be a real rough area, but now they are cleaning it up. Making restaurants and nightspots out of the old factory buildings."

When Mas described the drugs that he had seen in the back room behind the red door, Lloyd nodded his head. "Your boys were probably selling Ecstasy. That's the popular drug in these clubs down here."

Ecstasy, *hiropon,* didn't make much difference to Mas. Names and chemicals could be changed, but drugs had the same general effect. To give temporary sweetness to a life that was bitter and hard to take. In Mas's case, he was lucky that he preferred the bitter to the fake sweet.

It was early morning, and that wasn't doing Hell's Kitchen any favors. It was like shining light in a drunk's face: the area, rather than menacing, seemed pitiful. Pedestrians moved in slow motion, as if walking too fast would cause their heads to roll off.

They passed a couple of brick factory buildings, syringes and torn condom packages scattered on the sidewalk. Mas then pointed down an alley, toward a faded red door. "Thatsu it," he said.

Just as Mas had, Lloyd moved the trash can next to the door and climbed on top so that he could see through the window above the door. Mas sidled up to the trash can, waiting for Lloyd's scouting report.

"I just see a man sleeping on the couch."

"Whatsu he look like?"

"Actually, he looks kind of familiar. Brown hair, porkchop sideburns—you know, like Elvis." Lloyd told Mas to knock and call the teenager over to the door. Mas didn't know if this was a good idea, but he complied.

Mas hammered the door with his fist.

There were noises of someone moving around in the room and then a shuffling of feet.

"What?" A voice slightly muffled by sleep, yet still undeniably male and young. "Who the hell is it?!"

Mas placed his mouth near the crack in between the door frame and the door. "Mas Arai. Itsu Mas Arai."

"Who?"

"I was here dat day. Wiz Phillip Ouchi."

Mas grimaced as he saw Lloyd reach for the metal light fixture above the door. Who did he think he was? Yojimbo? Some lone-gun bodyguard?

Mas could hear the locks being loosened.

The door opened a crack, just enough for Mas to see Riley's bloodshot eye, and then *BOOM!* Lloyd's long legs smashed open the unlocked door, knocking Riley down onto the floor of the back room.

Lloyd had landed on Riley's legs, and now his long fingers were around Riley's thick neck. Mas looked around the room, and he grabbed the first weapon he could find, a state-of-the-art hedge clipper, and pressed down on the handle so the clipper's metal jaw opened.

Riley was gagging as Lloyd pressed down on his Adam's apple. "I want you to stay away from my wife. And the rest of my family." Riley pulled at Lloyd's arms—the teenager had more muscle, but Lloyd had more heart. Lloyd's hands remained in their position underneath Riley's chin.

Riley coughed and strained for air. He desperately exchanged glances with Mas, who knew that this *hanatare*, a runny-nose punk, wasn't worth killing. In fact, the boy was literally a *hanatare*, because two lines of snot were streaming out of his nostrils.

"I thinksu you betta let him say sumptin'," Mas told Lloyd.

As soon as Lloyd let go, Riley dropped his head, gulping down big breaths. He coughed, letting strings of mucus fall to the floor. "This is screwed, man. I didn't mess with your wife."

"You know who I am."

"Yeah, I've seen you at the garden." He bent down again, and then made a sudden move for the cushions on the couch. Lloyd beat him to it, and a gun clattered onto the ground. Mas scooped it up, and before he knew it, he was pointing it at Riley. Mas had held guns before in his life. One was a distant relative's shotgun in Watsonville. When they weren't harvesting lettuce or picking strawberries, Mas went with a second cousin to shoot at geese, ducks, and pheasant at a nearby farmer's ranch.

And later, in Texas, as Mas traveled to different labor camps during tomato season, he had an opportunity to handle a coworker's pistol, which they took turns aiming at empty beer cans. That was a wild gun, whose force bruised Mas's hand in spite of the thick calluses that padded his palms like gloves.

But this gun's handle was as smooth as polished stone. It was compact and neat, a streamlined weapon that any man would be proud to own. Lloyd must have felt Mas's excitement, because he gently took the gun from his father-in-law's shaky hands and held it in his own.

Riley knew he was really beat this time, and leaned back against the wall.

By now, Lloyd had noticed the expensive garden equipment lined up on the other side of the wall. "You ripped us off. That equipment is from the Waxley House." Lloyd held the gun tighter and aimed it toward Riley's head. "You're the one who killed Kazzy."

"Listen, listen." Riley raised his hands. "I explained that all to Phillip. I found the guy there. He was already dead, okay? I saw the gun and I was going to keep it, but when I heard the cop cars, I threw it in the trash can down the block. I wasn't paid to deal with that."

"Why were you in the garden in the first place?"

"Phillip paid me to vandalize the garden, that's all. I don't know what the hell why. Maybe he was getting back at his dad, okay? I used to have an internship at his company. Phillip would come in, thinking he was all that, and then the old man would overturn his decisions. Maybe he was sick of it, I don't know. Anyway, I got in a little trouble—borrowing too many office supplies—and I got fired. Then, out of the blue, Phillip calls me. Says that he has a little job for me to do. It was easy. Just go to the Waxley House late at night a few times and make a mess. Dump trash. Tear down the branches. I was doing that kind of stuff in junior high.

"But killing Kazzy—that's not anything that Phillip

proposed. And I wouldn't have done it if he had. I have a good thing going here. I don't need to kill people to make money. I just have the gun for protection."

"How about the equipment?"

Riley's face looked sheepish and, for once, more his age.

"For my girlfriend's dad. She wanted it as a birthday present. I guess he likes to garden."

Lloyd lowered the gun. "Well, I guess we'll hang on to this right now. You return the equipment back to the garden, and we won't tell anyone that you stole it."

"So when can I have the gun back?"

"We'll see," said Lloyd. "We'll just see."

Mas didn't think that it was a good idea for Lloyd to go into the Ouchi Foundation board meeting with a gun in his pants pocket, but there was no stopping him now. Lloyd was pretty quiet and reserved for a *hakujin*, but now an aggressive part of him—maybe a past generation of hunters who wore coonskin caps—was coming out. Men like Tug and Lloyd, with their sedate, decent exteriors, had pushed down their dark sides for so long that their primitiveness was more concentrated and pure and, as a result, more dangerous. When their anger was unleashed, you had to take a step back and stay out of their way.

As they approached the Waxley House, Mas was shocked to see the state of the sycamore. Someone had taken what looked like a chain saw to the poor tree. Stripped of branches on the right side, it seemed as though it could topple over at any time. Perhaps that was the state of the Waxley House as well.

Mas followed Lloyd into the house and then into the dining room. The fry-pan–faced attorney sat at the head of table. Becca was at his right and Phillip across from her. Miss Waxley's back was toward them, and to her right was Penn Anderson, his orange hair uncharacteristically drooping down like a wilting plant. To her left was Larry Pauley, who looked like something wild had been unleashed inside of him. He wore a wrinkled long-sleeved dress shirt over a pair of jeans ripped at the seams.

Phillip was the first to say something. "It's not right for him to be here." There was an annoying thin shrill to Phillip's voice. "His wife has been charged in my father's murder. There's a huge conflict here."

"Don't talk about me like I'm not in the room," Lloyd said. "I have every right to be here, according to Kazzy's will."

"Kazzy's not around now. We're the board, and we should decide," Phillip pushed back.

"Did they decide that the garden should be destroyed?"

Becca, who had been nervously fingering one of the three earrings dangling from her earlobe, became alert. "What?"

Lloyd laid his cards on the table. "You paid a teenager to vandalize the garden."

"I don't know what you're talking about." Phillip stood as straight as one of the shovels in the toolshed.

"Some kid named Riley."

"Riley?" Becca asked. "Didn't K-*san* fire him for stealing from the company?"

"Listen!" Phillip exploded, the volcano finally erupting. "Our father was pouring millions into this place. It didn't make any good fiscal sense. Ouchi Silk is on the brink of bankruptcy. Who wears silk anymore in America?"

"So you hire a criminal to deface our garden." The siblings were going at it—two crocodiles facing off, their tails whipping back and forth.

"There was no stopping Kazzy, Becca. He was like a man possessed. He had to restore this whole place like he remembered it, sixty years ago. Why? Mr. Waxley is the one who kicked him out of here in the first place."

Miss Waxley then reared her head and joined the fight. "I won't allow you to talk that way. Our family is the one who gave Kazzy his start. Our foundation, don't you forget, has also poured good money into the garden. My father was just trying to get Kazzy on his own two feet. And look what happened! Perhaps Kazzy owed his success to my father."

Before the two families clawed each other further, Lloyd stepped in. "I didn't come here for this. All I want are the financials."

The group stared at Lloyd, trying to comprehend what he had just announced. Penn looked like he was going to dissolve into his chair, whereas Larry seemed to rise up, an *obake* coming back from the dead.

"If I'm officially on the board, I want to see the financial statements," Lloyd repeated.

"What?" Penn followed Larry's lead and stood up as if he

were a marionette whose strings were being lifted by his puppeteer.

"The quarterly statement since the foundation was created. Tax filings, et cetera."

"That's not going to happen. You have no right to any of those documents," Larry said, pointing an overstuffed sausage–shaped finger at Lloyd.

"That will take some time to photocopy," said Becca.

"Well, then let's start off with the past quarter."

Becca glanced at the attorney, and he nodded his head. She disappeared, and Mas could hear her shoes clomp up the wooden staircase. The phone rang, and then, a few moments later, Becca came down. "It's Mari," she told Lloyd. "She says it's an emergency."

Lloyd left the room, and Mas felt desperately uncomfortable. Becca, Phillip, Miss Waxley, and Penn had all positioned themselves in different corners, like the same poles of magnets repelling each other. Larry, on the other hand, planted himself right in front of Mas. "You two aren't going to get away with this," he said. Larry's breath was warm and *kusai*, like Mari's old dog Brownie when he was sick with distemper.

It was just business records; why was Larry so concerned? Mas didn't back down, and stared back at Larry's face. The vein underneath the scar on his forehead pulsed, making his flesh look like a crawling spider.

Lloyd reappeared and asked Mas to meet him outside. His eyes were moist, and in the hazy sun, his pupils resembled the broken patterns within a kaleidoscope.

"Takeo needs a blood transfusion. I need to go to the hospital now. Can you wait to get the financial statements? We'll call you at the apartment and tell you what's happening."

Mas nodded.

"And put this"—Lloyd slipped something heavy into Mas's coat pocket—"in a safe place. But no target practice, okay?"

"*Orai.*"

"I'll tell them what's going on."

"I wait here," Mas said. Lloyd went back into the house and then reemerged, gripping Mas's shoulder briefly before he headed for the sidewalk.

A few minutes later, Larry stormed out, almost knocking Mas down from the porch—a giant bowling ball crashing into a lone pin. He uttered no threats or apologies. He moved quickly and forcefully down the walkway and up the sidewalk. If Larry was indeed a gambling man, he would seek relief at the tables or racetrack, Mas figured. The problem was that Larry was already acting like a gambler on the losing end of a bet. That kind of transparency would lead to further losses.

Becca came out with a stack of papers in a manila file. Mas took them without saying thank you or good-bye. He wanted to get away from the Waxley House as soon as he could.

❖ ❖ ❖

Back at the underground apartment, Mas had to find a hiding place for the gun. It was so beautiful, Mas wanted to keep stroking it, but he didn't have time to be an *aho*. He first put it in the bottom desk drawer. But wasn't that obvious? Next was a drawer in the bedroom underneath Lloyd's boxers. Another stupid idea. Finally, Mas decided on the *okome* canister on a shelf in the kitchen. There wasn't that much rice left, but enough to cover the gun. Mas pushed down on the tin cover, hoping that out of sight meant out of mind.

Next Mas had to contend with the papers, an inch thick. He arranged the financials in piles. This was a familiar task, as he met with his tax man, a former gardener, once a year before April fifteenth. Before their meeting, Mas would sort out receipts, check stubs, and invoices, attach related pages with paper clips, and calculate the totals with an adding machine Chizuko had bought from a now defunct discount chain called Fedco.

Mas chewed on some peanuts left over from his plane ride and surveyed his work. He had placed income all together in one pile; he wasn't concerned about incoming funds. But expenditures, that was another story. Becca, whether intentionally or not, had gone beyond just providing financial summaries. Instead, Mas had copies of receipts and checks, all signed by Larry Pauley and Penn Anderson.

Sitting at Lloyd's desk, Mas paid special attention to the bills for gardening supplies and services. He used to help his ex-friend, Wishbone Tanaka, with his lawn mower shop on rainy days in Los Angeles. He was familiar with various gardening and pesticide companies, their prices and policies. Adjusting his reading glasses, Mas blinked hard and tried to focus. The rows of numbers seemed to merge into one another. Mas felt his eyelids drooping. He rested his head on the stack of papers. Just for a minute, he told himself.

The phone rang, jerking Mas awake. He was still at Lloyd's desk, and he could tell it was morning, because light was coming through the edges of the curtains. He must have slept a good six hours. The financials that had served as his pillow were wet with Mas's drool. His reading glasses had dug into his face and left impressions on his cheeks. Wiping the drool off the side of his face, he answered the phone on the fifth ring.

"Dad," said Mari, "we need you now."

chapter twelve

Mas sipped some orange juice through a straw and bit into a cookie, one of those Danish ones that came stacked in white cupcake holders and arranged in a round aluminum tin. Actually he didn't care much for these cookies, as he usually regularly received at least three tins from various customers each Christmas. He preferred those pastel pink, yellow, and green swirls that he bought from a Dutch bakery in Bishop on his way home from fishing in Mammoth Lakes. That was everyone's take-home gift, *omiyage*, to the ones who had to stay behind in Los Angeles.

But the nurse had told him to make sure to eat and drink before he left the blood donation room. "Need to maintain your blood sugar level," she said. So Mas dutifully poured himself a drink and forced himself to finish a flattened-pretzel–shaped cookie topped with large sugar crystals.

The nurse was pretty good with a needle. A rubber tie at his elbow, one slap on his forearm, and Mas was filling a bag full of blood. He had done this at least one time earlier, and hated the fact that his blood would be churning in someone else's body. But this time it would be his grandson's. Both of them had type AB; AB people could receive from anybody, but could only give to other AB types. He did feel some apprehension. "Don't wanna hurt Takeo more," he said to Mari. "Who knowsu with the *pikadon*."

"Dad, the Bomb happened over fifty years ago. Anything you may have, you gave to me, and I've already given it to Takeo. Aside from Lloyd, we're all radioactive. Haven't you noticed that we glow in the dark?" Mari grinned. Her humor was biting, but today it made the news that Takeo needed a blood transfusion go down a little easier.

Both Mari and Lloyd didn't trust the general blood supply and had called everyone they knew to donate. Apparently Takeo didn't need much, but they wanted to stockpile, just in case. Mas didn't realize how many friends they had in New York. Most of them were *hakujin*, with unkempt frizzy hair (gardeners or filmmakers? Mas wondered), but some were black, Chinese, Sansei, and Puerto Rican. They all bent down to hug Mari and kept an arm around her shoulder. Mas could almost see all the *kimochi* that was being woven around his daughter and son-in-law like bolts of fabric, cocooning them from harm. But Mas knew those cocoons, no matter how saturated with love, were still fragile and vulnerable; anyone could still tear through and reach the soft parts.

He wished that he could join in. Add to the layers of support. But it would be like ballroom dancing, or kissing. No self-respecting Kibei would partake of such practices in public. If he did, wouldn't he just dissolve, lose control and a sense of himself? If he opened that floodgate, there was no telling how much of him would bleed out. Instead, he could help his family in practical matters. Make sure that there was food on the table, ample life insurance in case he dropped dead too early, and a house, bought and paid for. That was Lloyd's job now, but Mas wasn't in New York City for no reason. While Lloyd and Mari needed to keep a watchful eye over Takeo, Mas had to tend to the other matters that would keep them together.

Mas had lost track of the days of the week, so he was surprised to see a security guard, not the floppy-bow–tied receptionist in the mausoleumlike lobby of Waxley Enterprises. *Mochiron*. Of course. It was Sunday, not a day of work, at least for white-collar types.

Mas didn't know what to do. This had been a waste; he should just go back to the hospital and be with his family. But he felt that he needed to get a better sense of Larry

Pauley. Maybe take a second look around his office and photos of his prized Thoroughbred. Mas waited by the side of the door and saw a couple of Latino men unloading a carpet shampoo machine from a white van. They spoke a different kind of Spanish than Mas was used to, but he still could make out enough words, and, of course, when language failed, you could always read people's faces. And one of them was obviously irritated. A third man had not shown up. Mas watched them struggle with their cleaning equipment, and finally stepped in. "*Ayuda, ayuda,*" he offered, lifting two buckets. "I go in, anyways."

They first protested, and then shrugged their shoulders. So a *loco japones* was going to help them, they probably figured. What did they have to complain about?

Mas let them lead the way through the lobby, lowering his face as they passed the security guard, who obviously recognized the two regular cleaners. They entered the freight elevator, whose walls were covered with a gray padded blanket. While the elevator rose, the two men spoke to each other, talking about some local soccer tournament the day before. They stopped on the third floor, at which Mas carried out the buckets filled with rags and cleaning products.

"*Gracias, gracias,*" they murmured, as Mas hit the Up button for the regular elevator.

Getting out on the eleventh floor, Mas was relieved to see no one manning the receptionist's desk. But as he walked down a corridor, he felt the presence of another human in the maze of cubicles. Sure enough, Mas spied hair, the color of a paper bag, frizzed out like cotton candy. As the woman rolled her chair back, Mas finally saw the rest of her. A *hakujin*, wearing jeans and simple striped shirt.

"Excuse me, sir, can I help you?" she asked. Rather than afraid, she seemed curious. Here Mas's size and age were obviously an advantage.

"Ah, Pauley. Mr. Pauley," Mas managed to spout out.

"Mr. Pauley isn't here."

"Left sumptin' in his office last time," he said, and then charged through the door to the hallway on the left.

With the cotton-candy–haired woman practically tailgating him, Mas charged into Larry Pauley's corner office. It was dark, but Mas could still see that the walls were empty, no painting of the galloping horses, only a clean blank space where it once was hung. Larry Pauley must have been in this office for a long time for the paint to have faded. The beer steins were also gone.

One leg of the desk had been broken and the window that overlooked Central Park was now boarded up.

"I told you that Larry Pauley wasn't here anymore." The woman pulled at her hair. "I guess he didn't take leaving too well."

By the time Mas returned to the hospital, most of Mari and Lloyd's shaggy-haired friends had left the waiting room. Mari was walking in the hallway, carrying a steaming cup of coffee.

"Where've you been, Dad? I was looking for you. Didn't know if you wanted a bite to eat from the cafeteria."

"Howzu Takeo?"

"Good, real good. Lloyd's with him. Tug's around, too. I think the transfusion has really perked Takeo up. We started off with Lloyd's supply—he gave about a week ago. Apparently, I can't give any blood right now." Mari's eyes became wet and shiny. "I'm anemic, Dad. Low iron."

No wonder Mari's color looked bad, thought Mas. Here he thought it was just age, but it was actually some medical reason.

Mari sipped her coffee and then leaned against the wall. "Seems like I can't do anything right for him now."

"Youzu a good mother."

"You think? I'm trying. I really am. Lloyd says that I've been doing too much. After Takeo was born, I've tried to slow down, you know."

"Not be so *gasa-gasa*."

"Yeah. But that's in my genes."

"You like your mom."

"Actually, Mom always said that I was like you."

Mas shuffled his feet and looked down at his loafers. Mas knew that he had to mention his trip to Waxley Enterprises. "Izu try to see Larry Pauley," he announced. "I thinksu heezu fired."

"Why?"

"I dunno. I didn't get a chance to talksu to Lloyd, but I think itsu has to do wiz the books."

"The books?" Mari looked confused.

"I checksu all the bills: don't make sense. One lawn mower company belly-up, no around anymore. But still listed in the records."

"What?"

"And they put down chemical fertilizer, but I knowsu Lloyd use all natural. Don't make sense. Overcharge for bamboo. And *toro*, too. They pay two thousand dolla for dat. No way dat *toro* two thousand."

"So you think Miss Waxley figured that out as well? Maybe he's been doing that at Waxley Enterprises, too, huh. Maybe that's why he was fired." Mari furrowed her eyebrows. "Oh, I forget to tell you. Haruo called yesterday for you. Wanted our fax number. What's that all about?"

Before Mas could explain, he felt another presence beside him. The eccentric man he had met at the church, Elk Mamiya. He was a couple of inches shorter than Mas, most likely a pure five feet tall, so Mas could see right into his magnified eyes. Little globs floated in the whites of his eyes like curds in spoiled milk. Elk must not have been sleeping well.

"Mamiya-*san*," Mas said, wondering if some kind of health problem had brought the Nisei to the Brooklyn hospital.

"Heard about your grandson through the pipeline at church," Elk said. Gossip traveled fast in New York City, thought Mas, as fast as in Los Angeles. Tug must have mentioned the blood drive to the church ministers.

"Sank you, *ne*," Mas said.

Mari extended her hand. "Yes, we really appreciate your help."

"No, no, I'm not here to give blood." Elk shook his head, sparse tufts of white hair sticking out of his ears. "I'm here to tell you I figured it out."

Mari crinkled her nose as if she smelled something bad.

"I've been doing research into this Hirokazu Ouchi—"

"That's Kazzy's father," Mari said.

"Yes, an Issei, born in Nagano Prefecture. Married to Emily, an Irishwoman. Don't you think it's quite a coincidence that he died shortly after his wife died giving birth to a stillborn child?"

"What are you getting at?" Mari thinned her eyes.

"What I'm getting at"—Elk began to raise his voice—"is that somebody killed him off. Somebody wanted him dead, and then they killed off Kazzy." Elk turned to Mas. "I told you, back at the church. They're out to destroy us."

"Ah, Kazzy's father died in the 1930s. I doubt that has anything to do with Kazzy's death today." Mas didn't know why Mari kept talking to the man. It was obvious that he was not in his right mind. Mas had met his share of men who had fallen off the edge. Some had been scarred by the camp experience, others from surviving the Bomb. He didn't know why certain people were able to piece themselves together and even flourish, while the weaker ones languished like plants without water. It was a slow death, a process that Mas preferred not to watch, because it reminded him of his own disintegration.

Mari visibly frowned, and Elk apparently noticed. "So don't believe me. What the hell do I care?" Elk focused back on Mas. "I just wanted to warn you—watch your step. They're watching." With that, he left, the fluorescent lights reflecting blue on top of his bald head.

"Who was that?" Mari asked.

"Ole man from Tug's church." Mas was going to add that he was *kuru-kuru-pa,* but thought better of it. Elk Mamiya was apparently acting out of his convictions. He had come all the way to Brooklyn to protect a fellow Japanese American, and Mas should at least be grateful for that.

Tug then turned the corner, a cotton ball taped to the inside of his forearm.

"Uncle Tug, were you with Takeo?" asked Mari.

"Looking good. That's what I told the doctor."

"Yeah, Dr. Bhalla has been a godsend. Don't know what I'd do without her."

"Bhalla? No, this was a big, tall man. Couldn't really see his face, covered up with a mask. He had a scar on his forehead."

"What?"

"Yeah, he was with Takeo when I walked in."

"Lloyd?"

"No, no sign of Lloyd," said Tug. "Come to think of it, that struck me as kind of strange."

❖ ❖ ❖

Big and tall, with a scar on his forehead. Could only be one man. Larry Pauley.

Mari took off first, splashing her coffee onto the floor and wall. Her thin legs churned forward, her feet working so fast that her tennis shoes hardly touched the squares of linoleum floor. Mas followed through the maze of hallways and heavy unlocked doors. Women and men in pastel gowns holding clipboards watched them go—most likely not knowing if they should help or stop them.

They stormed through a wing of small rooms with large windows. Even though the door was closed, Mas could hear Takeo bawling. What did they say about parents and grandparents: that your ears became so in tune with your baby's cry that you could hear it when others couldn't. Takeo was lying on a high bed with metal sides, his face scrunched up and puckered like a pickled plum. Tubes were hanging loose, and the blood from the bag was dripping onto the floor. Multiple alarms sounded off in the room—some as soft as the beeping from a microwave, others as loud as the warning noise from a work vehicle backing up. Nurses and doctors crashed in, surrounding Takeo and eventually pushing Mari out of the way.

No sign of the giant gardener. Mas then spotted that the door of the bathroom was cracked open, not by a doorstop but by a size-eleven shoe, toe up. Sure enough, it was Lloyd—still breathing, but out cold on the tile floor.

With Mari and the team of doctors aiding Takeo and Lloyd, Mas ran out into the hallway of the neonatal ward. An old man, perhaps another grandfather of a broken child, was looking down the hall toward a stairway door that was swinging shut. Mas caught the door and entered the stripped-down stairway. He heard the echo of footsteps banging against metal stairs. Down, down. Mas followed the echo, his knees aching, his heels smarting, lungs low on air, until he landed up in the fancy, hotel-like lobby. Was it the tail of a white lab coat disappearing out the automatic doors?

Mas ran outside and then across the street. He wasn't quite sure if he was heading in the right direction. But then there was the white medical jacket, crumpled on the sidewalk next to the entrance of a Chinese restaurant. Mas knew enough not to touch the jacket. He went through the restaurant, a fancy kind with tablecloths and cloth napkins. As he stared into the faces of the diners, their backs stiffened. They probably thought that he was an aging busboy reporting for the swing swift or perhaps a senile old man who had lost his way.

Mas returned to Takeo's room, only to see his grandson cast on open seas, surrounded by doctors and nurses, their gowns the color of green toothpaste and after-dinner mints. "*Gambare, gambare,*" Mas murmured. Don't give up. Don't sink. Mari was constantly trying to swim toward Takeo, but the waves prevented her from moving forward. Lloyd, unconscious, was taken away on a gurney. And again, Mari was too far, her loved one unreachable. She looked as though she were underwater, and even to Mas, sounds were distorted, movements in slow motion. Before she collapsed, Tug, the tall angel, grabbed her arm, while Mas, the father, grabbed the other.

Mari rested on a couch in the waiting room, a cold pack on her forehead, while Mas and Tug spoke in the hallway.

"Couldn't catch him. No good knees anymore," said Mas, dejected.

Tug handed him a paper cup filled with water. "Drink this, and take a few deep breaths."

Mas kept on wheezing, and Tug theorized that perhaps decades of smoking were finally taking their toll on his health. If Mas weren't so worn-out, he would have snapped at his friend. He didn't need useless health advice when his daughter had almost passed out, his grandson and son-in-law attacked. Lloyd was now conscious but being X-rayed to make sure that his brains weren't scrambled from the blow to his head.

Both Detective Ghigo and Jeannie Yee were now on the scene. Ghigo said that they had an APB out for a dark-haired man named Larry Pauley. But hair could be colored and IDs falsified; Mas knew that much. And besides, had Larry been behind the shooting of Kazzy Ouchi? His style seemed more rough-and-tumble, while Kazzy's murder had been more calculated, with an attention to details.

Mas and Tug made their way to the waiting area. Jeannie paced the linoleum floor, her heels clicking, *kachi-kachi*, like the red and blue castanets that children pressed together while dancing in circles at the summer Obon festival at the Pasadena Buddhist Church. Instead of a shimmering waterfall, Jeannie's hair was uncharacteristically mussed up, a blue jay's nest. Funny that both she and Ghigo would show up at the hospital together, thought Mas.

"We'll pick him up," said Ghigo. "He had a large amount of money recently transferred to his personal account. He and Penn Anderson were using the Ouchi Foundation to embezzle money from Waxley Enterprises. Using their own business contacts as vendors, overpaying them, and pocketing the extra."

"The police traced the anonymous calls back to Penn," explained Jeannie. "He had a voice-altering device. He's been feeding all this information about Mari and Lloyd to divert attention from the missing money. He made such a production of hiding his identity that it seemed obvious that he was hiding something. I guess that it didn't hurt that he had been double-crossed by Larry. He's admitted the embezzling, and is willing to testify against Larry. He just doesn't want to be associated with any murders or attempted murders; he's said that's all Larry's doing."

"I need to see my son." Mari removed the ice pack from her head and tried to lift herself up from the couch.

"You hear docta; Takeo *orai*," Mas said. "Sleepin' now. Needsu his sleep." Ghigo had ordered two police officers to keep watch in front of Takeo's room.

"Yes, Mari. You need to rest a little. They could get you a hospital bed." Tug placed his huge hands on the top of the couch.

Mari shook her head. "I can go over to Lloyd's room and keep him company." Lloyd had a mild concussion. He'd been knocked out by a fire extinguisher. He hadn't seen his assailant, unfortunately, but several security cameras got pictures of Larry—his mouth covered with a mask, but that medical jacket, soaked in the scent of a designer cologne, had plenty of dark hairs. Good thing that Mas had pointed it out to the police.

"Maybe, Dad, you can get a few things for me from home?"

Mas nodded.

As Ghigo and Jeannie moved over to have a private discussion by a magazine rack, Tug clapped his hands together. "Well, good thing, Mas, the mystery's solved. It looks like that Larry Pauley killed Mr. Ouchi."

But Mas wasn't in a celebratory mood. He was far away, looking beyond Tug, toward the darkness of the street through the hospital windows.

It was past midnight before Mas reached the underground apartment, but people—some alone with their heads down, others in pairs making loud noises—were still walking the streets. You could never feel lonely in New York City, thought Mas, wondering if that was one of its main charms.

After he entered the apartment, he turned on the lamp. White papers littered the front of the fireplace. *Dorobo*, thief, thought Mas. He slowly retrieved them, realizing as he did that they were actually a product of the fax machine.

With the help of his reading glasses, Mas arranged them in order. The first page stated, FAX COVER SHEET/Kinko's. Kinko? Sounded like a strange Japanese name. But then Mas remembered that name on storefronts all throughout Los Angeles. A chain of photocopy services.

Underneath Kinko's was another name: Haruo Mukai. So Haruo had come through again.

There were three additional pages. All were from Asa Sumi's journal, although the script looked a little different. Instead of the neat hatch marks that could have been made by the end of a sharp knife, the handwriting was rushed, fluid like running water. The entry was dated February 20, 1931. *Yesterday was my last day at the Waxley House,* it began. *Even to think of it now, tears are running down my face. The morning began as usual, preparing fresh bread, jam, and fruit for breakfast. But no one came down. I wondered what was wrong, and then I heard Ouchi-san call my name.* Mas kept reading, sometimes unable to make out certain words, but continuing, knowing that something important was contained in there. He read the entry five or six times to let its weight settle in his gut.

Kazzy hadn't been killed to cover a man's greed, but a daughter's scorn.

chapter thirteen

Mas didn't sleep at all that night. He was a walking mummy, stumbling on the sidewalks of Park Slope, leaning against trees, watching a man wash his Pontiac at three o'clock in the morning. Everyone here was alive, completely engaged with what they were doing, whether it be corner-store workers setting out the new newspapers for the day, or people drinking coffee and long Mexican sugared donuts. He figured that the energy of the streets could help him think. To take pieces of paper, casual conversations, and chases—both physical and mental—and somehow pull them together into something that made sense.

Mas then knew that he needed to see the pond again. He walked more purposefully, ignoring the weight and weaknesses of his legs. A gray fog covered the top of the Waxley House, erasing the existence of the watchful rooftop dragons. He figured that the house would be empty. He entered the back through the side gate, hearing the woeful barking of a dog a few houses east.

The past few days of both sun and coolness had done wonders for the garden. The cherry blossoms were ready to pop open, and the long, skinny blades of the silver grass was fluffed out like a bouffant hairstyle. Mas greeted all the plants silently in his mind. You needed to talk to plants, but you didn't have to do it out loud like Becca.

Mas finally scooted down into the belly of the pond on his *oshiri*. The concrete was cold and wet from the morning dew, and Mas knew that it would take some time before his jeans dried completely. Mas crawled on his hands and knees to the spot. The carved message, left for who? Kazzy, the son? Or perhaps someone like Mas, a fellow gardener whose gaze stayed on small things, perhaps because that was all he was allowed to see. What had Kazzy's father used? The end of a stick? The end of a rake? Either way, the strokes were sure and strong. 子. Child. And 生. To live. CHILD LIVES. CHILD LIVES. Jinx Watanabe said that Kazzy's sibling had died in birth with his mother. But Kazzy's father knew different. So did the housekeeper, Asa Sumi. A baby had been born. A baby with pale skin. A baby girl, according to Asa's diary.

Mas didn't know if it was the result of a love affair, but he doubted it.

"Fixing something?" Mas knew who it was even before he looked up to see the varicose-veined legs of Miss Waxley. She was holding a small gun; how did a genteel woman like Miss Waxley know how to shoot? wondered Mas.

Mas raised his arms, like he had seen done in so many cowboy and detective movies. It was such a natural response. *I surrender. I give up.* But Mas knew that Miss Waxley would not honor his defeat without payment. The shot, he imagined, might go through his heart, or perhaps his head, like Kazzy.

They both knew the truth, so there was no use in Mas saying it out loud. But Mas did have one question. "Youzu old like me. Whatsu the use? You gotsu no kids."

"How can you say that? This is my life. The only life that I've ever known. All these years, I've wondered why my mother didn't show more love to me. I had always blamed it on her sickness, but then Kazzy comes to me, saying that he has proof that we are half brother and sister. The same mother. The Irish maid.

"I told him that he was wrong. What's this proof he has? And then he gives me a translation of the journal. That the Japanese housekeeper assisted in my birth. That she thought it unusual that the baby looked so white, with golden wisps of hair."

Kazzy must have sensed that there had been something mysterious about his father's death. They would probably never know what really happened. Mas suspected that Henry Waxley had played some sort of role in Hirokazu Ouchi's early demise, just as Elk Mamiya had hypothesized.

"I couldn't let him tarnish my father's reputation," Miss Waxley continued. "My family's reputation. He told me that he needed to tell his children, his grandchildren. That his own father had left this message, and to honor his father, he needed to let everyone know the truth."

"Whatchu father did can't hurt you, Miss Waxley. Thatsu his business, not yours."

"You should have left it alone, Mr. Arai. Just let it stay buried. But I saw you that day at the garden, looking at the writing in the pond. You were slowly putting two and two together."

The gun in Miss Waxley's hand shook—from either nerves or the old lady's weak muscles. "But the journal's gone, you see. Destroyed. Burnt to a crisp."

What about the copies? Mas thought. Then he realized that Miss Waxley wasn't operating out of logic, but of desperation. "Youzu wrote those notes. To Becca and Phillip. And Anna Grady. From K-*san*." It was so clear to Mas.

Miss Waxley nodded. "I was in the house when that gardenia was delivered. I saw it as my chance, my chance to get Kazzy alone. To stage his suicide. So easy. But then you came along, ruining my plans.

"I knew that it was a matter of time before you came here again. You couldn't let the poor plants alone, could you?" Her eyes shifted to the message on the concrete floor of the pond. "I hate this garden. What's written there, for everyone to see. My father's company has poured money into restoring this place. But Kazzy didn't care. He was going to keep going, whether I liked it or not. My life is mine; it's not for public display."

Mas didn't doubt that Miss Waxley was prepared to kill him. She hadn't just killed Kazzy, but must have also ordered poor Seiko's death in Fort Lee. And Mas was next on the list. He wished that he had hung on to Mari back in the hospital, like her ragamuffin friends. But she knew that Mas cared, didn't she? Flew all the way to New York? Gave blood for the grandson? Mas kept his arms outstretched like the man on the cross. His fingers trembled, and he didn't know if it was from holding his arms up so long or straight-out fear. He knew that he should keep his eyes wide open, remembering his last moments clearly, the still cherry blossom branches, the clumps of silver grass, the grayness covering the sky like a blanket. But he closed his eyes, picturing his daughter holding his grandson.

A pop burned in Mas's ear, and then a smell ten times stronger than burning incense. Mas opened his eyes and Miss Waxley was screaming, tumbling toward him like a crazy bird trying to land. Mas rolled to his left, and Miss Waxley fell headlong on the concrete bottom, the gun clattering nearby. Mas looked up and saw the outline of his daughter standing at the rim of the pond. "You okay, Dad?" she asked.

Mas felt his chest, his shoulders, even his head. There was no blood, no holes, no missing parts. He was completely intact, whole.

chapter fourteen

The wayward bullet, this time, had not landed on the dirt floor of the shed, but in the trunk of one of the cherry blossom trees. It was indeed Mari who had saved him, cracking Miss Waxley's head with one of the garden rocks and then pushing the old woman four feet down onto the concrete floor. Luckily, the busybody neighbor had seen Mari run into the garden; curiosity had gotten the best of him. He had witnessed Miss Waxley brandishing the gun and spouting out her confession, thereby becoming Mari's ticket out of jail.

"Howsu you know I'm here?" Mas was resting on the back stairs, his hands still trembling.

"I was worried when you never came back to the hospital with my things," Mari explained. She had gone to the apartment, found the fax, and promptly called Haruo, who gave her a quick translation of the fax. He was the one who suggested that Mas might be at the garden. "He told me that you would need to be around plants to really think."

Like always, Haruo was watching his back, more than three thousand miles away.

In minutes the police arrived. If Mari hadn't saved Mas, the police would have been investigating a murder-suicide. Mas figured that after he was shot, Miss Waxley would have turned the gun on herself. The point wasn't that she escape prosecution but that her secret end where it started, at the Waxley House.

Paramedics checked out Miss Waxley's broken body and confirmed that she was indeed dead, her skull cracked, with her sticky blood settling underneath her. She was a tough *baba*—an old woman with a single-minded purpose—to hide the fact that her father had had relations, most likely forced, with an Irish maid. And that union had resulted in her, a woman whose perceived family lineage was so revered and precise. The Waxley family ended with her, but the irony was that the extended family tree would continue on, with the Ouchis.

Mari and Mas took turns sitting in the dining room of the Waxley House, telling their stories to Detective Ghigo, his bald partner, and their attorney, Jeannie. Mari went first, because she was considered the main suspect. After her turn, Mas was called in. He kept his eyes on the attorney as he told them about reading the journal and putting two and two together. Seeing the words on the bottom of the pond had sealed it, and then he had come face-to-face with Miss Waxley and her gun.

"But how did she know that you knew anything?" the bald detective asked. "She could have just let your daughter take the fall and kept out of it."

Mas said nothing. If you attempted to hide something, you had a sixth sense about who was going to rat you out. Miss Waxley had had that feeling about Mas.

After Mas was released from their interrogation, he joined Mari in the living room. She was on the cell phone, talking to Lloyd, no doubt. "Everything's okay," she was saying. "Yeah, Dad's fine."

The front door opened, and it was J-E, Miss Waxley's driver. Instead of a suit and tie, he wore a faded sweatshirt, shiny blue exercise pants, and, of course, the red-soled shoes. Also, another addition—a beanie cap that hid his eel-like hair. "I saw all the cop cars. Is everything okay?" he asked.

Mas pointed his finger at J-E's head. "Youzu the one in Seabrook. Impala, *desho*?"

J-E turned quickly to leave, but Mari, dropping her cell phone, wrapped her arm around his. "You're not going anywhere."

"Okay, okay." J-E tried to shake Mari off. "I followed you

guys. But I wasn't going to hurt you. 'Just scare them,' Miss Waxley said. I didn't know what the hell this was all about. She told me that she would fire me if I didn't follow through. She didn't want you to find something at that museum. That's all I know. I couldn't go through with what she wanted. It was bullshit, and I told her so. And then she fired me."

"When?" Mas asked.

"Four days ago."

Before Seiko Sumi was thrown off her balcony. Mas didn't think that the driver would commit such a bloodthirsty crime, but you never knew. Sometimes the most harmless-looking ones were the most dangerous. After J-E was fired, Miss Waxley had to find another henchman. And that most likely came in the form of the sumo wrestler, Larry Pauley.

"You better talk to the police," Mari said, leading the driver to Detective Ghigo.

Mari and Mas sat on the back stairs outside the Waxley House. It was like a replay of Kazzy's death. The coroner's office arrived, and so did the detectives and police officers. The body was wrapped and carted away. New police tape was affixed onto two pine trees across the concrete pond.

In a matter of hours, the cherry blossoms had finally opened in full force, weighing their branches down with pink flowers. "They would have to open now," Mari said.

"Thatsu the way it happen," Mas said. "No control nature."

"Do you believe in God, Dad?"

Mas paused. Decades, or even months, earlier he would have said no, that he believed only in Mother Nature. But there was something out there working hand in hand with trees and plants, he had to admit. "You *orai*?"

"I feel so terrible." Mari pressed her wrists against her eye sockets. "I killed someone. Another human being. I mean, I know that it was to prevent her from hurting you—but still. How can I live with that?"

There were no answers. Mas remembered when he abandoned his friends after the Bomb fell. He felt as though he had killed them, too. And that guilt burned in his gut for close to a lifetime. "Day by day," Mas said. "Just thinksu about Takeo. Thatsu best thing."

The sides of Mari's mouth turned upward, but Mas noticed a fluttering in her cheeks, as if it was difficult to keep a smile on her face.

The back gate opened and the two Ouchi siblings walked in. Becca was wearing a T-shirt at least a couple sizes too tight and a torn-up pair of jeans, while Phillip was in a tailored knit jacket. "Is it true?" asked Becca. "It was Miss Waxley?"

"Yes," Mari said. "She killed your father, and she tried to kill mine."

Phillip was a walking, talking skeleton. "I can't believe it," he murmured. "I can't believe it. Why?"

"Sheezu gotta secret," Mas said. "Secret she don't want

nobody to know. Dat her mama is not Mrs. Waxley but Kazzy's mama."

Phillip took a few steps back. "What are you saying?"

"That Miss Waxley was K-*san*'s half sister." For once, Becca was quick in connecting the dots. The realization hit hard, though, because afterward she didn't speak for some time.

"Kazzy must have found out recently when he read Asa Sumi's journal. She was a housekeeper who helped Emily at the Waxley House," Mari explained. "I guess he wanted to tie up all the loose ends in his life before he died. He probably wanted to let you both know the truth."

Mas pointed to the *kanji* on the side of the pond. "Kazzy's daddy try to leave message. 'Child lives.' Asa Sumi wrote dat they tole him the baby died, but he knew the baby was alive."

"What he probably didn't know was that the baby's father was Mr. Waxley," Mari added.

They all remained quiet for minute, deeply affected by how family members could wound and sometimes even destroy each other.

"I knew that this damn garden was cursed, Becca," Phillip finally said. He ran his hand through his graying hair and paced the length of the pond. "We should cover it over, like it was before."

For once, Mas felt sorry for Phillip. Maybe he had misjudged him. Mas knew what it was like to be ignored, your work not fully appreciated. He probably had been struggling to keep Ouchi Silk, Inc., the family business, alive. It was on its last legs, and while his father was the one who had built it up, Phillip would be the one to watch it fall down.

Mas knew that it was his time to step in. He went back into the house and brought a plastic bucket from the laundry room.

"What are you doing, Mr. Arai?" Becca's black makeup was smeared underneath her eyes.

Mas filled the bucket with water from an outside faucet and motioned for Becca, Phillip, and Mari to come to the far northern side of the pond, by the stone *tsukubai*.

Phillip knelt by the stone water basin. "What's that? I never noticed that before."

"*Tsukubai,*" Mas said. "Makes your hands clean."

"I think they use it for the tea ceremony, right?" Becca said, wiping tears away on the back of her hand.

"It's part of a purification rite," Mari said. "That much I've learned from my husband."

Mas didn't know much about purification, but he knew that somehow the pond, with all its bloodstains and bad memories, needed to be made clean again. Although the police tape warded them off from disturbing any evidence, they at least could wash themselves of its curse.

Mas poured the water over the hands of Phillip, Becca, and finally his daughter. Mari took the remaining water from the bottom of the bucket and shook it off on Mas's hands. The bandage had fallen off of Mas's cut a day earlier, and Mas was surprised to see that the skin was already starting to fuse together again.

The back door opened and there emerged the neighbor, Howard Foster, who had completed his interview with the police. His hands on his hips, he made a strange noise with his tongue and teeth, as if he were calling chickens for their next feed. "I told you. I told you that this would end up a disaster," he said, shaking his head. "You should have never unearthed this pond." He walked up to Phillip. "I've been talking to my bank. I think that I can make you and your sister a fair offer. Once you're ready, give me a call."

Phillip stood above the *tsukubai* and folded his arms. "I won't be making that call, Mr. Foster, because we are keeping the house."

"And the garden," Becca added with finality.

❖ ❖ ❖

Before Becca and Phillip left the garden, Mas pulled Becca aside. "Youzu chase Anna Grady away," he said.

"What?" Becca's right eyelid fluttered like a butterfly trying to make its escape.

"Youzu don't want her to marry your daddy."

Becca swallowed and looked away. "I finally got K-*san* to myself, you know. After all these years. We shared the same passion for gardens, plants. I can't tell you how many times we visited the Brooklyn Botanic Garden together. We even had pet names for each one of the bonsai in their collection. Do you know some are hundreds of years old?"

This woman has too much time on her hands, Mas thought.

"And then he tells me that he's met someone. And it's

serious. He was talking about marriage, Mr. Arai, after only two months. I had to put a stop to it." Becca explained that she had hired a private investigator to look into the background of Anna Grady, formerly Anna Miller, both in the U.S. and in Estonia. "She had been married once before, but that wasn't a big deal, with K-*san* married three times. But what the investigator found out overseas was highly damaging: Anna's family had aided the Nazis during World War Two. What if that news got out? K-*san*'s reputation would be at stake."

Mas wasn't that sure of that. "Ova fifty years ago. Nobody care."

"That's what Phillip said. But K-*san* would have cared. I know it. He prided himself on helping teach military intelligence officers to help end the war. What if people found out his new wife was a Nazi? What kind of PR mess would that be?"

Mas shook his head. Anna's country had been pulled apart by different world powers. The only reason her family probably had turned to one was to get away from the other.

"I threatened to tell K-*san* if she kept up the relationship. She refused to break it off, almost spit in my face. Before I could do anything more, K-*san* ended it. I was so happy at first. But then his mood became so dark. He must have known that he was dying then. I'm sure that's why he decided to call it quits with Anna. He didn't want her to feel that she had to hang around while his body wasted away." Becca hid her face in her hands. "He must have really loved her." She lowered her hands, black makeup smudges like ash around her eyes. "Do you think K-*san* would have forgiven me?"

Mas didn't answer. He didn't know Kazzy Ouchi, or even much about forgiveness. He did understand emptiness and regret, however. Having those feelings in common, they stood silently at the open gap of the pond, imagining what it would be like for it to be finally filled with clear water and brightly colored fish.

After the police told them that they could go, Mas told Mari that he needed to make one more stop, one more task he needed to do, before returning to the underground apartment.

"I have *yoji*," he said.

"Want me to come with you?"

Mas shook his head. "But there's sumptin' you and Lloyd needsu to do. Your own *yoji*. Tell Lloyd to give Ghigo *okome* can."

"Our rice container?"

"Let Lloyd handle," Mas said. His daughter had gone through enough for that day.

Mas returned to the same Parisian flower shop, and indeed the same girl was working behind the counter.

"Hel-lo," the girl said very deliberately, and Mas figured out that she still thought he was an inspector from Japan.

"I needsu gardenia."

"You want to send some gardenias?"

Mas nodded. "One dozen," he said, taking out his credit card. "To Fort Lee."

For the next couple of days, Mas really tried to take it easy. Both Lloyd and Takeo were discharged from the hospital, so the whole family was again in the underground apartment. Mas, however, couldn't help but be *gasa-gasa*. He first began cleaning the moldy bathtub with an old toothbrush and then tried to do something with Lloyd and Mari's pitiful garden. Finally, Mari moaned. "Dad, you're so restless; you're driving us crazy. Get out of the house, why don't you? You're going home in a couple of days. Go sightseeing with Tug."

Mas was not wild about sightseeing, because what was the point? He usually wanted to get from point A to point B with the least wandering. Straight lines were the best, the shortest distance between two locations.

But Tug was a lot like Chizuko. They liked to see things beyond the most direct route. To heed his daughter's plea, Mas agreed to wander this time. "You have to see the Statue of Liberty," Tug said. "Up close."

As they approached the landmark on the ferry, Mas first noticed that the statue seemed squatter in real life. He thought that the green lady's figure would take his breath away, overwhelm him with her sheer size and grandeur. Instead, she seemed more comforting, like a distant female relative who regularly sent you treats in the mail. But the color—the greenish tinge much like the rusty copper end of an old hose—that was another story altogether. That was indeed incredible.

Upon reaching the small island, they debarked from the ferry and stood at the foot of Lady Liberty. Dodging the lenses of cameras aimed by Chinese and European tourists, Mas couldn't really take in much of the statue, aside from the folds of her skirts. Tug explained that they could take an elevator to climb three hundred fifty-four stairs to the statue's crown, but again, Mas thought, what was the point? Then Tug took him to the edge of the water so that they faced the skyline of Manhattan.

Tug told him about all sorts of Nisei who had made it—men and women who constructed skyscrapers, built sculptures, created paintings, and established trading empires.

The Nisei who flew away from the Pacific Coast were indeed a different species. They could stretch their wings without fear of being clipped or captured. Even Takeo Shiota, an Issei, had made a name for himself. But then Mas remembered how Lloyd had told him that Shiota had been left to die in an internment camp. Why? thought Mas. Why would a gardener who placed a giant orange gate in a pool of water be a threat to anyone?

Mas remained quiet on the ferry ride back to Manhattan. The wind whipped through his hair, causing the sides to stick straight up like the ears of an aging bat.

"There's one other place I want to show you," said Tug.

Mas's legs were so *darui*, weak, that he thought that his feet and knees would detach from their joints. But again, no *monku*, no complaints.

They took the subway, and from there, more walking. The sun seemed to drop all of a sudden, painting a silvery glow in the gray skies. At least the sidewalks were pristine, not a crack or a bump from an overgrown tree root in sight. The drapes of the exclusive apartments were wide open, showing off the units' contents—antique lamps and polished tables. Mas would be worried that revealing all that wealth would invite robbers, but this was an area so rich that any evildoers would instantly stand out. In fact, Mas was surprised that an undercover policeman didn't pop out from a hiding place to question him. He was, however, with the best alibi he could ask for, the all-American Tug Yamada.

They finally stopped in front of one of the multilevel apartments. "This is New York's Buddhist church," said Tug.

"Ha—" Mas kept his mouth open as he checked out each floor of the concrete building. Didn't look like any temple he had come across before. Even the Seabrook Buddhist Temple seemed more sacred than this.

Tug explained that he'd visited this temple a couple times in 1946. Outside, it couldn't compare with the grand temples in California, but inside was the familiar smell of incense and the golden altar, Tug remembered. Christianity had touched Tug by then, so he had hidden his dead friend's worn Bible underneath his coat while he listened to the familiar chant of the priest.

"Look, Mas." Tug pointed to a huge statue of a Japanese man standing behind an iron fence outside the neighboring apartment. The height of at least two men, he wore a curved, umbrella-shaped hat and cloak. He held a staff in front of him like a candle that would give off light. "This is new to me."

"Izu see dat before," Mas murmured. Some kind of *erai* leader, but he couldn't place the name. Wasn't that the same kind of statue standing on the grounds of the easternmost temple in Los Angeles's Little Tokyo?

Tug walked over to a plaque. "This statue is originally from Hiroshima. Survived the bomb, like you."

Then Mas faintly remembered seeing the statue a couple of miles northwest of Hiroshima's ground zero. How had it come to be moved to New York? thought Mas.

At first the statue looked totally out of place, fenced in behind an iron gate on New York's Riverside Drive. But the longer Mas stared at it, the more at home it seemed to be.

chapter fifteen

And the older a Japanese garden, the more natural it looks, and added years serve only to increase its glories.

—Takeo Shiota

Mas walked through the long plastic strips hanging from the doorway of the grocery store. The Korean shopkeeper was perched on a stool next to the cash register this time. Maybe business was slow this morning, thought Mas.

"Haven't seen you in a couple of days," the shopkeeper said as Mas approached the counter.

"I really goin' home now," Mas announced, drumming his callused thumbs against the counter's rubber surface. "Tomorrow."

"Good to go home."

Mas nodded.

"Talk to my sister last night. She says it's seventy degrees over in L.A."

"Oh, yah." It would be good for his muscles and joints to feel the beating of the sun again. Yet a part of Mas was going to miss the coldness. It made him move around more than he ever would, even in spring.

"Marlboro?" The shopkeeper started to reach for a carton of cigarettes, but Mas shook his head. He remembered what Takeo's doctor had said. *You need to cut back or quit altogether, Mr. Arai. Don't you want to see your grandchild graduate from high school?* That was a ridiculous challenge; Mas didn't even know if he could count that high, but what if he beat the odds, confounded all the handicappers and prognosticators at the local lawn mower shop? Instead he reached for a package of Juicy Fruit gum. A jumbo pack almost as wide as a deck of cards. Seventeen sticks should keep him busy on the plane. And in terms of overdosing on sugar, who cared about that? Since he had no teeth anyway, it didn't make much difference.

He took out a dollar, but the shopkeeper pushed the money back toward Mas. "Free," he said. "On the house."

Mas got on an underground train on his way to the Eighteenth Street station for Joy's exhibition opening. Lloyd had plotted Mas's path on both subway and street maps so carefully that Mas thought that each footstep had been calculated. Neither Lloyd nor Mari could make it, because of Takeo, so Mas was supposed to be the Arai-Jensen household representative.

As he sat in the train car, Mas thought about what it was really going to be like when he returned to the house in Altadena. He had spoken to Haruo earlier, updating him on all the news, including the latest, that Larry Pauley had been arrested at the Canadian border. He had been carrying one hundred thousand dollars in cash and was on his way to purchase a Thoroughbred reared in British Columbia.

Haruo had news of his own. "When you get back, there's sumbody you gotsu to meet," he said. "Izu gotsu a new friend."

Mas's ears perked up. He had heard this tone of voice before. He knew what it was about even before Haruo went further.

"She's a routeman. You knowsu, buys flowers at the Market and delivers them all ova the place. Sheezu been doin' dis ever since the fifties."

A routeman? Must be a big, strong woman, one who could easily toss Haruo from one side of the room to another. But then Haruo was partial to strong women, as all Japanese American men were.

"How's Tug doin'?" Haruo had asked.

Sitting in the train car on his way to the art gallery, Mas honestly wasn't sure. Tug had said some strange things last night, that Joy would never get married and have children like Mari. *How do you know?* Mas had asked him. *Joy still young. Has time.* But Tug had just nodded his head sadly, saying that it wasn't in the cards for her.

Mas ended up at the gallery a little late—he had taken a couple of wrong turns, in spite of Lloyd's detailed maps—and sure enough, there was Tug, wearing a light-blue suit and a red and blue striped tie. With all the cigarette smoke from the young people waiting outside, Tug looked like he was emerging from a mist from the heavens.

"Sorry Izu late," Mas apologized.

"No problem," Tug said, opening the gallery's glass door.

The pervading color was black, which made Mas feel that he was at a funeral reception. He thought that he had seen a flash of red in a corner, but that was actually a windowpane lit up from the back. As he got closer, he noticed that red raindrops bled down the glass. The artwork was aptly labeled, *Blood Rain*. Mas, who had seen enough blood on this trip, moved to a ceramic hot dog and bun the size of a small sports car, and then a mound of trash, complete with sanitary napkins and empty beer cans.

"Whatsa point?" he asked Tug about the trash installation. "Dis on every street corner."

"The guy's famous, I guess." Tug read the label. "Selling for three thousand."

Three thousand? Could pay one third of my new credit card bill. Mas imagined throwing down fresh grass cuttings and a rusty Pennsylvania push lawn mower. How much would these thin *hakujin* pay for that?

More black clothes, but no sign of Joy. There was an

African American woman with a huge wrapped yellow headdress the size of a beehive. And a *hakujin* woman dressed in an old black kimono cinched at the waist with a piece of dyed blue fabric. Mas grimaced. Although this woman maybe didn't know any better, the kimono she was wearing was strictly reserved for men and for funerals. And the belt was *furoshiki,* a piece of cloth that Chizuko had used to wrap around bamboo containers of *musubi,* rice balls wrapped in black seaweed. When Mas brought that to Tug's attention, he merely shrugged his shoulders. "Don't matter, Mas," Tug said. "This is America."

Besides Mas and Tug, there was another Asian face—a young woman wearing a pair of *monpe* pants, the pantaloons, cut at the calves, that Japanese peasants wore in the rice paddies. But instead of straw *zori* slippers, the woman wore military boots, not that different from the ones Tug had probably had in Europe. Mas feared that Tug was going to try to make conversation with the girl. She must have sensed it, too, because she disappeared in the crowd of black as soon as Tug made eye contact.

Waiters came around often, offering glasses of wine and strange appetizers. As usual, Tug declined the wine, with Mas accepting each one of Tug's rejects. The same went for the Ritz crackers topped with caviar, sour cream, and avocado. Who would have known such a strange concoction to taste so good?

"Wherezu Joy?" Mas asked.

"I don't know," said Tug. His military-trained eyes surveyed the crowd, searching, searching.

The two friends finally landed up in a corner, surrounded by X-rays illuminated by metal light boxes.

"This reminds me of Dr. Hayakawa's office," Tug said, referring to a gastrointestinal specialist in Pasadena who had yanked out Tug's gallbladder last year.

While doctors' offices always made Mas feel cold and alone, this X-ray gallery felt warm, like a line of fireplaces glowing from the middle of the wall. The X-rays were cut up and brightly colored in fluorescent paint. One light box held a montage of head X-rays, with a negative of a girl in the center.

Mas lowered his reading glasses from his head to his nose. In the photo negative, the girl's teeth were black, the pupils of the sloping eyes white.

"Who's dis?" Mas asked.

"It's Joy."

One light box after another reflected parts of Joy's life. X-rays of broken arms, a teenage Joy playing basketball. X-rays of a fractured leg, Joy on the steps of the Medical University of South Carolina. Mas couldn't look at Tug's face. He didn't understand what the X-rays meant and wasn't sure that he even wanted to.

Apart from the light boxes, there was another feature in Joy's exhibition. A metal contraption that attracted more people in black to wait in line to peer inside.

"Dat part of it?" Mas asked.

Tug examined the side of the machine. He explained that it was an old-time Mutoscope, similar to ones set up in the penny arcade on Disneyland's Main Street. By cranking the side handle of the scope, you could flip through a series of cards, creating a moving picture. A movie screening for a private party of one.

Tug and Mas stood in line behind the African American woman in the beehive headdress. After she was through, she turned and looked over Mas's head to smile at Tug. "Wonderful, just wonderful," she said, readjusting her makeshift hat and turning her attention to the wall of trash.

"Go ahead, Mas."

"No, you go," Mas insisted. It was Tug's daughter, after all. They continued like this for a couple more rounds until it dawned on Mas that Tug was afraid. He needed a friend to be the guinea pig viewer.

Mas took a deep breath and then pressed his face against a viewer shaped like an underwater diving mask. He cranked the handle and saw Tug as a boy on the chili pepper farm with his four oldest brothers and sisters. The old photograph was black-and-white, and then suddenly his overalls were colored a bright blue, the chili peppers green and red. Then the static figures became an animated cartoon, the chili peppers thrown in the air and then segueing to an image of Heart Mountain, Wyoming, the landmark peak within the internment camp. Smoking like a volcano, Heart Mountain erupted, spreading thick red and black lava, which carried a photo of Tug in his Army uniform. Lil appeared, so pristine in a white cotton blouse and her hair permed and curled close to her face. In the background was her barrack in Arkansas, a tar-paper shack that transformed into a giant jaguar. Didn't make sense, but Mas kept cranking. And finally there was Tug again, wearing one of Lil's full-length aprons and holding one of their carving knives. Lil was next to him, her hands on his shoulder. Thanksgiving dinner, about five years ago, judging from the style of Lil's eyeglass frames. Suddenly they moved, no more apron or knife, no more turkey. They were ballroom dancing, something Mas wouldn't dare to do. The dancing couple dissolved into two smiles fluttering like butterflies. Then blank. Mas continued cranking, and the movie returned to the chili pepper farm.

He let go of the machine's crank and stood up straight. "Nice," he said. "Real nice." Tug hesitated and then leaned down to the scope. He was cranking like a madman; he must have viewed the movie two times straight. Mas didn't know what the short film meant, but somehow it made him feel happy. And on this trip, you had to grab at any kind of remnants of happiness.

The person behind them began to cough, and even Tug realized that his time was up. He removed his face from the viewer. The line had gotten longer, at least fifteen people deep, but Tug had to experience an encore and went toward the end of the line.

"I wait here," Mas said, opting for another glass of wine by a display of a basketball covered with Barbie doll heads.

Tug was third in line when a familiar voice called out a few feet away: "Dad." Surrounded by four women, Joy stood by the broken-arm X-ray light box. Circles of her two braids—one hot pink, the other blue—were pinned to the sides of her head. She wore a shimmering light-blue dress with a plunging neckline held together by a circular brooch.

"Hey, we match," she said, laughing and pointing to her father's light-blue suit, his tie, and even his round Optimist Club tiepin. Tug got out of line to talk to Joy, but then a group in black walked in between them. Taking another drink of his wine, Mas watched as Tug desperately tried to make his way to his daughter's side.

When Mas walked into the apartment, his face hot and stoplight red from the successive glasses of alcohol, he was enveloped by a wonderful aroma from a pot boiling on the stove.

"Whatchu making?" he asked Mari, whose hands were stuffed in oven mitts.

"Corned beef and cabbage. Lloyd's favorite."

"No, that's your favorite," Lloyd said. Mas had to agree. Every St. Patrick's Day, they had gone to the Japanese Catholic church just east of Little Tokyo to eat corned beef, cabbage, and sticky rice in Styrofoam bowls on plastic trays outside on tables covered with butcher paper. They had gone at the invitation of friends, but soon it was a tradition that Mari insisted on every year.

Chizuko also made her version throughout the winter, long, peeled carrots floating alongside a slab of red meat and cabbage. One year, Mari had gotten her tonsils removed, and seemed content eating her special diet of 7-Up and ice cream—that is, until she saw the steaming pot of her favorite food and burst into tears.

"Rememba after you got your tonsils out—"

"Oh, yeah." Mari smiled, lifting the meat and vegetables with a pair of tongs. "I can't believe you'd remember that. I was only about six years old."

For a moment, Mas felt normal. The corned beef was tender, falling apart in his mouth without much effort of his dentures. They laughed, the noise and the scents filling the corners of the underground apartment. Takeo was safe in his crib, sleeping, hopefully not being terrorized by any nightmares.

After their early dinner, Lloyd insisted that Mari go to the gathering at the Teddy Bear Garden, the community garden trapped in an enclosed triangle.

"Get out of the house. Breathe in fresh air. It's just a few blocks away."

Mari was still wary about leaving Takeo, who was now awake and lying on a blanket on the floor. "Well, I'll at least change his diaper before I go," she said.

"No, Mari, I can handle it. You just go."

"Izu help Lloyd," Mas added.

Mas knew the drill now from babysitting Takeo. Fresh diaper—disposable paper ones with stickers, not cloth and safety pins like in Mari's baby days. Take off the dirty diaper and clean *oshiri*. Lloyd pulled up Takeo's legs and wiped his bare butt with a Wet One.

"*Ara*—" Mas pointed to the blue-black mark above Takeo's behind. He hadn't noticed that before.

"Yeah," said Lloyd. "I guess he's more Japanese than *hakujin*."

❖ ❖ ❖

The bald man, the night gardener, remembered Mas as he and Mari approached the gate of the Teddy Bear Garden. "Yes, the gardener from California," the man said.

"My father," explained Mari.

"I had no idea. Well, welcome to the family. Have something to eat, something to drink."

They stood in line, holding small empty paper plates and napkins. Mari seemed to know most of the people, and Mas recognized a few of them from the blood drive at the hospital. They ate chocolate cake on a damp bench, and Mas could sense that Mari, her eyes darting back and forth at the crowd by the barbecue, wanted to make more conversation with her friends, yet stayed behind with him.

"You pack everything?" she asked.

"Yah." There wasn't much to pack. Lloyd had gone over to the Laundromat and washed Mas's underwear, socks, jeans, and long-sleeved shirt. All that was rolled up and pushed into the hard plastic shell of the yellow Samsonite.

"Who's going to pick you up from the airport?"

"Haruo." Mas wasn't looking forward to all the stories he would have to listen to on the hour's drive back to Altadena.

"It's good that Haruo's there for you, Dad."

"Um," Mas grunted. He stacked Mari's finished plate on top of his and made his way to the garbage can a few steps away. He passed a couple of women who didn't look like the rest of the crowd. Instead of jeans and knit scarves, they wore pressed slacks and gold jewelry.

"Who's that?" he heard one woman ask the other.

"Oh, he's connected with the Waxley House. He's their little Takeo Shiota," one of the women said.

Mas bared his top dentures. He wanted to snap at the women, but he would never dare to do so. He turned toward the bench, and there was Mari, her head tilted back, a small green sycamore leaf in her hands. Her mouth was wide-open, the short staccato of laughter starting to ring from her throat. It sounded somewhat familiar to Mas, yet different, like an old tune that was made new again.

the rest of the crowd. Instead of jeans and knit scarves, they wore pressed slacks and gold jewelry.

"Who's that?" he heard one woman ask the other.

"Oh, he's connected with the Wade-Gerhardt House. He's their little [illegible]," one of the women said.

Max flared his own nostrils. He wanted to snap at the woman, but he would never dare to do so. He turned toward the bench, and there was Mary, her head tilted back a bit, her [illegible] in her hands, her mouth was wide open, the [illegible] of laughter [illegible] from her throat. It sounded somewhat familiar to Max, yet different, like an old tune that was made new again.

ABOUT THE AUTHOR

NAOMI HIRAHARA is the author of *Summer of the Big Bachi*, the first book in the Mas Arai mystery series. A writer, editor, and publisher of nonfiction books, she previously worked as an editor of *The Rafu Shimpo*, a bilingual Japanese American daily newspaper in Los Angeles. She and her husband reside in her birthplace, Southern California. For more information and reading group guides, visit her Web site at www.naomihirahara.com.